THE SET UP: 1984

CLASSIFIED UNTIL 2064

A novel by
Gretchen Eick

The Set Up, 1984: Classified until 2064

Blue Cedar Press
P.O. Box 48715
Wichita, KS 67201 U.S.A.

First Edition
10 9 8 7 6 5 4 3 2 1
ISBN 978-1-7342272-5-3 ebook
ISBN 978-1-7342272-8-4 paperback

Includes Discussion of Sources and Study Guide
1. *Operation Bishop drug bust. 2. 1984. 3. Iran-Contra.*
4. *U.S./U.K. foreign 5. Middle East. 6. International intrigue.*

Editor Laura Tillem
Cover by MD. Hasanur Rahman

For David James Crighton

Table of Contents

Characters

David Bennie, 20, an unemployed Scot trained as a boat mechanic

Brian Baker, 30, the playboy son of an Oxford don and his Greek wife

Keith Brown, 38, from a poor British family from the London Docklands, owner of a carhire shop whose hobby is boats

Georgina Graves, 28, businesswoman girlfriend of Brian Baker

Janet Morris, 38, grammar school teacher, Keith's partner and mother of Teddy, their four-year-old son

Niko Karras, 26, Greek Cypriot by birth whose family fled to Lebanon and then became refugees in Rhodes, Greece in 1975, where he works as a trawler like his father

Sally Eliades, 21, British girl whose father was Greek, who tried to run a bar in Rhodes, Greece

Tom Hill, late forties, British uneducated loner, carpenter and radiographer working Mediterranean boats

*William Casey, 70s, Director of the CIA in the Reagan Administration

*Oliver North, 40, Marine working at the National Security Council during the Reagan Administration

*Bob Anderson, former Secretary of the Navy, Deputy Secretary of Defense, and Secretary of the Treasury in the Eisenhower Administration and an oil and gas businessman

*Clark Clifford, corporate lawyer and lobbyist, counsel to presidents Truman, Kennedy and Carter Secretary of Defense for President Lyndon B. Johnson, chairman of First American Bankshares, the largest bank holding company in the Washington, D.C. area

*Max Hugel, businessman and Deputy Director of the Central Intelligence

Agency for Administration (DDA) and then as Deputy Director of the Central Intelligence Agency for Operations

*Adnan Khashoggi, Saudi Arabian businessman and arms trader

*Bruce Rappaport, Ukranian born Israeli international businessman in oil, shipping, and finance, a founder of the Israeli Military Police

*John Shaheen, formerly part of Office of Strategic Services, predecessor of CIA, and president of Golden Eagle Refining Company and Macmillan Ring-Free Oil

* Indicates an actual historical person. Only North is still living.

Part 1 - The Set Up

Chapter 1

David, the beloved youngest child, sailed along on the confidence that comes with being the baby of the family. He had left school at sixteen but he was not lazy. The apprenticeship program at British Steel in mechanical and production engineering that he joined saw him excelling, even winning a prize for his performance—the only one offered that year. He expected to move directly from the apprenticeship into a choice job with British Steel. He expected his life would be easier than his parents' lives had been. He had expected the world to add him to its ranks of the appropriately employed. Instead, his apprenticeship delivered him the scrounging life of the unemployed. It was not his fault. In September 1981, one month before the apprenticeship program was to end, all the apprentices were informed that there would be no work available at British Steel for them. David was eighteen and a recession had crippled the British economy. There were no jobs.

Still exuding the optimism of the young, he decided to see the world and for six weeks he wandered through Holland, Belgium, France, Germany, Italy, Spain, Yugoslavia, Spain and Greece, having a glorious, carefree time. Surely he would find work when he returned to the U.K.

When his funds ran out, he returned home, moved back in with Mam and Dad and lived on the dole while he looked for work. He was desperate for a job and applied everywhere he could. He even applied for a position with the British Antarctic Mission, although he knew it was a long shot. Confronted with the sagging economy, he seriously considered joining the Royal Navy as his brother had done.

David came from a family that had faced more than its share of life's challenges. Living along Scotland's northeast shoulder, money was hard to come by. The Bennies found compensation for their lack of wealth in the love and good humor that bound them to each other. They stuck together no matter what.

David had heard nothing from the British Antarctic Mission, but when he stopped by his parents' house on a Sunday evening in time for supper, Mam told him a call had come in for him from someone in London. They'd left a callback number.

It was warm in the small cottage, especially warm for April. Mam was cooking something that smelled fishy in a large pot on the stove. The odors of fried onion and potato floating on the air reminded him that he hadn't eaten since a hurried bowl of porridge ten hours before—but the chance of employment got him up from the table and to the phone.

He dialed the number Mam had scribbled down. A low female voice told him there might be a position for him if he could be in London by one p.m. Monday—tomorrow! Anxious to make some money, he said he'd be there, though it was nearly impossible. London was a good twelve hour drive even if he had a car. He momentarily felt guilty about asking Mam or Dad for cash, but this was a necessity. As the indulged wee one of the family, he'd learned early how to manipulate his folks. He turned from the phone and asked his sister if he could borrow her car to go to a job interview in London. He knew that if she said Yes, Dad would have to drive her to her job. He calculated, correctly, that Dad would rush to offer his own vehicle to David for the drive to London to save his sister inconvenience. Dad would happily take the bus to his work.

Dad followed the script as David had expected he would, even offering David money for petrol. Bless his parents. They always came through.

David had no time to consider what to wear to this hastily set up job interview for a position that remained as murky as an oily puddle. As there was no time to lose, he wolfed down a bowl of Mam's special soup, grabbed a satchel, and tucked in a comb for his shoulder length hair, deodorant, his toothbrush, toothpaste, and a towel. He grabbed his denim jacket, his sunglasses and the satchel, hugged each parent goodbye, and dashed off to start the long road trip south in Dad's car. Mam passed him a thermos of hot tea as he rushed out the door.

He pulled off the motorway when he was an hour outside London and caught a cat nap in the car for a few hours. Then he ploughed through the unfamiliar London traffic to the office building in a fancy hotel complex near the Thames. Very little cash remained from Dad's handful of bills; the petrol stops had eaten up most of his reserve. He certainly did not have the cash to park the car in the hotel's garage.

He found himself bouncing from amusement and elevated good humor to anxiety and back. This was at worst a lark, something new to add to the unusual experiences he collected like some folks collect people. But what was he to do with Dad's vehicle? He decided to ask the doorman, who wasn't much older than David himself. He pulled the aged VW up to the apex of the half circle drive and stopped. He read panic and disapproval in the doorman's face. Okay, he could use that.

"Excuse me, sir," he began. The man's badge said, "Andrew" so he resurrected his Doric, the Old Scottish that had been his first language, as he explained that he'd been called to an emergency by his granny who was staying in the hotel. He'd driven all night and in his rush had neglected to bring his wallet. Such an embarrassing situation. Could Andrew suggest any place he could park his car while he ran up to see Granny?

Andrew looked him over. The way the young man in the dinged, disreputable VW dressed supported his story—shorts and sandals with a denim jacket and long hair pulled into a ponytail. Aye, it must be an emergency. Folk who entered these doors did so in high end suits with Calvin Klein ties and matching handkerchiefs peeking from their breast pockets. Andrew rode the bus to work each day, but his supervisor drove and parked in the parking garage beside the hotel. His boss had called in sick this morning, so his parking slot should be available. He doubted anyone would be checking a tired VW parked in that reserved space on the top floor of the parking garage next door. He explained how the young man could find the spot—D-18—and wished him luck, then shooed him out of the drop off circle as an elegant Mercedes pulled in. D-18. He hoped it was a sign. D for David and 18 for his age.

David parked Dad's car, ran his toothbrush around his mouth, pulled up his shirt and applied deodorant, locked the VW, and walked quickly back to the hotel entrance. The slip of paper on which he'd written where to come for his interview was in his shorts pocket, and he unfolded it as he strode into the lobby, moving toward the lifts and pushing UP. He was the only rider heading to the ninth floor, so no one witnessed his turning the wrong way and having to retrace his steps to locate the room. When he knocked, he thought he recognized the female voice that called to come in. He turned the knob and pushed the ornate wooden door with its opulent decorative moulding forward, following it into the room.

The room appeared to be a waiting room. Half a dozen men, most of them roughly his age, were, well, waiting. The pretty blonde girl behind the desk looked terribly busy as she moved back and forth responding to the buzzing intercom, answering the phone, and rifling through the filing cabinet, mostly coming up empty handed. She seemed stressed. He approached her desk and waited for her to turn from the filing cabinet, trying to insert himself into the moment between her one task and the next to tell her who he was. "Yes, thank you. Take a seat." She replied without looking at him, though he caught her eyeing his naked legs as he followed her instructions and moved toward the chairs. Girls were always admiring his legs. Why else would he wear shorts in the frigid temperatures of London in March?

He chose the empty chair halfway between the entrance and the other door off to the right that the girl kept anxiously glancing at. As he settled into the upholstered armchair, he noticed the other men arrayed around the room, each seated with an empty chair between him and his neighbor, each of them dressed carefully in a dark suit, white shirt, and blue narrow-striped tie. Only one deviated from that uniform, and his deviation was barely perceptible: small British flags flocked across his blue tie. David was clearly the outlier among those waiting to be interviewed. The humor in the situation struck him, along with the ridiculousness of his own behavior, driving like a bat out of hell twelve hours to London for a job interview dressed as a beachcomber. Oh well, chalk it up to inexperience. He could relax and observe, which he liked to do anyway.

The intercom buzzed and the girl reported quietly that David Bennie had arrived. To his surprise he half-heard a male voice directing her to send him in. She stood and ushered him to the door on the right, opening it and announcing his name, "David Bennie" before returning to her tripartite responsibilities.

This room was a well-appointed office. Satiny ivory damask drapes just touched the lush, discreetly patterned carpet. Two large tan leather side chairs with a low glass-topped table between them flanked a heavy mahogany desk at which sat an overweight man, past his prime but obviously with the means to enjoy his stage of life. He wore a classy wool blazer with an Oxford emblem on the upper left pocket, a pale blue silk shirt—at least that's what David guessed it was, never having been in the presence of silk shirts before—and pricey-looking leather shoes. The absence of a tie grabbed David's attention. The man leaned across the desk, extending his right arm, a shiny Rolex slipping forward from his shirt sleeve. He must be left handed, David observed.

"Sit down. I'm Christopher Bailey. Happy to meet you. You're a Scot, right? Tell me what experience you have had operating large boats."

David sat across from Mr. Bailey, resting lightly on the chair, expecting this to be a brief and unproductive interview. "Yes, I'm a Scot. I worked on a fishing boat several summers as a lad. I've completed my apprenticeship with British Steel in engineering, but I've not a lot of experience operating large boats. In fact, sir, none at all--yet."

"Are you a drug user?" Mr. Bailey was watching him closely.

"Well, Mr. Bailey, I've used my share of marijuana and, like most of my generation, I've done a bit of cocaine now and then." David was certain that would be it. Clearly, he was not qualified for this position.

"Can you be in Malta by tomorrow night? Any obligations that would keep you from an immediate start?"

David was stunned. "I can be there, though I'll have to scare up the cash to pay for a ticket. No obligations to anyone, other than getting Dad's car back to Aberdeen. What is it you be wanting me to do?"

Christopher Bailey, a man obviously used to getting his way, waved off the question. "Okay, then. You're hired. You'll be working aboard the largest of my yachts, *The Welsh Falcon*, as watch captain. You'll sometimes contribute your engineering know-how to help keep the engine fit and running well. It will bring good pay, more than you've expected, but your pay won't come until you bring the boat back to London. Then you will receive a tidy lump sum. He continued, "Oh, and did I mention that you will be responsible for playing the bagpipes? I'll be joining you on board in several of your port stops, and I'd like to have a piper announce my arrival."

David thought Bailey was kidding, but in the interests of honesty he hastened to assure Mr. Bailey that he was not a piper. Bailey's animated face fell from its cordial smile, and shadows showed up in the cracks and crannies of his face so you could tell he was nearly a pensioner. "No matter, lad. I was just pulling your leg. Sound like a job you can handle?"

"Yes, Sir, but may I ask a question?"

Mr. Bailey cast David a look that might have said he was reconsidering his offer. David kept going. "Why are you hiring me, sir, since I have so little experience?"

Mr. Bailey's smile returned like the sun coming out. The man was quite remarkable, and his confidence and power attracted David.

"Because you're honest, the foundation for a good working relationship in my line of work. Also, because you're a Scot. Do you speak Gaelic?"

David, still mystified but intrigued, nodded.

"There's something about a Gaelic speaker running *The Welsh Falcon* that feels right, don't you think? Yes, this will be good! Then we will see you in Malta, David Bennie, tomorrow evening. Suzie will have an air ticket for you within the half hour." He walked David to the door, instructing Suzie to book a ticket for Mr. David Bennie. Then he turned to the young men in suits arranged around the waiting room—to a man they looked confused and uncomfortable—and told them they could leave. He'd filled the position they had applied for.

David waited for confirmation of his ticket--Aberdeen to Malta, one way--then made his way out of the hotel, grateful that Andrew the doorman was on break but ready, if need be, to attribute his broad grin to Granny's nearly miraculous recovery. He edged Dad's tired VW out of D-18 and let it roll down the ramp on fumes to save gas. Then he located the M25 beltway that encircled the city and exited onto the M1 heading north, leaving a trail of sooty exhaust behind him. He still had no money, but at least he had a job and a plane ticket to Malta. He could add another international location to his "Been There" list.

It was the start of his career at sea.

He'd never taken an international flight before. He shifted his weight from sandal to sandal as he waited to board with the eclectic collection of passengers. There were a few overdressed "mature" women wearing gaudy jewelry and too much makeup discreetly scanning the waiting room. He winked at one to check out his theory that their roaming eyes sought male attention. When she smiled at him too demurely for her age, he smiled back, his theory confirmed. Several "Suits" with slightly greying expensively cut hair, leather briefcases and roller bags bestowed brief, disdainful glances on the others in line, resting their eyes on each just long enough to communicate dismissal, as if to say: You have no value in the scheme of my world. The effect was much like Her Majesty's slow-moving sideways tilt of her hand in the Royal wave. Several younger men, also Suits, talked animatedly about last night's football match, slipping into the conversation where   in the stadium they had seats thanks to their employers' largesse. They probably thought they were veiling their competitiveness, but to David they were as obvious as three-day-old fish. He found them amusing. These were power people, easily identified by their mannerisms and speech patterns. If you didn't recognize their importance, he was certain they would be happy to tell you. David stood out like a defiant third finger. He smiled, recognizing his own power to challenge theirs simply by being himself.

Just last night his sister had phoned from the States for her weekly check-in, and Mam had gone off about what was happening to working people as the rich got richer and more powerful across the world. Trisha told them of the latest craze in the states, a new TV series called *Lifestyles of the Rich and Famous* that was surging in popularity. It was the 1980s, Dad reminded them, and the power of elites was ascendant. You only had to look about to see the re-emergence of the fur coats that no one would wear in the socially concerned 1970s. Dad was on a tear. "The resurgence of unregulated capitalism and the *conspicuous* consumption raging across the Western world is worrying, of course. The rich are in for astounding good times, judging by the victories of conservative politicians like Mrs. Thatcher in 1979, American President Ronald Reagan in early 1981, and West German Chancellor Helmut Kohl in 1982. But a body'd be daft not to notice what's happening in this country with all the slackers living off the dole and not lifting a finger to better their lives!" His face was ruddy with emotion. Of course, he made an exception for his son being on the dole.

Sometimes his parents' knowledge of politics awed David. They were working people, supporters of the Tories, and they paid attention. He listened to them carrying on about the working class leaning on the government for assistance and then wasting the money they got from "our pockets" to purchase knock-offs of Armani suits and Louis Vuitton shoes that cost a thousand pounds, which they found outrageous!

David loved to watch them play off each other's arguments, most recently when Mam's brother Jamie called from Canada the night before David left and had the temerity to criticize Mrs. Thatcher. The pulse in Dad's forehead was pounding like a drum.

"Maggie Thatcher's the best Prime Minister we've had in decades, she is. She'll put the whole country to rights and make all these lazy slackers get off their duffs and get a job!" Dad had said.

"Not all of us working people behave like that," Mam had replied. Mam's face was red and her eyes shot sparks. "You've got an example in your own house of a right hardworking young man who's not been able to locate work."

Uncle Jamie had reminded them that working folk like them couldn't afford to go on like this on international phone calls or they'd have no money for porridge, never mind expensive shoes. They'd all laughed at that and said their quick goodbyes. It was one of the things he loved most about his family, their ability to laugh at themselves even when their political passions were noisily engaged. Ah, he did love them!

The stewardess called for general boarding now. He crammed his canvas duffel bag into the overhead bin before sliding into his window seat. His going off to work for Mr. Bailey, who was obviously a most prosperous man, had pleased his parents, who practiced a kind of deference toward the financially successful. He smiled at the disconnect between their respect for the moneyed class and disrespect for laboring people who weren't laboring. Then, exhausted by two days driving to and from London, he crashed into sleep.

When he arrived in Malta, David went straight to the marina where hundreds of posh yachts were tied up and where his brother had told him he could always find cheap lodging.

There was *The Welsh Falcon* tied up at the pier. There were crewmen from all over the world, it seemed, and all the languages they were speaking reminded him of the Tower of Babel. He located the captain of *The Welsh Falcon* and presented him with his papers, including a note Charles Bailey had brought out to his secretary just before David left his office in London. "Give this to the chief mate," he'd instructed, passing it to David. "He'll take care of you." David's stomach was flip-flopping as he followed the captain onto the boat. He was entering a new world cut off from the family and locations that had nourished him. Too late to reconsider, he thought. He stepped onto the gangplank, the wind whipping his long hair across his face so that for a moment he couldn't see where he was going. Little did he know that he was unwittingly entering the pages of history.

Chapter 2

January 15, 1984: Brian Baker let the hot shower pummel his tired body overlong. He had to think, and this was his most private place to do so. His skin turned red and redder and still he remained there, the fury of the scalding water pounding him into submission, forcing him to focus on serious problem solving.

Brian had rarely been forced to do anything. He was his mother's youngest and only son and resembled her with his dark Greek good looks and charming smile. By contrast Brian's very English father, a don at Cambridge in mathematics, was always serious, like so many in his generation. They had attended the best universities in the U.K., each boasting long lists chiseled into their hallowed walls of those who perished in The Great War and World War II. When you belonged to the generation that just missed being artillery fodder by accident of birth, taking life seriously was a default response.

Not so Brian's generation, Love Children of the Sixties. Many of his classmates had abandoned all responsibility for leadership. They figured what with nuclear weapons, Cold War and genocides, there was little chance human beings would get it right. They might as well party on. If the likelihood of a better tomorrow had burned up in the Blitzkrieg, in Hiroshima and Nagasaki, or in the ovens of Auschwitz and Dachau, they might as well go up in smoke burning tobacco and weed.

Brian's father drew the opposite lesson from the history that had played out across the world during his childhood. He dedicated himself to the Never Again philosophy and worked furiously and silently at it. His wife and children paid the tab for his over-commitment, and each of them resented it and him.

Brian turned the shower tap back to a gentle drizzle. No question about it. He must find a way out of this mess without involving his father.

Or his mother. If he confided in her she would surely tell his father. Mama, like so many immigrant women who follow a foreign husband to his home country, of necessity relinquished her own meaning of "home." Though she spoke the language of her acquired culture fluently, when you came from somewhere else, you could never be confident that you understood the ways of your adopted country. Which intensified your dependence on the relationship that bound you to this new, persistently foreign place. She might resent her sacrifices and Papa's ignorance of them, but she was still dependent on him. Yes, she would tell his father, preparing herself for his disappointment in their son, a disappointment her husband would never speak of. Instead of naming it, Father's disappointment would leak subtly from his eyes and the set of his mouth when the family was together. Disappointment that inaudibly whispered to Brian's mother and her son "you are not one of us."

What should Brian do?

He turned off the taps and reached for the oversized white bath towel, rubbing his hair and wrapping it around him. He sat on the toilet, head in hands determined not to leave this room without a plan.

He had a friend from secondary school, with whom he'd gotten into and out of lots of trouble. Archie had street smarts. He'd been admitted to St. Peters School in York as a charity student, raised by a single mom with few resources. And Archie rose to the occasion brilliantly. He rapidly acquired dirt on each privileged boy in their class and used his inside information to keep them supplying him with marijuana, cash, and other perks beyond his means. Archie was Brian's role model. Brian admired Archie's ability to get what he wanted using an infinite number of devious strategies. He hadn't seen Archie in several years but quite by accident had run into him in a shop on High Street yesterday. Now Brian's brain fastened onto the notion that Archie would know what he should do.

Brian and Archie had formed a special bond at St. Peters, maybe because neither of them gave a damn about what was expected of a St. Peters man. It was liberating not to care, especially when you had a friend watching your back. In the years since graduation, Brian had twice helped Archie out of a scrape with the law, so Archie could be counted on to be discreet and helpful in return now.

Brian dressed and phoned Archie from his room to set up a meeting. Archie suggested they meet at the Bentley Golf Club in Essex for an early lunch, say 11:30, before the regulars started to arrive. Brian dressed in a wine, gold and cream colored cashmere sweater and soft gold wool slacks, topping the combination with a Harris Tweed jacket that subtly combined the three colors. That should look prosperous enough. Appearance is important. Then he left the house and drove to Brentwood, planning what to say to Archie. He stopped at a pay phone en route to the Golf Club and phoned his broker to instruct him to sell his stock in Sinclair Computers. immediately, never mind the loss. He didn't want to risk someone listening in on the extension at the house. Thirty-minutes later he eased his silver Mercedes into the long and winding driveway that led to the Golf Club, parked, and walked up the steps with a confident smile pasted on his face. Archie met him in the lobby, and they shook hands warmly.

The Bentley Golf Club was impressive--lavishly polished woodwork, supersized marble fireplaces, and stags' heads mounted high above the wainscoting. The deep greens and rusts of the décor and the taxidermy trophies defined Modern Manhood. Brian scanned the room looking for nubile young estrogen carriers among the wait staff, distracted now by a sudden urge to exercise his overactive testosterone. Archie threw him an amused look. "Still the same Brian, I see. There will be time for pussy after our conversation, I assure you."

Archie guided him to the left where the Stag Room opened to a wall of windows looking out on the thick grass carpet where men—only men—hit small white balls about. Brian had never had the patience for golf. He was an instant gratification man, which explained his difficulty switching from admiring the short-skirted waitresses to refocusing on why he was here. A pint of ale, crusty bread, and French onion soup thick with Stilton cheese would help. They made catch-up small talk until the food arrived and the wait staff left them alone. Then Brian laid out his predicament.

"My grandfather—my Pappous--left me a tidy fortune about a year ago. I invested almost all of it in Sinclair Computers. Sir Clive Sinclair is a friend of my father and it seemed a wise move. The company's based in Cambridge. It's Britain's leading computer company."

Archie interrupted him. "Their Sinclair Spectrum mass market computer is supposed to have the best color graphics in the business. I plan to get one of their latest Quantum Leap models. 'The first home computer with a 32-bit CPU.'"

"Yes. Everyone wants a Quantum Leap. They announced this week that it will go on sale days ahead of Apple-Macintosh's 32-bit CPU model. Britain's most successful computer company was primed to break new sales records."

"So what's not to like about that? Sounds like you've done well," Archie's wide grin disconcerted Brian. "You're going to be a very rich man, my friend."

Brian looked out the window at the golf course, his eyes out of focus. He drew in a deep breath, then continued, his eyes on his water glass. "Yesterday evening Sir Clive phoned me himself to warn me that there was trouble ahead, serious trouble. He had not planned adequately for the demand the QL was generating. Orders were flooding in and overwhelming their ability to produce enough QLs. He was working around the clock to manufacture more, but it was impossible to train enough workers to fill the immediate demand. The papers are running a story tomorrow about the debacle. What seemed an incredible success story is about to become a nightmare, driving customers to Apple and 'poisoning the well' for our product. Sir Clive told me he expects to lose just about everything. I am one of their biggest single investors and, because I'm a family friend, he wanted me to be forewarned. I've got my broker trying to sell now, but he said the leaks of the story are already producing panic selling of Sinclair stock."

Brian's distress was evident. "Archie, I need a way to recoup. Fast. I can't tell my parents that I've lost almost all the money that Pappous left me. My father must believe that I got out of Sinclair just in time. Which means I must find a way to make up my losses in a hurry. I came to you because I know you have your finger on all the most important pulses."

Later Brian would marvel at how rapidly Archie had processed the situation and arrived at a full-blown solution, using information Brian must have told him about Brian's family when they were teenagers. Spot on Archie summoned the details and spun them into a Plan. Not until much later would Brian understand just how convenient Brian's problem was for Archie and his employer.

"Your father served in the colonial office in Cyprus as a young man, correct?" Archie asked him.

Brian nodded.

"Your mother is a Greek Cypriot whose family are well connected in the eastern Mediterranean, correct?"

Brian nodded again.

Archie leaned back in his chair, fingers folded together in front of his chest. His intelligent eyes studied Brian, and Brian felt like he was sitting the toughest of exams.

"First: The most profitable business today is drugs. The network is international and opportunities for making major money abound. The best cannabis in the world these days comes to Europe from Lebanon. Lebanese Gold, they call it. Cyprus is just across a small channel from Lebanon. But I don't have to tell you that. A smart person with connections in that area who knows what they are doing can make a killing in a very short time."

A golf ball slammed against the brick wall to their right with a muffled whack, just missing the window. They both startled and shifted their focus to the young caddy coming to collect the ball. Then Archie continued.

"Second: Britain is ripe for picking. We're way behind America. In the past year transnational gangs in the U.S. have set up a very sophisticated distribution system. They have gangs in every city west to east, and drug use in the States is skyrocketing, while here in merrie olde England our young pine for pot more than they do for pints." Archie smiled at his clever alliteration. He still exercised the charm of a young Bad Boy.

"Our market is barely tapped, and it's primed to take off." He paused too long, then continued. "East of here the Docklands of Essex are experiencing hard times, 16,000 young men out of work and ready to do anything that pays. There's a natural workforce here and a natural center for importing and distributing the stuff. We're only 47 miles from London and a hop across the Channel to Amsterdam, Brussels, Paris, and access to all of Europe. So far Customs hasn't wised up to the opportunities that urban blight and growing poverty in Essex provide for drug smuggling." Archie was gleeful as he seemed to devise a plan on the spot. He had always loved a challenge, especially one that let him thumb his nose at convention--and dabble in sketchy activity that verged on criminality.

"You need two things: A legitimate business close to the Docklands where the 'product' can be stored, and from where it can be distributed throughout the U.K. and Europe. And you need yachts. They can be quite disreputable— you don't want them attracting attention. You make the contact with your suppliers, pick up the product, and your yachts transport the product to the market—Essex. From there distributors take over getting it out to buyers."

Brian's mind had begun reeling during Archie's first point. He grabbed a napkin, never mind that it was linen, and his fountain pen scratched against the warp and bled into the cloth as he scribbled notes. Archie waited for him to catch up, waving a male waiter to the table for a cappuccino and ordering lemon posset for them both. The waiter returned, gliding across the plaid carpet like he was on wheels, depositing the coffees and possets, and gracefully exiting. He could probably tell that Archie did not want to be disturbed, for which Archie was certain to reward him with a handsome tip.

"Look around you, Brian." Archie resumed. "What do you see?"

"A club where the rich and powerful meet up?" Brian was stretching his brain to guess where Archie was going with this.

"Okay. An elite members-only club between the Docklands and the world's biggest financial center, which is also the hub for the U.K.'s highways. A legitimate business….And you, my half-Cypriot friend, have contacts in the region that produces Lebanon Gold, the latest jewel of the illegal drug trade. The possibilities are endless." Archie leaned back in his captain's chair so that it balanced on its two back legs. Brian felt a spasm of anxiety, anxiety that Archie—or he himself?—might fall. But the chair remained inexplicably stable. Brian's grandfather might have said it was a sign.

"You asked for my best problem solving, my friend, and I gave it to you. The rest is up to you. You can take it or leave it."

"But I have no idea how to start such a 'business.'" Brian heard the fear in his own voice and cursed himself for never rising to Archie's level of daring, always being the "me, too" in their relationship. He got himself together, summoned the confident exterior that those who grow up with wealth and position suckle with their mothers' milk, and attempted a parry move to even the odds between them. "Are you wanting to go into this business with me?"

Instead of deflating, Archie smiled larger than ever, as though he was just waiting for this invitation. "I'm already heavily invested in Bentley and I have friends who are regulars here who we could lean on for protection should Maggie's War on Drugs start sniffing around. I can help you make the Lebanon/Cyprus contacts, and together we'll tap some hungry men in the Docklands. What do you say?"

It was late afternoon before they left the Golf Club. Brian's linen napkin had acquired a half dozen contacts scribbled in Archie's barely legible hand, including a chum from Archie's childhood with some experience delivering yachts and who, according to Archie, had once been involved in quasi-legal activity. The January afternoon sky was streaky pink and orange in the west, over London, and pinpricks of yellow sodium streetlights were blinking on across the city. Brian pulled the Mercedes visor down to shield his eyes from the gaudy horizontal light charging across the sky as he headed west on the M25 to the M11 that led him straight north to Cambridge. He felt greatly relieved, at least for the moment. He had a plan and a partner.

Over dinner he told his father that he'd pulled his money out of Sinclair and shifted it to the Bentley Golf Club just in time, feeling wary that Sinclair might have over-hyped the Quantum Leap. Judging by his father's rare smile, his father seemed pleased.

Chapter 3

A month before Archie and Brian's first meeting, on a grey morning in mid-December 1983 in a secret location east of London, five men met in a basement office of what looked like an abandoned stone warehouse. Despite the derelict appearance of the building, the room where they met was posh in a controlled, masculine way. Two large, brown leather couches faced each other across the length of an intricately designed crimson Persian rug. A stout cherry wood desk loomed imposingly between the couches. Opposite the desk at the far end of the rug sat two stolid captain chairs with leather seats framed with bronze brads. There were no cushions on the couches and the desk held only a telephone, intercom, blotter pad, and a bronze cylinder containing a handful of pens and several precisely sharpened pencils. The room exuded minimalism, self-control, and power.

The men were all assigned to a special task force that was having its first meeting in the office of the senior official at Customs and Excise (C&E). In addition to the Customs and Excise official, there was a man representing the British Secret Services, MI-6, and the Chief Inspector for the Chelmsford police. The other two were Americans, one from the U.S. Embassy and the other from the CIA, a.k.a., the Agency.

The host from C&E seated himself at the desk and extracted a notebook and pen from its middle drawer. The others also took seats. The Americans lowered themselves onto the sofas facing each other, leaving the hardwood chairs for the remaining Brits. The man from MI-6 scowled involuntarily at this assumption of privilege. The others missed his subtle change of expression as all eyes were on the taller of the two Americans who cheekily pre-empted their host as he was about to convene the meeting.

"Can you provide some coffee," the American from the Agency announced in an authoritative, peevish voice. It was not a question. The three Brits were put off by his rudeness. Their eyes commiserated: *Typical CIA*. When the host asked the room, "Coffee or tea?" the other two Brits—though they might prefer coffee—responded, "Tea, white, thank you." They would show this American what proper manners were and affirm the superiority of their British traditions.

The host leaned toward his intercom holding down the button for his secretary. "Cecily, can you bring us three white teas and two coffees, please? Thank you." Then he took the lead away from the American, by introducing the official from the American Embassy and the CIA man to the Chelmsford police inspector and the man from British intelligence. He did not supply a name for the CIA man. He invited his fellow Brits to introduce themselves. While they were doing so, Cecily appeared with a tray and made the rounds delivering their hot drinks. She slipped out the door, efficient and invisible.

Introductions completed and business cards exchanged, their Customs and Export host asked the Embassy official to explain why they were gathered.

This American was shorter and more portly than his rude CIA colleague. He was also diplomatic. He smiled broadly and thanked them for leaving their important work to come out on such a damp and chilly morning. "Gentlemen," he began, "we are joined in an operation that will be of great benefit to our respective nations and to Israel, a close ally to both of our governments.

"Let me explain: The United States and UK have two primary foreign policy goals, stopping the expansion of communism and defeating Muslim terrorists. Right now our primary battleground for fighting communists is in Central America, where Sandinistas guerrillas have overthrown the anti-communist government of Nicaragua. The center of Muslim terrorism is Lebanon, where nine months ago the U.S. Embassy was blown up. We lost more intelligence officers in that attack than ever in our history. Three months ago, suicide bombers drove two large trucks loaded with TNT into the U.S. Marine Barracks and the French multinational force barracks in Beirut, killing 241 American servicemen and 58 French soldiers.

Taking his time the man from the American Embassy poured cream into his coffee, picked up his cup, and leaned back, stirring ever so gently before lifting his eyes to his CIA colleague seated across the rug from him who picked up the cue. His speech was more clipped than the man from the Embassy, and he talked like he was in a hurry.

"Lebanon has experienced civil war for the past eight years. Syrians, Israelis, Palestinians, Sunnis, Shi'as, Christian Phalangists, the Lebanese National Army and 43 private armies all are fighting in Lebanon. Israel props up the Christians. Syria and Iran aid the various groups of Muslims. And the Russians support Syria. *Which makes Lebanon pivotal in both the Cold War and our fight against terrorism.* It is in our governments' interest to keep Lebanon *divided*—we don't want consolidation of the various Muslim armies, and we don't want any alliance of Muslims and Christians. Either would endanger our primary ally in the Middle East, Israel."

He continued, "Lebanon is also the primary source of the hashish, or cannabis resin, which has been flooding Britain in recent years. Lebanon's Palestinian guerrilla groups, along with the Syrians, are the source of that hashish. They grow it in the Bekaa Valley and distribute it from Damascus and from Tripoli in northern Lebanon--not to be confused with Tripoli, Libya. Those drug sales fund the Popular Front for the Liberation of Palestine or PFLP, a radical group of Palestinians. These drug sales also fund the Syrian government. It bears repeating that the PFLP is a major promoter of terrorism and Syria is allied with communist Russia."

The CIA man had an annoying habit of pausing after each sentence and surveying the room to see if these foreigners understood him. His colleague from the Embassy made a mental note to caution him to not talk down to the Brits.

Now he stood and began to pace, walking on the outside of the rectangle of furniture. They had to swivel their heads to watch him. Four heads pivoted as one following him around the room.

"Our sources have learned that Lebanon's popular Muslim Prime Minister, Rashid Karami is organizing secret negotiations between the Muslim militias, Palestinian groups, Christian Phalangists and Syria to reach a peace agreement predicated on expelling Israeli troops from Lebanon by next October. A successful peace agreement that requires Israel to leave Lebanon would hurt the interests of both of our governments." He paused, longer this time to let the impact of his statement make its mark on his audience.

"You may or may not be aware that Prime Minister Karami is from a powerful Muslim family, one of the thirty elite families who control Lebanon. His home territory is Tripoli, on the northwest coast of Lebanon, the center of the drug trade. Karami's influence is considerable. He has been prime minister many times and is well known for his independence. He refuses to maintain a private army, though virtually all the other prominent families have them, and he is adamantly against Israel's presence in his country. He has the charisma to be able to pull off such an unprecedented peace agreement.

"Our task is to squash this peace initiative and discredit both Hafez Assad, president of Syria, and Rashid Karami, Prime Minister of Lebanon." The man from MI-6 cleared his throat. The CIA man turned to him and nodded. The Brit picked up the narrative.

"Our assignment is to set up a major drug deal by a group of low-life Brits who will purchase drugs from Palestinian radicals on Karami's turf, off the coast of Tripoli, Lebanon. We orchestrate the capture of the smugglers here in London with lots of bells and whistles and a great deal of press. We'll organize a Hollywood style drug bust that ends Britain's cannabis trade with Lebanon. That loss of revenue will undermine Karami's peace agreement and cut off drug funds to the radical Muslim terrorists and to Syria. I trust you need no more explanation."

Except for the persistent barking of a dog on the street outside, the room was silent.

The Chief Inspector for the Chelmsford police looked at their Customs and Excise host with raised eyebrows. This is above my pay grade, his face said when their eyes met.

"Of course, I don't need to remind you that this is a delicate, top secret project for both of our governments." The MI-6 man made eye contact with each of the other men and then took his seat.

The Chief Inspector from Chelmsford had wondered why he was included in this high level group. Now he thought he understood. His question was still necessary to confirm his assumption. "Am I correct in assuming I am here because you are planning to make this drug bust in my area of Essex? And we will know in advance where the drug smugglers will land in Essex and be there to capture them?"

"You've got it! What's not to like in such a plan?" The CIA man smiled for the first time.

The Chief Inspector wanted to say more. Setting up a group to attempt drug smuggling sounded to him like entrapment, which was illegal in Britain. In the U.S. as well, he believed. But to raise this might make him seem a security risk. Everyone knew laws could be bent when the cause was important enough to those in authority.

"Operation Bishop will be the biggest drug bust ever. You will all be heroes. Karami's peace deal will be impossible after this exposure, and the drug smuggling to Britain from the Bekaa Valley that funds the terrorists will receive too much public attention to survive. No more drug money to Russia's Syrian allies or to the radical Palestinian terrorists, who dominate Bekaa drug production and distribution. And Israel can remain in Lebanon. Lord knows, after the attacks on the U.S. Embassy, on the Marine Corps barracks, and the French forces, we need Israel on that frontline."

"Logistics?" asked the host.

"Obviously we and MI-6 have contacts in Syria and Lebanon collecting info, and there are plenty of not so bright unemployed young men in the Docklands of Essex for our local agent to recruit. The recession has left them desperate for work. They can't have their pints, their weed and their smokes if they're not making any money, right?"

His smile assumed that those in the room were of one mind: The men they would recruit to carry drugs through the Mediterranean to Essex would be local losers whose incarceration would benefit Britain.

"You in Customs and Excise will need to begin now to monitor those recruited, to collect evidence against them so that once they're captured in the act of bringing in the drugs, we will have an airtight case to put them away. We want records on them from now until they deliver their cargo. Understood? Airtight documentation. You will report to our host, who is the point person for Operation Bishop. He will communicate details to you as they develop. Any questions?"

There were none. Four pairs of eyes watched the CIA man stand, nod to the host, and exit the room. The meeting had taken only forty-five minutes.

Chapter 4

K eith pushed open the door to his living room in Chelmsworth, outside of London, and sang out, "I'm home!" His and Janet's four-year-old, Teddy, came barreling through the doorway from the kitchen to tackle him like a Rugby star, his namesake stuffed bear gripped under his right arm like a football. His other arm wrapped Keith's knees in a grip that always surprised his father by its anaconda strength. Keith reached down and lifted the boy, raising him onto his shoulders so that the top of his head barely missed scraping the ceiling of their duplex. Teddy buried his hands in his Dad's thick mottled grey and blonde beard, pulling out the occasional strands of white. It was their daily ritual of connection.

Janet standing in the doorway, wiped her hands on a paper towel and smiled her greeting. She hoped her eyes showed how glad she was to see him. She had not wanted to marry Keith when she discovered she was pregnant, but she did want him in her life and their son's life. Her fierce independence he had misread as rejection, which had led to altercations over the years they'd been together. A week and more ago they'd had some serious conversation, Keith acknowledging that sometimes he didn't feel loved by her and Janet reminding him that when her elder sister's husband left her, while Janet was still in grammar school, and her sister had to go on the dole to put food in her kids' mouths, Janet had promised herself that she would always be prepared to go it alone. Never would she let what her sister went through happen to her. It wasn't that she didn't love Keith. It was just that she had to protect herself—and Teddy—from being too vulnerable to the affection of any man, even this crazy bear of a man whom she deeply loved.

The conversation had helped them both. Since then she intentionally worked at showing him that she loved him.

There was something about Keith tonight that was different, however, and she asked him about it. He suggested they talk after Teddy went down to sleep, and they'd moved on to eat supper and play Chutes and Ladders with the child before story time.

When Teddy's eyelids gave up their struggle to stay open, Keith and Janet moved quietly down the stairs, both avoiding the wheezing step that experience taught them might startle Teddy awake to beg for "just one more book, Mummy." No sound from Teddy's room. They made it to the front room and closed the door to the hall. Keith's face was flushed and glowing. He looked like a big kid with a story he couldn't wait to tell.

Before they settled in, Janet remembered to relay a message from his old friend Archie Avery. Archie and Keith had grown up in the same rundown neighborhood in the worst part of Maldon, just off the docks. Their paths parted when Archie received a scholarship to St. Peters School, but they'd never lost touch. Keith said when your childhood is as rough as theirs was, the ties you make last forever because no one else can understand what you came from. She'd never appreciated that reasoning. Her own childhood was hardly the lovey-dovey tales of children's books, but she didn't say that. Let him hold onto his memories of deprivation. They might motivate him to make Teddy's and their lives better.

Keith sat on the loveseat and threw an arm around her, pulling her to him, hip to hip. She could feel the warmth of his thigh against hers and read his intentions.

"First tell me what has you so wound up". She turned toward him, eyes focused on his face so she wouldn't miss anything. He was one of those people who could with ease and regularity exaggerate—or even lie—a habit he seemed to modify when he felt her closely observing him. She had that kind of power, for which she was grateful.

Keith looked at the wall across from the loveseat, his eyes finding the photos of her parents that hung there in cheap gilded frames from Tesco. Her parents were much younger then but already looked weary. He drew in a long breath that lifted his thick eyebrows and turned to face her, taking her hands in his.

"Archie reached me at the shop. He was calling about a proposal for me to handle a job for a friend of his. It would bring us….wait for it….*fifty thousand pounds*."

Now her eyebrows lifted and her eyes resembled chestnuts, rich brown, round, glossy, and deep, like he could walk through them right into her soul. He was hit with a wave of gratitude that she was in his life, glad that they'd been able to work through the problems that percolated to the surface of their lives without disturbing the roots of their mutual caring. "God, I do love you!" His words embarrassed him, and he turned away to refocus his thoughts. She kept holding and patting his hand. Her eyes never left his face.

"Archie has a friend who's doing business building a trade that will be based here in the Docklands. There will be several boats hauling goods here from the Mediterranean, and he thinks I'm the person to manage the whole operation. It will mean some travel, flying out there to make arrangements with the sellers, selecting the boats for the fleet, hiring crew, sailing the first boatload through the Mediterranean and to Essex. And it will mean finding someone else to tend the dealership from June through mid-October--but if it goes well, they'll probably want me to handle future shipments as well. This could end up making us a very comfortable living."

She was nodding Yes, restraining her usual cautionary first response. "So you're to do the trial run for the business?"

He nodded, smiling.

"What's your cargo?"

Usually he wouldn't lie to her, knowing how she saw through him. Strictly speaking, Archie had not named what he'd be bringing back to Essex. Keith chose his words carefully. "I'm not sure. Maybe small coffee tables and chess sets inlaid with mother of pearl. You know, the kind you were showing me last week in that upscale shop in Colchester. Samples. To see if they sell, I believe." Funny how easy it was to be inventive. Later, she would recall this moment and the odd look on his face as he answered her.

Janet looked across the room, trying to control the mix of excitement and distrust she felt at this unexpected good news. She allowed excitement to displace distrust. She wanted to be encouraging. Keith had enough people in his life who liked to rain on his parades.

"Maybe you can bring a table for me, too? I do really like that Middle Eastern inlaid wood furniture." She was already imagining what they would do with the extra money. Keith's car repair shop had done well enough for him to invest in a car hire business in Chelmsford, just down the street from the car repair shop, but both places were mortgaged, and he certainly had never brought in fifty thousand pounds in a year, much less in three-and-a-half months. She could probably balance teaching with running the shops while he was gone, if she left Teddy with her mum. That extra income might pay off the car hire place, especially if he made more than one run. Still, to her knowledge Keith had only occasionally ferried yachts for people. This sounded a lot more demanding than his past experience, but she decided not to voice her concerns. Instead, she smiled encouragingly.

"I'm glad you're up for this," Keith told her. "I'm to meet up with Archie's friend at the end of the week. They'll be wanting me to make a trip there in a couple of weeks to scout things out." He pulled her to him and hugged her, liking the feel of her nipples against his T-shirt and relishing the warmth of her response. For the moment they set aside further conversation about Keith's pending job opportunity. Something more urgent called.

Chapter 5

By an accident of history Nikolaos Karras was born in Beirut, Lebanon, on February 2, 1958 rather than in Cyprus. His family told and retold the story: How his Cypriot mother, hugely pregnant with him, had been about to answer the front door of the home of the Baker family for whom she worked in Cyprus. How her employer had called her to the kitchen at just that moment: "How long until the moussaka will be done?" How she had returned to the kitchen to reply and then, turning back toward the front hallway, had been lifted off her feet and thrown backward against the kitchen cabinets when something—later identified as a hand grenade— exploded on the doorstep. The force of the explosion demolished the entryway, spewing shards of wood and glass along the hall and into the living room. Thank God she was only bruised, but had she not turned back to the kitchen to respond to the question, or had she moved back into the hall a moment earlier....

She had pulled herself together, holding her heavy belly. The baby was still moving inside her. She could not stop shaking thinking of what could have been. Amidst the turmoil swirling around her—her employer screaming for help and a mix of police and neighbors swarming through the gaping mouth of the house—she knew one thing for certain. She must leave Cyprus as soon as possible. She could not allow the fighting going on in her home city to harm the baby she carried. She would follow her parents, who had left for Beirut, Lebanon, just a week earlier, taking her two young children with them to escape the civil war.

The half-British, half-Cypriot Baker family she and her parents worked for were nice people, which left her conflicted. She believed Cyprus should be independent, but she didn't carry generic anger toward all British people. She pretended sympathy when her employers criticized the EOKA guerrillas and kept her husband's membership in the illegal Greek-Cypriot nationalist army secret. If her baby was, as she hoped he would be, a boy, he would be named Nikolaos, meaning "Victory of the People," in honor of their struggle for independence.

Consequently, two weeks after the explosion that had terrified her, in December 1957, she and her unborn child became refugees of Cyprus's civil war, fleeing her country's war for independence from Britain and leaving her husband behind to fight with the EOKA guerrilla army. They sailed across the strait to Lebanon in a small fishing boat Mr. Baker hired to carry them to safety. She would give birth in a foreign country away from her husband and the land they loved, but her mother and father and her children would be there beside her.

The birth had been difficult, primarily because the baby was so large, ten pounds, and had an especially large head. She had feared it would tear her body apart as she pushed it out. The baby was a boy! Thanks God, she and Nikolaos both survived.

Her husband would join them when the war for independence ended.

Her parents didn't discuss the war or the reports that her husband smuggled out to her. Her parents remained loyal to their British benefactors and prayed for the Baker family, grateful for their assistance in helping her and their grandchild to escape the violence.

Seven months after her escape to Beirut--in July of 1958--civil war spread to Lebanon. U.S. Marines landed in Beirut—the first overt U.S. military action in the Middle East. Fourteen thousand U.S. troops spread out across Beirut. Lebanon's Orthodox Christians welcomed the Americans, fearful of a possible alliance between Muslim Lebanese, Egypt's President Nasser and Syria.i But by the end of the year Lebanese of all religious persuasions settled back into living together, and the U.S. troops departed. Niko, of course, was too young to remember any of this.

When Niko was two he met his father for the first time. The war in Cyprus had ended and Cyprus was independent. Now that Lebanon had settled into a tentative peace, Niko's mother preferred to remain in Beirut with her parents, so her husband moved to Lebanon to join his family.

Life was generally calm for their family for the next fifteen years while Niko grew up. When he graduated secondary school, Niko began working alongside his father in a trawling business.

Cyprus's war for independence had uncorked the genie's bottle. War had blown across the Mediterranean Sea, landing in neighboring countries like airborne seeds of fast-growing weeds, virtually impossible to eradicate.

Niko turned seventeen in 1975, just as Lebanon quite literally exploded into civil war. Israelis, Christian Lebanese, Muslim Lebanese, Druze, Palestinians, and Syrians all fought each other. In Beirut, which had been "the Paris of the Mediterranean," residents huddled in crumbled buildings and besieged embassies for visas to emigrate. Niko's mother was among them, along with her aging parents, three children and husband. They were the lucky ones. They received permission to go to Greece. There, in Rhodes, they started their lives over once again.

The primary thing Niko's mother learned from living through war in Cyprus and Lebanon--the thing she fed baby Niko from the time he nursed at her breasts--was the need to take care of yourself, no matter what it took: There is no one right way in war time. Survival is the only essential. *You must stay alive.*

For Nikolaos that meant getting along with people: Christians and Muslims, colonists and anti-colonists, communists and capitalists, Greeks and Turks. Reject ideologies. Walk with a foot planted in each camp. Make friends on all sides. That is how you survive.

This good Greek Orthodox boy loved to listen to both Christmas music and the Muslim call to prayer. He made friends of Muslims and Christians. And he acquired a working knowledge of Arabic, English, and Turkish. As a young adult working the boats from their home in Rhodes and moving about the water world of the Mediterranean, those linguistic skills made him valuable.

Chapter 6

The old man was preoccupied as he entered his office. One hand ruffled his thin white hair before his fingers began tapping out a tattoo on his desk. Sophia always complained that he fidgeted. Yes, he did, especially when he was focused, and now he was definitely focused, thinking through an idea he had heard in the past hour. He was an entrepreneur and appreciated creative new ideas. He had wanted President Reagan to reward him with Secretary of State for all he did to help Reagan win the election to the presidency in 1980. But instead Reagan had asked the white haired, bespectacled Irish American to become Director of the CIA. At the time it was a major disappointment, but William Casey had a history of turning disappointments into opportunities. Two years into the job, he was in his element expanding covert activities and figuring out how to work under the radar of Congress and the media. His favorite project was the CIA program to overthrow the leftist government of Nicaragua in Central America. His CIA recruited, equipped, and trained "Contras," guerrilla armies in Honduras and Costa Rica, to accomplish this.

Most men in their seventies would be enjoying retirement, but not Bill. He was proud of the fight his agency was making against communists and terrorists across the globe. Sitting at his desk his eyes found the wall map with all the colored pins, each identifying the location of a covert operation--in Central America, Africa, the Middle East, and Southeast Asia, so many damned countries he couldn't remember them all. Afghanistan, Angola, Cambodia, Chad, Ethiopia, Libya, Nicaragua, ...? Covert ops were like war games. Unfortunately, the damned leftists in this country aided by the press were determined to shut down his Contra war against the Nicaraguan government. Hardly a week passed without stories in the press that undermined the Contra operation, stories of air strikes on the airport in

Nicaragua's capital, of destroying oil storage tanks, of mining Nicaragua's harbors. Of course, the *New York Times*, *The Wall Street Journal*, and *Los Angeles Times* were quick to trace these covert actions to the CIA.

Opposition to U.S. government funding of this guerrilla army kept steadily growing, rooted in the churches, including his own beloved Roman Catholic church. They had convinced Congress to make it illegal for the U.S. government to use taxpayer funds "for the purpose of" overthrowing the government of Nicaragua." His spies on Capitol Hill were reporting that Congress was likely to ban all aid that would assist the Contras directly or indirectly by early fall. He paid attention to that intelligence, planned for it, planned ahead. He was already creating an infrastructure to keep his guerrillas fighting communism regardless of what Congress voted as policy. But the young man at today's meeting had presented an interesting possibility for finding additional funds for the Contras. American politicians wouldn't imagine we'd link Iran and its scary Ayatollah, who resembled an Old Testament prophet in his flowing grey beard and flinty, glaring eyes, to the Contras. So preposterous. Might it be feasible just because it was so out of the conventional realm of possibilities?

What he heard today at the meeting of the Special Situation Group had his brain buzzing. The President established the Special Situation Group to come up with creative new ways to counter the dramatic uptick in terrorism. Today one of the Vice President's men had made an audacious proposal: "Why not link the Middle East and Central America, achieve your foreign policy objectives in Central America *with help from the government of Iran*, the #1 promoter of terrorism in the Middle East? *Use Iranian money to fund wars against communists in Central America.* Iran needs weapons for its war with Iraq. Offer Iran an opportunity to purchase weapons from us at a healthy mark-up, secretly, of course. Iranians get the latest military technology, and what they pay us we channel to the Contras without Congress knowing. We may even get Iran to throw in the release of our highest value American hostages. It's the perfect play."

The room had gone totally silent as everyone processed this proposal. It was preposterous and brilliant. Of course, Iran was at the top of the U.S. terrorist list, meaning under U.S. law nothing could be sold to the Iranians. But Britain, our closest ally, had used arms sales to Iran to achieve the release of some of their hostages. *If the Brits arranged weapons sales to Iran, if the U.S. and U.K. worked together, and if secrecy could be maintained... .* If we jack up the price we charge the Iranians for the weapons, our profits provide another way to continue to fund the Contras if or when the feeble-minded Congress prohibits all U.S. government aid to them.

Casey had been intrigued. Predictably, the State Department opposed it. Which meant their staff might leak it to the media if the intelligence agencies pursued it. It was hard enough keeping his own people on board with his expansion of covert programs. Ever since Congress had investigated the CIA in the 1970s, the Agency had been shackled to a set of principles not appropriate for a country fighting communism and terrorism around the globe. So many good agents whose anti-communist, anti-terrorist credentials were second to none, *the real Americans*, had left the Agency, fired or retired. Reformers had "cleaned house," brought in a new officers and analysts. Well, no one would be able to accuse Bill Casey of running a weak and wimpy Agency. Casey's covert operations were so covert that only a hand-picked few intelligence men knew about them. Congress certainly didn't know. He smiled wryly. Well, he would pursue the proposal from the man in the VP's office. Just must ensure only a few people he trusted knew about it.

The following week Casey met with Prime Minister Thatcher's personal secretary. It was a productive meeting. The Brits had previously agreed to supply mercenaries to assist in training the Contras--a public-private sector partnership, not publicly acknowledged, of course. Now the Brits agreed to participate in negotiating arms sales to Iran. The money laundering would be the easiest part with the Bank of Credit and Commerce International (BCCI) in eighty countries affiliated with the biggest banks in the world—Bank of America, Lloyds, Barclays. BCCI could transfer millions in dollars or pounds instantaneously without leaving a trail! Everything was falling into place.

An important part of this geopolitical operation was cutting off drug revenues from Lebanon's Bekaa Valley. Those drug sales paid for terrorist activity against Israel and the West. And according to the director of British intelligence, Brits purchased more Lebanese Gold cannabis resin than anyone other than the Mafia. That minor operation we're running, the drug bust we're setting up outside of London--Operation Bishop?—that will cause the terrorists serious financial losses, disrupt their lucrative drug business, and keep Lebanon in chaos. Prime Minister Rashid Karami's peace talks will have no chance of getting anywhere.

Casey allowed himself a moment of self-satisfaction. No CIA director since Allen Dulles has been more successful, he thought smugly.

Chapter 7

Three weeks after his conversation with Archie at the Bentley Golf Club, Brian Baker flew to Athens and then took a local flight to Rhodes, the Greek island off the coast of Turkey and Syria. With him were Keith Brown, who Archie had recruited to manage the project, and two women, Brian's current "squeeze," Georgina Graves, and Keith's longtime partner, Janet Morris.

On the surface it was a holiday trip to Greece. Brian had secured rooms at a luxurious guest house beside the sea on the outskirts of Rhodes Town, using a credit card Archie supplied. The four spent their mornings on the beach. In the afternoons they split up. The women visited historical sites while the men went off, presumably for a pint of ale. Janet assumed Keith was using some of that time to look for a seaworthy yacht of the right size to replace his boat, *The Sallykins*, for his first import venture. Janet was correct.

Sallykins was a rundown bag of a boat which he'd bought cheap from a man he met on the docks in Essex. He had intended to use *Sallykins* as a "starter" yacht for recreation. However, she was physically challenged, requiring a lot of renovation without any promise of being seaworthy in the end. Now that he'd signed on to import goods from the eastern Mediterranean, he needed a better boat. Pouring more pounds into refurbishing *Sallykins* would not be cost effective. Better to trade her for another vessel. Having gone out on *The Sallykins*, Janet agreed.

Their second day in Rhodes, Keith brought Janet to the marina in Rhodes Town to show her his new purchase, *The Robert Gordon*. Janet commended herself for assuming correctly what Keith had been doing during his afternoons away from her. It was reassuring to discover how well she knew him.

She wanted to board *The Robert Gordon*, but Keith dissuaded her, pointing out that she'd be in the way. He'd hired workmen to service the yacht and they had considerable work to do in a short time. It was best to leave them to it. She thought *The Robert Gordon* looked a mite questionable, not many grades above *Sallykins*, it seemed to her. But she didn't say anything.

Personally, Janet was more comfortable with mediocre vessels. More home-like than the first-class yacht Brian rented for them to take out for a day's excursion around the Lebanese, Syrian and Turkish coasts. They did have a lovely time pretending to be moneyed people, but Brian's lifestyle made her uneasy. She was lower-middle class herself and unused to lavish displays of wealth. To her, such displays put people who had less in a one-down position. Why did the proletariat tend to blame themselves for their lack of material success? Was it because the oligarchs encouraged blaming-the-victim? At least some of us don't get drawn into their narrative, she thought. She knew from her own life that people could work all their lives and not do better than staying abreast of last month's bills.

She kept thinking about the children she taught from lower income areas of Chelmsford. They would never in their lifetimes experience this luxury or see the world from this privileged vantage point. It wasn't fair, and she expressed this to Keith that night as they cuddled on the king size bed in their room on the fancy yacht.

Keith told her to let go of her prejudice against the rich. Just enjoy this getaway. It wasn't like Brian and Georgina would be their new best friends. It was simply a grand adventure for this one time. Anyway, Brian was picking up the tab!

By day four she'd managed to follow his advice and found herself enjoying their leisure jaunt immensely. Her moral inconsistency embarrassed her when she thought about it, so mostly she didn't think about it.

Their five days in Rhodes were lovely. She and Georgina wandered the walled Old City, the oldest inhabited medieval city in Europe. They got lost in its maze of 200 unnamed streets. There were mosques and churches, a Jewish quarter, and an ancient temple to Venus, mute testimony to the adaptability of the people on this island through centuries of military and political occupations by Greeks, Romans, Byzantines, Turks, and Brits. Their last day the women went off to tour Lindos, leaving early in the morning so they could climb its acropolis before the heat set in. The walls built by the Crusaders in the 1300s met them first, enclosing the ancient town with its narrow alleys and whitewashed buildings. No cars in Lindos, only donkeys padding along the cobblestones as though they had not a care in the world. Janet took photos of the donkeys, the sea, the Greek ruins, and the sea birds from atop the acropolis to show her class, and to show Teddy, who was staying with her mum back home.

When their holiday ended and they parted from Brian and Georgina at Heathrow, Janet realized that she'd never caught their surnames. She decided now was not the time to ask. She shook hands with Brian and air-kissed Georgina's right cheek, thanking them for the fun adventure, and turned away. Like Keith had said, Brian and Georgina will not be our new best friends. She promptly forgot them as she saw her small son running toward her wearing an elated grin and holding out a wilted bouquet of carnations in cellophane that his granny had bought for him to bring to the airport. The carnations flopped back and forth keeping time with his short, chubby legs. Even strangers turned to smile at the adorable lad's delight in his mum's return.

Chapter 8

Brian Baker's excursion to Rhodes with Georgina, Keith Brown and Keith's girlfriend Janet left him feeling more confident about this business venture. They'd located a new yacht and arranged for the yacht to be delivered to Majorca, Spain, where they had lined up an acquaintance of Keith to build compartments below deck in the fore section to hold the cargo. Keith would fly to Majorca to oversee the work on the boat. Archie had told Brian that Spain was the best place to organize the operation because Spain had no regulations and a policy of no extradition. If you were deemed suspicious by Her Majesty's Government, you would not have to worry about being deported to the U.K. That's why they made their preparations in Majorca and Palma.

Archie said Customs people referred to the Spanish coast as "Costa del Crime" because so many smuggling operations of all sorts originated there. Archie sounded very knowledgeable about such operations.

As a kind of trial run, Keith and Brian had sailed to the eastern end of the Mediterranean while the women were sightseeing in Rhodes. That was where Keith would eventually pick up the cargo—off the coast of northern Lebanon.

To please his mum and Archie, Brian told Keith, he needed to spend one afternoon while they were in Rhodes with the family who had worked for his parents in Cyprus when Brian had been a toddler. According to Brian's mum, the Karras family, had moved to Rhodes in 1975. The grandparents were no longer living, but Brian's mum had stayed in touch with the mother of the family and urged him to visit them while he was on holiday in Rhodes. "You'll gain perspective on your early years when we lived in Cyprus. Ask her to tell you the story of how she nearly lost her life while employed by us."

The Karras family lived in a fishing village about twenty kilometers northeast of Rhodes, so Brian had hired a taxi one afternoon while Keith was shopping for a replacement yacht.

Mrs. Karras appeared delighted to see grown-up Brian. She ushered him upstairs to the second floor where a terrace extended over the lower part of the house. The view as he entered the terrace caught him by surprise. Shadows flickered across the room teased by sea breezes that rustled the canopy of grape leaves that shaded the terrace. Rows of red geraniums lined up on the balcony sill on two sides of the room. They drew his attention to the vista the terrace opened on, the hillside and the village below, then to the horizon where sky met sea. The scene was saturated with color—red geraniums with their dark green ruffled leaves, flat roofed whitewashed stone cottages bunched together along the hill's narrow stone streets, the greys and greens and purples of the rocky hillside descending to the turquoise sea, and the white triangular sails of fishing boats busily moving in and out of the small harbor. The scene so entranced him that Brian was slow to notice the man seated behind him to his left in a dark blue armchair.

"This is Brian Baker, whose family I worked for in Nicosia," Mrs. Karras was saying to the man. She turned to Brian, "This is my husband. He's recently out of the hospital so I've told him he must rest and let our beautiful portion of this island heal him." Her eyes shone with affection for the man. As she and her husband looked at each other, their connection was unmistakable. Brian felt moved and a bit uncomfortable in the presence of this intimacy.

Mr. and Mrs. Karras treated Brian like their own son, plying him with *baklava*, *melomakarona*, and *bougatsa* that reminded him of the days before Christmas when his granny was still cooking alongside his mum, turning out these same Greek delicacies. They sat on the terrace under the pergola with its profusion of grape vines, while the sun shifted position, alternately concentrating and dispersing the shadows. Mrs. Karras recounted her vivid memory of the explosion that, but for a few seconds, could have killed her and her unborn child in her last days working for Brian's parents in Cyprus. She told the story well, and he listened attentively.

A breeze caught the door to the patio and banged it against the wall, startling them and drawing all eyes to the doorway. There stood a noticeably handsome young man Brian guessed to be in his mid-to-late twenties. "The perfect ending to my story," Mrs. Karras said laughing, "You see before you the other person who experienced that explosion, my son Nikolaos."

Niko shook hands with Brian, kissed both of his parents, and pulled up a chair next to his father. Brian noticed Niko reach for his father's hand and squeeze it before turning his attention to their guest. Brian felt a twinge of jealousy. He and his father never kissed or held hands. Their absence of affection was a sign of the distance between them. Brian had not thought about that before, but here, in the presence of so much caring, he felt acutely what was missing in his own family life. He forced himself to focus on the conversation. Mr. Karras and Niko were talking about boats. Niko operated a trawler but said he was disappointed in its profitability. That caught Brian's attention. Niko arriving at his parents' home just then might be a lucky break.

Or was it Destiny? Brian had hoped to use his family's ties to the Karras family to identify one or two young men who worked boats for a living who might be up for signing on as crew to bring their cargo through the Mediterranean and on to the U.K. And here was Niko with the qualifications he was looking for. Brian's grandfather would say, "Destiny leads him who would follow it." Pappous liked to quote Greek philosophers.

As the conversation continued, Brian learned that Niko spoke some Arabic and Turkish. Having someone on the crew who knew Arabic could be most useful if they had to communicate with the suppliers, although Archie had assured Brian that he would handle all such communications himself. "Best for you not to know some things, my friend," Archie had reminded him.

When he said good-by to Mr. and Mrs. Karras, Niko walked back to the marina with Brian, giving Brian a chance to speak to him about possibly crewing with a British skipper named Keith for the next several months. He offered Niko 20,000 pounds for the trip. He could see Niko was intrigued. It was quite good pay for three months' work. By the time the two men parted, and Brian climbed into the taxi that would return him to the city, Niko had enthusiastically agreed to take the job. They set up a way for Keith to communicate with Niko. Brian said Keith would send him an air ticket to Majorca in the coming week, and Niko would fly there to join the third crewman, a pal of Keith's who hailed from the Docklands but was now making the ports of the Mediterranean his home. Keith, Keith's mate, and Niko would probably complete their crew.

As they said good-by, Brian made it clear to Niko that his own role recruiting Niko must remain a secret; Brian was only helping Keith and didn't want any other involvement. Niko agreed and they shook hands. Apparently, Niko was comfortable operating on a handshake and a promise. Brian's mother had spoken with pride about the integrity of the Greeks, how you could depend on them if they shook your hand. Good. Archie had stressed that Brian should be invisible once this initial "holiday" in Rhodes was over and the staffing arrangements made. He could count on his family's connection with Niko to protect his invisibility.

Late that evening when they rejoined the women, Brian watched Keith telling them about his day. Keith carried himself with confidence and good humor. He seemed bigger than his short and stocky body. Interesting how perceptions distorted things. Archie was another of those men whose oversize personality magnified his size. Maybe if you grew up poor in the Docklands, like Archie and Keith, developing your "hale and hearty" was a survival skill. Brian felt a surge of gratitude for Archie, his confidence and street smarts. Brian knew he could not handle any of this without Archie. The man had balls and smarts. And he certainly had saved Brian's ass.

Archie had known Keith since childhood and had assured Brian that he could trust Keith to manage the operation. Keith seemed to be a good bloke. That he was paying off a car hire business and a car repair shop was an unanticipated bonus. It made him highly motivated to earn a bundle of cash. It also solved the question of how to transport the product once they docked in Essex.

Vans hired from Keith's shop would transport the cargo from where *The Robert Gordon* tied up to the Bentley Golf Club. There it would be stored in the secure, air-tight rooms below ground that Archie had had constructed in the basement of the Club. Keith's repair shop could make alterations to the vans to complicate attempts to trace them. The whole arrangement appeared to him to be coming together quite nicely.

That Keith had personal ties to Archie and Niko had personal ties to Brian's family would ensure they would do as they were instructed and would not betray Brian and Archie, should anything go wrong. And Niko speaking Arabic and Turkish would provide extra insurance when the boat was in Turkish and Lebanese waters. Brian smiled to himself as he watched Keith entertaining the women with more of his stories. There is a certain thrill to this whole business that this rich kid from Cambridge has only experienced through James Bond films, he thought.

On the Tuesday after they returned from Rhodes, Brian pulled into the Golf Club shortly after three. He and Archie had a few details to discuss. They had agreed they would no longer communicate by phone, fax, text, email, or post, only face to face. The War on Drugs declared by U.S. President Richard Nixon eight years ago had spread to the U.K. with a vengeance. The alarmist tabloid press warned that the numbers of Brits using cannabis was escalating rapidly—20,000 convictions for possession last year alone, up by 25% from 1980. The upside of those figures was the potential profitability of this operation. The downside was increased vigilance on both sides of the Atlantic against drug smuggling.

Brian exited his Mercedes and took the steps to the main entrance two at a time. He and Archie were meeting in the newly constructed storeroom below the kitchen where the walls had no ears. They sat, each on a step stool, in the cavernous, gloomy room, and Brian passed Archie his flask of Glenlivet. It always helped to start their conversations with a bit of lubrication.

With Archie he could review his checklist of all the details that needed to be handled before the yacht left Palma in Majorca, Spain for Rhodes and the Lebanon coast. He could also express his anxiety.

"Did you read the story in the Times about U.S. universities being ordered by the government to destroy all of their research files on cannabis? It's true!" Archie was wagging his head back and forth and snorting derisively. "How ridiculous! Even Queen Victoria took the stuff for her monthly female 'distress,' prescribed for her by the Royal physician! What a crock of shit! Parliament blows off the conclusions of the Home Office's Select Committee that cannabis is no more harmful than tobacco or alcohol and instead bans it from any and all medicinal uses. Bloody stupid! But I guess their wacky overreaction plays to our benefit. Illegal substances make for a great return on investment….Now, what details have you taken care of so far?" Archie reached for the flask.

Brian recounted the connections he had made on the trip to Rhodes and how confident he was that Niko and Keith would work out very well. Keith had selected an old mate of his for the other crew member. The man was about to begin reconstructing the cargo hold of the boat that Keith had acquired. Keith knew he'd be provided 100,000 pounds cash upon the arrival of *The Robert Gordon* in Essex. With this he would pay the crew, after the cargo was unloaded and they'd taken the yacht to Amsterdam. "We sailed the area where they will meet the suppliers, but I'm still fuzzy about that part. How do we contact them and who are they?"

Archie smiled. "You're going to remain 'fuzzy.' I keep telling you, the less you and I know, the more deniability. We're leaving those details in the hands of professionals who supply cannabis resin every week to buyers all over the world and know what they're doing. I'll provide the purchase price. And I'll get Keith the number to the safe deposit box in Tartus, Syria just before he meets up with them. He'll pass it on to the suppliers. No cash will change hands directly. I'd prefer doing this in Beirut, but things have been so chaotic there the past two years, what with Israel's raids on the PLO refugee camps in West Beirut, that I can't risk it. Beirut used to be my favorite city in the whole world, but it's starting to resemble London during the Blitz. Unfortunate. However, chaos is beneficial to us."

Brian wasn't sure how, but he decided not to ask. He noticed Archie's reference to "us," but, although he wondered who "us" referred to, he didn't pursue it.

That evening Brian opened his *Evening Standard* to read that the United States had evacuated all of its diplomats, their families and its Embassy staff from Lebanon. The U.S. government took this step in response to the March 16 kidnapping of William Buckley, an American suspected of being the CIA station chief in Beirut. Brian called the Club and left a message for Archie to meet him for breakfast the next morning. He needed to know how this would affect their plans. Archie greeted him, hale and hearty as ever, and they sat at a back table in an empty hole-in-the-wall coffee shop whose heyday, if it ever had one, must have been thirty years ago. They were in the Docklands. Brian had forgotten how derelict the area had become--abandoned storefronts and warehouses, roofs caved in, windows broken and boarded, rutted streets and cracked sidewalks strewn with discarded crisps bags, cigarette packs, used condoms, and empty lager cans. The people on the streets walked with their bodies curled inward against the spring chill. They appeared worn and dilapidated, too, like discards for the charity shop.

Over coffee while waiting for their ham and eggs, Brian asked Archie what Buckley's kidnapping and the American evacuation would mean for their operation.

"Absolutely nothing. Our project will be nowhere near Beirut and neither will our sources. The Americans will be shitting their pants after the bombing of their embassy and marine barracks and now this, but, trust me, that has nothing to do with us. It's best not to go into it. I can assure you it will not affect us." Archie shifted position, sipped more coffee, and altered his facial expression, making it clear that he wanted to change the subject. "How are you and that blonde girl friend of yours getting on these days?"

Brian wondered if there was anything Archie did not know. Archie had never met Georgina. He doubted he had described her to Archie as a blonde. Ever since he first met Archie he'd marveled at what Archie knew. He wished he was as knowledgeable. He obviously exceeded Archie in some ways, mostly due to his parents and the opportunities they'd provided him. But one thing he'd learned from Archie: Privilege is no guarantee of superiority. He trained his attention on one more thing he needed to clear with Archie.

"I thought I'd make another holiday trip, this one to Majorca, just before the start of the operation to be sure it is all under control. Do you see any problem with my doing that?" After losing a considerable amount of money in his first big investment, Brian was uncharacteristically attentive to the details of this operation.

Archie took his time answering. "I think you can go. But I wouldn't meet with Keith. Just talk with him by phone from a phone box. Customs is on the prowl for any suspicious activity. They're working with the Drug Enforcement Agency of the U.S. which is working with the FBI and learning new tricks from them. The U.S. even has a Drug Enforcement regional office in Cyprus now. They're turning up the heat, but we are several steps ahead of them."

For as long as he'd known Archie the man had liked to display how much he knew. Here he was again. What did he mean that "we are several steps ahead of them?"

Archie was dispensing more advice from on high. "You might take a different girlfriend, one who's only interested in a temporary good time, on your 'holiday' to Majorca. You'll like Palma. I think it will soon be a major destination playground for the Rich and Famous—lovely beaches, lovely women, and an autonomous community free from financial regulation by Spain. A good place to do business discreetly and with little oversight—as good as Panama or Delaware in the U.S." Brian set aside his momentary annoyance at Archie's cleverness. The man was looking out for him. And everything seemed well organized. Brian would use his own judgment about which woman to bring with him to Spain. Archie didn't need to know everything.

After breakfast they drove to the Club where Archie showed him the obscure back entrance to the newly constructed storage area and explained that no staff would be around when the cannabis was brought here. He'd had the doors sealed with rubber flaps to ensure the smell would remain here below ground. With the kitchen directly above, the only smells that would reach diners in the Stag Room and other eateries of the Club would be of tasty concoctions by their new chef who, he confided with a wink, was himself from Lebanon.

Brian drove back to Cambridge hugely relieved. It was going to come together, he was certain of it. Whatever Archie had a hand in turned to gold. Always had. He couldn't be happier about his new legitimate business as a silent partner with Archie in The Bentley Golf Club. He hadn't needed Archie to suggest that he hang out there, chatting up the regulars and cultivating his image as a charming, wealthy young man, son of a Cambridge don. What's not to like in spending his time that way?

Chapter 9

The plainclothes officer leaned against the glass walls of the International Departures terminal at Heathrow, observing the motley crowd packing the queue to go through security and reach the gates. It was July 15th and hot in London.

There were elderly couples, stooped and leaning on canes, anxious young mothers pulling roller bags with one hand and holding onto their youngest child with the other, handsome women professionals wearing purposeful expressions, business people of both genders in conservative suits and shiny shoes, and long haired teens and twenties toting enormous backpacks from which aluminum cups and the telescoped poles of their pup tents rattled and clattered. The officer smiled to himself, eyes scanning the crowd and then moving back to settle on one person or two he intuitively sensed merited closer examination. Anyone watching him might have said his eyes moved like the sea, forward and back, up close and far away, up close and far away again.

He liked his work. He was a "good guy" fighting Evil and getting to do it mostly by observing people. That was something he'd done well throughout his life. As a child he paid attention to his parents' behavior, watching for Mum's anxious face and detecting when he needed to get her out of the room because Dad had had too much to drink and was on the edge of belligerence. Professional close observation like this did not disturb his gut the way his childhood sleuthing had. He made a game out of it, making mental checklists of what would be the best disguises for people engaged in illegal activity.

Take that dark eyed, dark haired, handsome gentleman with the gorgeous blonde hanging onto his arm, touching him frequently and turning to give him her full attention whenever he spoke. The woman's long hair bounced, full of light, when she turned her head, and her face broke into a full, toothy smile so effervescent that you had to smile back. The young man granted her only minimal attention. His ego hovered like an aura around him, overpowering even the charms of his escort. Interesting, that.

For a moment the officer was distracted by a short, feisty gentleman wearing plaid shorts and a polo shirt, a man probably in his late fifties and probably prosperous, judging by the finely tooled leather shoulder satchel he carried, the gold that flashed from his necklace, and the large onyx and lapis rings he wore. He was arguing loudly with a flight attendant, insisting that the second bag waiting beside him on the floor—larger but also of lavishly tooled leather—must go with him as a carry-on. No, this man was too obvious, called too much attention to himself to be suspect.

When he looked back, the young couple were gone. He scanned the queue and found them up ahead waiting in front of the Royal Jordanian Airlines counter. He sauntered to the counter, hovering within ear shot despite the clucking of tongues and sighs from those whose queue he had jumped. When he heard the attendant say, "You are all set for your flight to Larnaca, Mr. Baker," he left the queue and melted into the crowd waiting in the seating area. After making notes in the spiral notebook he kept in his left breast pocket, he moved to the gate area for Royal Jordanian Air Flight 2666 to Larnaca, Cyprus.

Customs monitored flights to and from Spain, Lebanon, and Greece. Those countries were natural centers of illegal activity because they imposed little regulation on the movement of goods. That facilitated the flow of drugs from the eastern Mediterranean to the U.K. and Europe.

Showing his badge discreetly to the flight attendant staffing the gate, the Customs and Excise officer ascertained the names of the handsome young couple before intuition told him they were approaching. He melted back into the cluster of passengers waiting to board the bus that would take them to their plane. No one noticed him slip away.

That afternoon back in his office, he ran a check on Brian Baker. No convictions and only one arrest, for drunken driving when he was eighteen. Still, he'd keep an eye on the man. His intuition was usually right.

He liked his job. Customs and Excise rewarded its agents when they captured smuggled goods—up to 40 pounds in a merit bonus for each apprehension. That was a good amount of money. He knew some of his unscrupulous peers would divide what contraband they found into three or four batches and claim each batch as a separate apprehension to earn forty pounds for each—a bonus of 120-160 pounds —but not him. He appreciated the job's other rewards, like the relationships you developed with contacts at the airports and at the seaside, the people who reported to you unusual activity they observed. Even some of the skippers became extra eyes and ears.

His assignment for the past two years was drug interdiction. All the oversight agencies talked to each other: immigration, intelligence, police, Customs and Excise. With drug smuggling bringing in massive money, sometimes even the top intelligence agencies, MI-5, MI-6, and the Foreign Office, got involved. The ingenuity of the smugglers fascinated him. It was no game for amateurs, that's certain.

Part 2 - The Transfer

Chapter 10

Brian had altered his plan to go to Majorca. Since he would only be speaking with Keith by phone, he could as easily do that from Cyprus, so he traveled to Larnaca, Cyprus, instead. Georgina went with him. Archie didn't need to know.

On this summer afternoon he strolled the Foinikoudes promenade along the southern end of the island away from the medieval castle they called Fort Larnaca. In his crisp Dockers and Calvin Klein polo shirt topped with a New York Yankees baseball cap he looked the quintessential privileged American tourist, which was the look he wanted. That was why he'd taken Georgina sightseeing all morning—Saint Lazarus Church and the Pierides Museum as well as the craft shops where she'd made many purchases. When she begged off more walking in the heat, he'd flagged a taxi to take her back to the hotel.

Feeling sentimental, he decided to try to locate the villa his parents had lived in when he was too young to remember much. They'd left Cyprus in 1958, shortly after the explosion at the front of their house, to return to Britain. His dad's homeland was a safer island. His parents had planned a family trip back here to visit their old haunts as a reward for Brian graduating from St. Peters--which they all had feared he might never accomplish--but the Turkish invasion of Cyprus had forced them to cancel that plan. All these years later here he was trying to locate his first home. As he walked the seaside promenade and looked up the streets that grew inland, some things felt vaguely familiar: The tall palm trees lining the boulevard, the paper-thin blossoms of bougainvillea spilling shocking pinks and purples everywhere, the feel of the heat at midday, the sun burrowing into his shoulders. He recalled a young woman who had been vaguely important to his three-year-old self. He wondered if she might have been Niko's mother, Mrs. Karras, the woman he had spent a lovely afternoon with in Rhodes.

It was perhaps a bad idea to depart from his tourist charade. Perhaps it would be better to return to Fort Larnaca and find a phone booth there to call Keith. But memory pulled him on. Yes, he recognized this place. In fact, there was his street. He turned and walked toward #26. Inside the decorative wrought iron fence, set back from the road, stood the square, two-story home with a flat roof. A tiled swimming pool was barely visible in the rear. The house was blazing white where the sun reached its stucco walls, and clusters of ancient palm trees moved not at all in the stillness of the muggy afternoon. The place looked smaller than he remembered. No sign of life. His anticipation deflated. He was disappointed that he felt no sentimentality about this house, this yard, only regret that whatever he had known as a young child living here was not available to him, not now and probably never. He shook off his melancholy, turned away, and jogged back to the promenade, retracing his steps back to Fort Larnaca. His watch told him he would be a bit late for the appointed call to Keith.

A phone booth leaned against the café attached to the Fort, its paint faded and blistered. He collected his Cypriot coins before entering it, pulled out of his pocket a dog-eared slip of paper, and dialed. Keith picked up on the second ring. Their conversation was pedestrian and formulaic:

"How are things?"

"Well."

"The kids?"

"All three are ready for their holiday. Going sailing end of July."

"Travel safely."

"Pricier than I expected here. Nearly done working on the new property."

"Maybe Grandma and I can help out. Ring us up when you get home."

"Will do."

"Regards to Cousin Martin."

"Bye."

"Cheers."

Translation: *The Robert Gordon* was costing more than anticipated and Keith needed money. They would leave for Rhodes probably the last week in July. "Cousin Martin" identified Chelmsford as the drop off point. That nothing followed "Cousin Martin" meant postal code CM0 Burnham-on-Crouch, which, decoded, identified the first digits of the phone number Keith was to call on arrival. "Ring us up" provided the remaining digits.

Brian hung up. He bought a coffee from the café and had a look at the part of the Fort where they'd executed people when it had been used as a prison. Then he hailed a taxi back to the hotel.

He was cool. All would be well.

Chapter 11

Keith had made notes on his conversation with Brian. He went over them now, leaning against the concrete barrier that marked the entrance to the Palma marina. He'd told Brian they would be ready to sail in a couple of weeks, by late July, and Brian had confirmed where they would deliver their cargo: Chelmsford, River Crouch, off-loading at CM0, the Chelmsford postal code, and calling the coded phone number from the marina there.

When he was in Rhodes with Janet, Brian, and Brian's girlfriend, an anonymous man had come up to him at a pub on the marina and slipped him an envelope with the cash he would need to trade his boat *Sallykins* for *The Robert Gordon*. The same man gave Keith a key he was to pass to the supplier. Brian told Keith the supplier would know where the safe deposit box was that the key fit. There would be no handling of cash. It was safer that way. Lord, he couldn't even imagine how much cash would be exchanged for a yacht full of cannabis resin!

He had followed Brian's instructions, traded his boat for the more seaworthy *The Robert Gordon*, and his crew were properly refitting it now to receive its cargo. He needed only to take on a cook in Rhodes, someone who would not participate in the transfer of cargo or know anything about it. The fewer people who knew the better, and the more money for the three of them.

The refitting was coming along well, and Keith's two crew members seemed sound and reliable. They stayed to themselves, but they tolerated each other, which meant they wouldn't gang up on him. He felt confident of that.

Niko Karras was familiar with the area off Tripoli and spoke—or understood—Arabic. Brian had assured Keith that Niko could be counted on because of Niko's connection to Brian's family. Keith's mate, Tom Hill, was a school dropout, but Keith had known him for years and trusted Tom's long experience maintaining boats and sailing the eastern Mediterranean. Both men clearly wanted the work. When he'd told Niko and Tom that they'd receive twenty and twenty-five thousand pounds, respectively, for this trip, the prospect of that much money overrode any questions they might have asked about the operation. He'd never spoken with them together, just in one-on-one conversations, and he'd left it to their imagination what kind of cargo would net that size of a reward. Better all the way around that way.

He could hardly believe his luck to have happened onto such a sweet deal. Him, Keith Brown, an average bloke from a third-rate area who'd barely made it through school. But his fortune had changed since he met Janet. He blessed her and sweet Lady Luck for that.

All right, then. They would sail *The Robert Gordon* back to Rhodes. On the night before they would leave for the waters off Tripoli, he would call the number Brian had supplied--the signal. And they would sail from Greece into those Lebanese international waters and wait there for contact to be made by the supplier. He wasn't sure how the suppliers would locate them. Brian had assured Keith he didn't need to know. It was all arranged. Keith had only to turn on the prow, port and starboard lights briefly at the set time the night before and the night of the transfer.

Keith tucked the Chelmsford phone number with the key into his waterproof zippered wallet and stretched, leaning back to feel the sun penetrate his chest and tighten the permanently rough and ruddy surface of his face. Majorca was a beautiful island. Just off Spain's Mediterranean coast, it basked in sunshine and quiet. With the money he would clear from this haul, perhaps he could bring Janet and Teddy here for Christmas holiday. He could hear Janet's voice cautioning him to pay off the car dealership first. His gut tightened thinking of her. He'd come to depend on Janet, though in this case he had not let her in on the full story. Wanted to protect her. Nevertheless, he wished he'd vetted the plan with her. She was a good one for thinking through details and solving problems. He wanted her to be able to depend on him. Could she?

He shook off the question, dismissing the times in the past when he'd been away sailing and given in to his need for a fuck. They were a good pair, solid as steel. He stood, turned right and walked along the Palma Marina, taking in the yachts lined up in their berths like greyhounds ready to race. His boat was up ahead, dry docked, and he could hear Tom hammering. Okay, then, bring it on, he said to himself.

Chapter 12

It had been a month since Niko had received a one-way plane ticket to Palma, the port city on the island of Majorca, off the east coast of Spain. He'd flown there to work on Keith's yacht, *The Robert Gordon*, joining Tom Hill, the first mate and carpenter. They were tasked with rebuilding *The Robert Gordon* from the inside out, reinforcing the hold and building storage compartments in the forward half, below deck. Keith's instructions were to refit the new yacht as rapidly as possible, aiming at leaving Majorca by late July. Then Keith, Niko and Tom would sail *The Robert Gordon* back to Rhodes, their point of departure for picking up their cargo at the eastern end of the Mediterranean. Niko had hoped to see his family while they were there, but Keith said there wouldn't be time for that.

The first mate, Tom, rarely spoke, just enough to grunt instructions to Niko with his gravelly smoker's voice and thick Cockney accent. However, he seemed competent enough as a carpenter. Judging by the way he rebuilt the cargo storage areas, *The Robert Gordon* appeared greatly improved. But Niko did not entirely trust him. Tom had the mannerisms of a person with a past to hide, nervous, even agitated at times, his fingers and his right leg always moving. Niko feared the first mate might have a criminal background. But Tom was Keith's friend. And Keith was their skipper. Niko kept his concern to himself.

Niko remembered his father's distrust of the British he had fought against as a young man in Cyprus. His father had passed that deep rooted distrust to his son. Niko found it hard to feel at ease being the only non-Brit on the crew.

Keith had asked Niko to sign on for the duration of this journey—5,000 miles. They would take the *The Robert Gordon* to Rhodes, from there to Lebanon, then back through the Mediterranean, around the Iberian peninsula, through the Bay of Biscayne and the English Channel to the U.K., and end up in Amsterdam. The whole operation seemed a bit odd to Niko, but the money was good, so he hadn't asked questions. He needed the money. His father had worked the boats all his life, but physically couldn't do it any longer. The Greek economy was experiencing another of its cyclical recessions and wages for trawling were decreasing while the price of basic necessities like food kept rising. Yes, his family definitely needed the money.

Apparently, Tom did, too, although Tom never spoke of having a family.

Tom had a piece of official looking paper saying he was a radiographer, which Keith made certain to tell Niko. Neither Keith nor Niko had that training. But the longer Niko was around Tom, the more he wondered how legitimate Tom's paperwork was.

The man seemed barely literate. Sure, he scribbled numbers down when he measured cuts for his carpentry, but when they were in port and went to a pub, Tom would ask Niko to order for him, even when the menu was in English. Everyone who worked the ports knew that you could get the required certificate proving your qualifications by passing cash under the table in half a dozen ports—including Panama, Liberia, and Cyprus. Tom probably finagled that certificate in Cyprus. Tom had mentioned that Cyprus was the place he used as his "permanent" home. Well, Tom may not have legitimate credentials, but he did seem to be able to use the radio. As long as the man could do the numbers off the radio, Niko guessed they could work together. Still, Niko was not comfortable around him. Too rough. But he would make it work.

It was the last week in July when Tom and Niko finished refitting *The Robert Gordon*. By then Niko had mostly let go of his unease around Tom. Proximity over time produces tolerance, his father used to say. It also helped that Keith had joined them. The man was jolly, one of those people who you instinctively like, though you may have second thoughts. On a warm summer morning the three of them set sail from Majorca, stopping at Malta, then on to Rhodes. There Keith went ashore to "conduct some business" and returned with a short, peppy girl, not particularly good looking, but a person who looked you straight on and whose eyes smiled. Niko liked that.

Keith said she was called Sally and would be their cook. When Tom mumbled a question about what experience she had cooking for a crew, she said she loved to eat and to cook and, from the looks of the galley, she'd be a vast improvement over what they'd been managing to produce. She was no nonsense. She had run a bar and had lots of experience in the kitchen. She wouldn't be intimidated. She smiled all the time she was standing up to Tom.

Sally was short and a bit chubby, a wholesome looking girl, and nice enough. Her presence on board made Niko more comfortable. She was friendly, talkative, and a damn good cook. Best of all, during her year running a bar in Rhodes, she had mastered the art of Greek cooking. She said it was in her genes. Her father was Greek. They'd talked the night she made moussaka, and Niko felt more relaxed after that. Now they were a crew of four—Keith the Captain, Tom the first mate and chief engineer, Niko second mate, and Sally the chef.

Niko and Sally hung out together when Niko was not on watch. Sally asked him to help her improve her very rudimentary Greek. If Keith and Tom were chums, Niko and Sally were on their way to that sort of relationship. Nothing romantic, of course. Niko was twenty-seven and Sally a half-a-decade younger. In fact, he protected her, like an older brother.

The boat's forward cabins were reserved for cargo and locked, leaving only three cabins for the crew of four. Keith's solution was to assign Sally to a bunk in the large captain's cabin with him. Niko's face gave away his disapproval of this arrangement, but Sally only laughed at his concern. "Lighten up, man. I'm a big girl. I can take care of myself, but there won't be no need to do so." She'd winked at him when she said that, then added, "Some days I wish there was a need, but blokes all tell me they respect me too much to take advantage. I'll probably be in me eighties and men will be telling me that!" He liked her sense of humor.

Sally had brought along a cassette player that operated on battery and kept the saloon filled with music while she cooked. Her addition to the crew raised their spirits. Keith and Niko could interact with her more easily than with each other. And Tom? Well, he stayed mostly to himself, whistling under his breath tunelessly. Niko suspected the whistling was his way to avoid conversation.

In Rhodes, Keith gave Sally three days of shore leave, a long weekend, telling her the men were going to sail to some of the other Greek islands for a "bit of diversion." He teased that her beautiful smile would only deter the Greek lassies who'd be flocking to the boat to court the men. He'd winked and grinned. She returned the grin with a comment about "all you randy sailors."

In fact, while Sally began an extended weekend off in Rhodes, *The Robert Gordon* was sailing from Rhodes for Tripoli, Lebanon, to pick up its cargo. Sally was not to know that.

Chapter 13

Two days before they were to reconnoiter with the suppliers, in the international waters off northern Lebanon, Keith and Niko were sharing watch duty on *The Robert Gordon*. It was late and Tom had already gone to his cabin.

Keith stood in the prow looking at the dark water swirling below them. He was assessing its power to drive them off course. Niko, behind him, was pacing, trying to walk off his discomfort. The sound of the soft, rhythmic slap of Niko's sandals on the deck bothered Keith. Then in a low voice Niko started talking about what he called the "out of control violence" engulfing Lebanon. It was their first real conversation. Keith's attention switched suddenly from the dark water to the intensity in Niko's voice. He did not turn around, but he was listening carefully.

Niko confessed that he was worried. This venture they were on might be really dangerous right now. Keith tried to recall what he'd read in the papers or heard on the radio that would alarm Niko. To be honest, he wasn't one to pay much attention to the news. That was Janet's role in their household.

"Are you referring to the American Embassy in Beirut being blown up last year?"

"That and a bunch of other things," Niko replied, "My father said the embassy explosion was heard ten miles away. More than sixty people killed. Six months later they drove a truck bomb into the U.S. Marine Corps barracks, detonated it and killed 241 soldiers."

Niko couldn't see Keith's face under the densely clouded sky. He could hear Keith's footfalls on the deck. They were both pacing now, like panthers, facing each other, heads lowered and swinging around when they reached the railing. He sensed Keith glancing over at him every few steps.

Keith had not anticipated Niko's anxiety. They all needed to be committed to this project.

Niko's words unsettled the night. "These Islamic Jihad guys know what they're doing. They've got kidnapping down to an art—they grabbed a department head at American University Beirut last February, the bureau chief of Cable News Network in March and a week later the CIA's top person in Lebanon—I think they call him their Station Chief. The CIA man was a pro's pro but they kidnapped him in the parking garage under his luxury apartment complex! Poor guy is probably being tortured right now, if he's still alive."

Niko clearly did pay attention to politics in Lebanon. "The Islamic Jihad says they'll keep on until there are no Americans in Lebanon."

"At least we're not Americans," Keith joked. It was a lame joke. He felt stupid hearing Niko talk. Niko obviously knew a lot more than he did about this. As the senior person in charge, Keith needed to understand what they were getting themselves involved in. *Why hadn't they had this conversation earlier?*

"Why do they hate Americans?" He felt exposed and embarrassed for asking. It was a question he shouldn't have to ask his second mate.

Niko looked out at the sea. Keith couldn't see his expression in the darkness. "You heard about what Israel did to the refugees in the camps outside of Beirut two years ago, right? The Israelis with their Lebanese Christian allies attacked Sabra and Shatila camps for forty hours, bombing them. Killed 800 people, whole families of Palestinians. The BBC called it the worst civilian atrocity in the Middle East. My family are Christians. We're not keen on the Palestinians, who my grandpa blamed for the crazy violence in Lebanon that forced him to move to Greece. But those were families…" Keith could see Niko's shadowy head slowly swivel back and forth.

"Israel had no right to invade Lebanon--Lebanon is a sovereign nation. No right to kill all those people. Israel couldn't have done that without its biggest supporter, the United States, giving them weapons and aircraft and, probably, the go-ahead. So Israel and its allies in Lebanon murder all those civilians and everyone in the Middle East knows the United States was either behind it or at least looked the other way. The U.S. even opposed criticism of Israel's action at the U.N...."

The air was not moving. Its dampness was a weight that hung on Keith. He wanted Niko to stop talking, but he didn't.

"I lived in Beirut through secondary school. Some of my friends there say that CIA guy who was kidnapped, he was working with Mossad, Israel's intelligence service. They say the CIA and Mossad were organizing an attack on Lebanon by U.S. Green Berets and Israeli troops. I don't know what I believe, Keith, but I have heard a lot of disturbing stuff. With all that's happening, it makes me nervous that we are meeting 'suppliers' off the coast of Lebanon. I mean, who are these guys we're working with? Won't the CIA and MI-6 be monitoring any activity in that area? I read in the newspaper that Israel was boarding all the ships off Lebanon's coast. Will we be boarded? And if we're not, why not?"

A shiver traveled down Keith's body from his forehead to his heels. What the hell are we doing? He felt dizzy with terror. "I don't know, Niko. I just know that we are too far into this to back out now. We have to go through with it."

There passed a long, awkward silence. Then Keith moved to Niko. He put his hands on Niko's upper arms and turned him so they were face to face. "You're not bailing on me, are you?"

Niko shook his head. "I'm just worried."

They could hear Tom, shuffling up the stairs to replace Niko on watch duty. That ended their conversation.

The next morning they returned to the marina in Cyprus and Keith went ashore early to a rundown pub a mile from the harbor. From a phone booth outside, he called the number he had been given. When a man with what Keith thought was a South African accent picked up, Keith, following his script, asked if he'd had a good night, enunciating clearly into the receiver. "Na'am," was the response and Keith clicked off. It was the signal. His heart was pounding.

That evening, Saturday, August 25, only the barest sliver of a moon punctured the darkness.

Now and again, it slipped out from behind the thick cloud cover like a child playing peekaboo. They expected to meet up with the suppliers off the coast of Lebanon at three a.m. the following night. Tonight's run would notify the suppliers where they would be waiting twenty-four hours later. By then there would be no moon. If they didn't show up, there would be one more night before the moon's girth would provide too much illumination to transfer the cargo without being detected.

They followed the Rules to Avoid Collision that had been in place nearly one hundred years. When they reached the pre-established location, they lay down anchor. They lit the white light on the prow and the red and green on the port and starboard sides for one minute only. The suppliers were to identify their location by this sign. Then almost total darkness descended. They remained for an hour and a half, then turned the ship back toward Cypress, not using the radio or lights until they were about a mile away from the marina.

The following evening mist further complicated visibility. They left the harbor at seven in the evening, as though they were heading out for a night of fishing. They lowered the anchor and sat in a random location for too many hours. Then they sailed toward the Lebanese coast. No problem with the darkness. The cloud cover obscured even the brightest star, and, without a moon, they could barely distinguish their own hands, much less other boats.

About midnight a small turboprop plane flew under the cloud cover above them. It wheeled south, flying along the coast of Israel, as best they could make out. Keith said it was one of the new Cessna 208 Caravans just out this year. Why would it be out in this weather? No one had an answer.

A couple of hours later they pulled up anchor and began moving toward their rendezvous point.

Chapter 14

The tension in the air weighed them down as they neared their place of contact. The summer night was warm and clammy, and Niko felt he was swimming in a giant mug of coffee, only the mug was turned upside down. He was trapped under the mug in the black liquid. It brought to mind a conversation he had had with his father.

His father had been trapped in his body since his heart attack, his blood vessels unable to carry enough blood around his body. He had described to Niko how he felt, "It's like I'm trying to swim in a thick, opaque sea with no idea where the shore is, feeling disoriented and so very tired." If there was one good thing from this night, it was that he could imagine what his father experienced every day. His eyes glazed thinking about the man and how strongly they were bonded. What would his father think of his son's involvement in drug trafficking? Niko suspected he would not approve. The family's need for income would not excuse participation in criminal activity.

A noise drew his attention now. A light sound like the scrambling of a hundred rats across the deck. Before them stood a group of fifteen or more gunmen carrying M-16s, Kalashnikovs and rocket launchers, all wearing black rain hoodies, pulled low to obscure their faces. The one in charge was speaking to Keith, and Keith was looking at him blankly. The man in charge turned to the others. Niko heard him tell them in Arabic that these sons of bitches wouldn't know their own asses needed wiping. Low grunts rippled through the group. Niko stepped forward whispering to Keith that he needed to act with confidence, show them the storage rooms in the cargo hold where the packages should be placed. Keith moved toward the men, and they moved to surround him. He must be terrified, Niko thought. Keith put up a good front, pointing to the steps down to the hold and motioning them to follow him there. A Coleman battery lantern swung from the ceiling in the hold. Its wobbling cone of light illuminated the storage areas.

At a word from their boss the men in black went into action, carrying the packages of cannabis resin wrapped in heavy white plastic and burlap from their boat. They swarmed across the deck and down the stairs into the hold of *The Robert Gordon* where they tossed their packages, not into the storage areas but onto the floor. Their rain hoodies flapped around their legs, and they resembled a passel of overgrown ravens, terrifying in their numbers and anonymity as they hurried back to collect more parcels from their boat, which was tied alongside *The Robert Gordon* and invisible in the thick darkness. Niko wondered if it was painted black to make it so. They moved quickly, disregarding Keith's pantomimed attempts to get them to place the cannabis inside the compartments in the hold. At first Niko, Tom, and Keith simply tried to keep out of their way. Then Niko gathered courage and moved down the ladder into the hold, where he began slinging the parcels into the opened compartments.

After about fifteen minutes, the hold of *The Robert Gordon* was cluttered with disorderly mounds of white plastic and brown burlap packages that were as tall as Niko. When no more were tossed down, Niko climbed up to the deck. He felt pleased that, despite his terror, his default calm enabled him to function without panicking.

The leader of the men in black moved up close to Keith and Tom and Niko, looking at each of them closely, as though memorizing their faces. He said something Niko thought was a threat. Keith shakily handed him something. Then the leader motioned his men back to their boat, and they pulled silently away.

Keith let out a sigh so long Niko thought he must have been holding his breath the whole time the men in black were aboard. Impossible, of course. Keith muttered that they should go into the hold and begin ordering the chaos. His hands holding the handrail trembled, as he pulled himself down below decks. Tom and Niko followed him.

Together they formed a "bucket brigade" to move the cannabis packages from the floor into the storage compartments Tom had constructed.

"Shit! This is so much more than I was expecting!"

Tom and Niko did not respond to Keith's exclamation. They continued piling the cannabis packages inside the storage chambers. It took more than an hour to get it all stowed away.

When they were done, the storage areas were bulging, and they were all exhausted and woozy. Tom fetched his hammer, nails, and rubberized rain tarps. He nailed the tarps inside the entryway to each storage area, stretching them tight to confine the smell of the marijuana within those spaces. Tom closed and locked the doors. That's when he realized he'd forgotten the paint. "Fuck!" His instructions had been to paint over the compartment interior doors with a high gloss paint that would seal in the contents and their smell. Nothing to be done about it now. All three men slid down to the floor, backs against the walls of the hold, their bodies limp with exhaustion.

A few minutes later Keith was nudging them, directing them up on deck. They must cast off now so they would arrive back in Cypress amid the activity of the fishing boats taking off at dawn. That would screen them from notice.

There was no further excitement that night.

Thank God.

Two days later Keith paced the deck of *The Robert Gordon*, the nails of his right hand digging dark half-moons into the palm of his left, anxiety distorting his face. Going through with it, seeing those men in black with their lowered hoods and alarming, glaring eyes, had magnified his apprehension a hundred-fold. He tried to dismiss his terror. Just do as you were told; it will be all right, he told himself. Around Niko, he forced a confidence that had deserted him. When he said for a second time that there was much more cargo than he had expected, Niko suggested they toss it overboard. Maybe it was all too dangerous.

Keith replied, "But you saw the way he looked at each of us. They will come after us if we change the plan."

Niko told them that the major powerful families of Lebanon are all involved in drug production and distribution. He had the feeling that the boss man who looked so closely at each of them may have been the producer of the cannabis, not just some middleman.

Keith said from now on they must never mention what their cargo was. "We don't know what is in the packages. It could be ceramic tiles for all we know. Let's keep it at that."

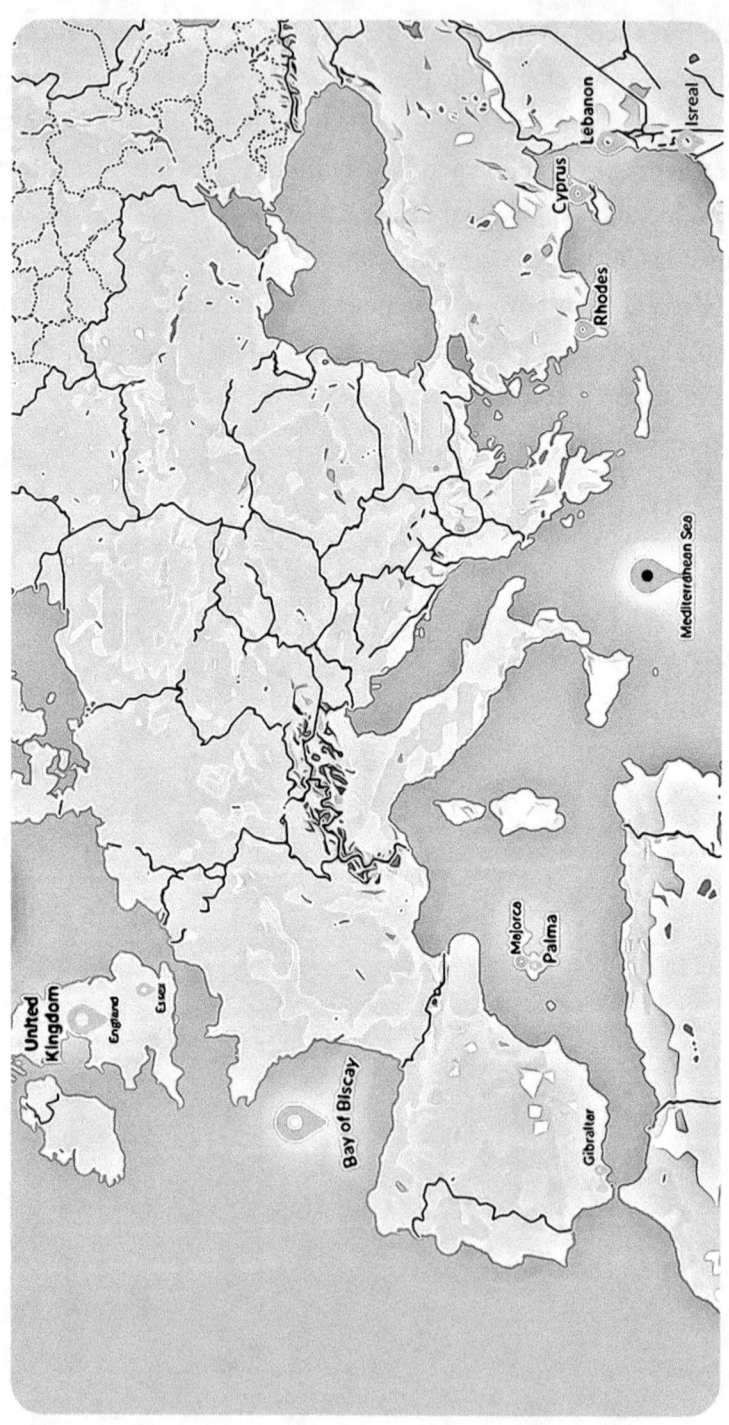

The Sir Robert Gordon, c. 1960

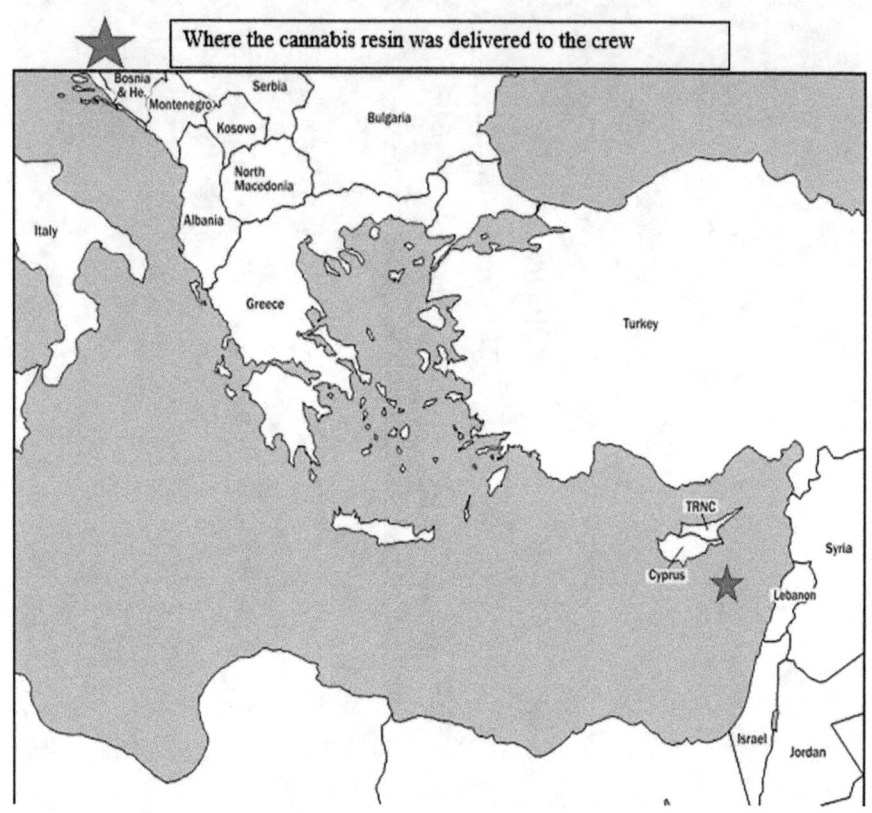

Where the cannabis resin was delivered to the crew

Chapter 15

They had safely brought the boat and its cargo back to Rhodes, sliding *The Robert Gordon* quietly into its assigned slip in the marina, *inconspicuous* and unnoticed, just as dawn was lighting the harbor sky. Keith went ashore. Following orders, he located an obscure bar at a distance from the marina. From there he placed a call to a number in Cape Town, South Africa. A thickly accented voice picked up, clearly not British. Keith and the man exchanged two words each: "Successful delivery" and "Four Crouch." Should any prying ears be listening, both clicked off before their locations could be traced. Then he returned to the boat. Uneasiness rooted in his brain and sent out runners in wild proliferation. *What was he doing?*

The sun sprawled across the marina, glinting off the profusion of white sails. Tourists were readying their boats for a day of sailing the Mediterranean. It was one of those beautiful summer mornings that insisted you notice how the white caps played tag with each other and the sea shimmered. Keith noticed, but only for a moment.

He bought a newspaper from the rack displayed at the entrance to a posh restaurant that overlooked the marina and carried it with him back to *The Robert Gordon*. Sally would soon rejoin them, but for now he had his cabin to himself. Sitting on his bunk below decks he scanned the front page.

The lead story featured the continued Islamic Jihad attacks on American targets in Beirut. The reporter wrote that nothing had been heard of the U.S. CIA Station Chief, William Buckley, abducted five months ago. Now Keith cursed his casual dismissal of the political situation in this part of the world. He had never paid attention to Middle Eastern politics. Running two businesses and being Dad to Teddy and partner to Janet had taken most of his time. There in the hold he read every article in the paper concerned with foreign policy in a futile attempt to make up his deficit.

Something else nagged at him. Why was he instructed to call South Africa? He'd understood this was a U.K. operation, a trial run bringing in cannabis to England to distribute across the U.K.

He gave the crew a break, to sleep late and visit the harbor bars until Sally rejoined them two days later. Her clattering noises brought a sense of normalcy—pots and pans banging, tea kettle boiling, spoons clicking against the sides of pans. He relaxed a little. She was making pizza and chocolate cake for lunch, and the musty fragrance of yeast dough rising mingled with the rich scent of dark chocolate to draw his attention. The sounds and smells of a kitchen were reassuring. They reminded him of home. For the next several weeks he needed to concentrate on bringing *The Robert Gordon* safely through the Mediterranean Sea, around Gibraltar, across the Bay of Biscay, along the English Channel and up the River Crouch. Unnoticed. Each of those posed challenges for a medium sized, middle aged yacht. Focus on the work ahead of us, he told himself.

He went ashore one more time before they left Rhodes. He had to report to Customs. In this port the customs agents did not board boats to check the veracity of customs declarations. That was why they'd used Rhodes, although, in fact, any number of the ports between Rhodes and London did not physically inspect boats that docked in them.

Keith's rules included no hard spirits on board, nothing stronger in alcohol content than ale. He loaded up on two cases of ale, weed and cartons of cigarettes. He'd stopped smoking when he moved in with Janet five years ago, but he needed the smokes just now. He'd smoke only these cigs and by the time they reached Essex would have weaned himself off smoking, he rationalized.

Their trip through the Mediterranean was slowed by a series of mechanical problems. They were delayed again with engine problems as they reached Gibraltar. These repairs would require a few days to complete. There Keith bought the September 21st *International Herald Tribune*, where he read that a car packed with 3,000 pounds of explosives had driven into the

U.S. Embassy Annex in East Beirut--where the Americans had relocated after their embassy had been bombed more than a year ago. The car bomb killed twenty-four people, including two U.S. servicemen, and wounded ninety, including the U.S. Ambassador Reginald Bartholomew. Since April 1983, there had been three acts of terrorism in Beirut that targeted U.S. facilities: the bombing of the embassy, the truck bombs that destroyed the barracks and killed 241 U.S. servicemen and 58 French soldiers of the Multinational Forces, and now the bombing of the U.S. Embassy Annex. The article said that the bombing was done by the Islamic Jihad or Hezbollah, a Shi'a Muslim terrorist group funded by Iran, the same group that claimed responsibility for the previous bombings of the U.S. Embassy and Marine Barracks.

Keith finished reading the story and then tossed the paper into a trash bin. Usually he would bring newspapers back to share with the crew, but this was different. No need to alarm Niko who seemed spooked enough. And Tom? The good thing about a bloke like Tom was that nothing much could get through to him.

Chapter 16

David Bennie's stint on *The Welsh Falcon* had led him to work on other yachts owned by an assortment of celebrities, thanks to the endorsement note Mr. Bailey had given him after his interview in London. The work had carried him around the Mediterranean multiple times. He had worked on the yachts of the world's most pampered people, ferrying millionaires from one watery playground and elite event to another, from the Cannes Film Festival to the Monaco Grand Prix to Palma's regatta race, Copa del Rey (the King's Cup). His bosses ranged from Alexander Salkind, the brilliant producer of the three Superman movies starring Christopher Reeves, to the billionaire Saudi arms dealer Adnan Khashoggi. It was exhilarating to move in such circles. He enjoyed observing powerful people in their native habitat. But after three years at sea, he was ready to see his family. They would undoubtedly appreciate his tales of the glitterati.

He performed his four-hour watches, made minor repairs to Mr. Khashoggi's boat, *The Nabila*, and tried to be helpful. But some days were bloody boring, especially when there was no wind and the boat bobbed about aimlessly on a quiescent sea that you could distinguish from a mirror only by the parallel dark marks that dented its surface, abortive swellings of water that never made it to becoming waves. Watching for whales and dolphins and other creatures of the sea was diverting for a while, but not for long. Some of the crew whittled or sketched to use up the time.

Others drank and/or smoked. No spirits on board, only cheap lagers, but when they'd come into port to take on fuel or make minor repairs, that's when the hard liquor took over their lives. The local police of the given port town would come aboard to read them the rules for crew in their town, which might delay their boozing briefly, but as soon as the police finished inspecting the boat, the crew would go off to find the very places the police had said were off limits.

Then there were the girls in the ports. They appeared in flocks, as if some neon sign had switched on announcing, New Group of Horny Men Just Arrived. Gaggles of girls in skimpy skirts and form fitting blouses wearing heels and lots of eye makeup would stroll the harbor front looking over the boats just in and assessing their human cargo. The girls were fully aware that men who'd spent weeks or months at sea were goners at the sight of unbearably high heels, lots of leg, and proudly protruding breasts. The eye makeup was a bonus, applied for those viewers who raised their eyes from the rest of the display.

Women would come aboard and pair off with the crewmen. Even on smaller boats they would find some space to work their magic on lonely young men. A few married men resisted, finding a phone booth from which to call home or writing amorous letters to their wives while they watched their single cohorts cavort.

Then it was back at sea. Some of the crew had shipped out together many a time and had become close, like soldiers in war sharing the same danger and spilling out their stories of home so that someone would know in case...

Some intimate details about each other you couldn't help knowing: whose snores sound like steam engines, whose farts woke you from the deepest sleep by their ferocious smell, who talked in their sleep, or cried.

But for more private people like David, the loneliness of being in such close quarters with people while knowing little about them, nor they about you, was baffling and brought blues that even too much whiskey or lager could not subdue. The bottle was at best an unreliable friend.

On this September day David could feel the blues winning. They had just tied up in Gibraltar, but he had no money for diversions. Not being paid until they arrived in Aberdeen, Scotland, was standard procedure, but their return to Aberdeen seemed more and more elusive, postponed and postponed as they were rerouted and rerouted. At first, he'd welcomed the changes in schedule as a break from the routine. But habitual delays and no money were tiresome and frustrating.

He'd not made close mates on *The Nabila*, so when the crew went ashore, he went alone, moving restlessly from bar to bar along the harbor, all too aware that his ability to drown his sorrows was nil due to the poverty of his pocket. He walked the Gibraltar marina in a dark mood, dragging his sandals on purpose, diverted by the protesting noise they made, until he remembered he had no cash for a new pair.

At the end of the slip was a smaller vessel, a yacht whose Scottish name caught his attention—*The Robert Gordon*. The name brought a surge of homesickness for Scotland and for his parents who he'd heard nothing about for some months, the mail being irregular and his destinations often unknown until they were at sea. Escorting the yachts of the rich and famous was not a job for one who liked to plan ahead.

A young woman was descending the gangplank from *The Robert Gordon*. She was short and plump with nondescript brown hair and a big smile that broke open her otherwise unremarkable face and reassembled it attractively. She was what Mam called "thrawn." He smiled at her. Having grown up with older sisters who thought he walked on water, he felt confident that she would smile back. She did.

That was how it started, both his platonic friendship with Sally Eliades and his connection with *The Robert Gordon*.

Sally was not a dock girl, although she had been drawn to the docks ever since she was a child because she loved the sea. She had never been attracted to the life of those women who thronged the docks to give momentary pleasure to homesick sailors. Those women's power came from manipulating men with their looks and their bodies. Not Sally. She liked to please men with her culinary inventions, but her true love was the sea. The walls of her bedroom at home in Kings Lynn were covered with photos of ships at sea. No Elton John or Def Leppard for her. No ABBA or Bee Gees or Rod Stewart or Bob Marley. The girl was single-minded. She loved the sea and was determined to live near or on it.

She told David she had signed on with *The Robert Gordon* in Rhodes, the only woman in the crew of four. She was their cook. David and Sally sat on the harbor wall kicking their feet against its unyielding stones and chatting as easily as children. David liked her independence, and, because he had family near Kings Lynn, she felt like Home.

When the crews of their two ships came stumbling back from the bars several hours later, they both received a royal teasing. It didn't matter. Their conversation had chased his blues. When he climbed into his bunk, his mind was chewing over a possibility: Maybe he could join the crew of Sally's ship. They were headed back to England, they had been plagued with mechanical problems he could fix, and they might even pay him.

The next morning he raced down to the slip where *The Robert Gordon* was still anchored, looked for Sally, and asked her if she thought they might take him on as crew, since he was experienced repairing engines and had previously sailed the unpredictable Bay of Biscay. She said she'd ask Keith, the captain. He should come 'round that afternoon.

When he did as she'd said, Keith was waiting for him. "We've only the four of us and Sally's our cook. I could use another experienced hand taking turns at watch as we cross the Bay of Biscay. What do you know about boats?"

"I've been at sea a few years now on several yachts. Before that I got my certificate in engineering from British Steel. All my life I've been around boats, and I've taken my turn fixing things with no adverse effects," David answered. He tried to strike a balance between displaying his competence and good humor.

"Well, then. We ship out tomorrow morning. Welcome aboard, mate."

That was all. David went back to gather his few personal items from *The Nabila* and returned that same afternoon to join *The Robert Gordon*. Things were looking up. He'd likely never see the pay owed him, but he'd seen the world, a good part of it, and *The Robert Gordon* would bring him home. Why not?

He mailed a postcard to his Mam and Dad on September 24th, before the yacht left port the next morning. He told them of his change of plans and that he expected to be home well before Halloween.

Life aboard *The Robert Gordon* was pleasant enough, except for minor mechanical crises and rough weather. He and Sally were roughly the same age and liked the same music, which she played daily on her cassette player. Niko didn't make much effort with him. Perhaps Sally was right that Niko felt displaced by David's arrival on board. With Sally and David hanging out together, Niko had lost his buddy. David simply did his job—two-hour watches and occasional repair work in the engine room. He stayed out of Keith, Tom, and Niko's way.

It was likely to be a nine-day trip from Gibraltar to England. Sally told him they'd had trouble after they left Rhodes. The boat ran out of fuel and had a malfunction with its radar that forced them to stop at the beautiful island of Ibiza, then again in Palma and yet again in Gibraltar. She told him their misfortune was his good luck. They probably would not have added him to the crew had it not been for these crises.

David was excited to be going home. Sally, too. Keith had promised her a ticket to see her Mum in London, along with her pay. He'd promised David a ticket to see his family in their new home in Corby, England, where they had moved after he left for sea. Keith said they'd not be paid until they brought the boat to Amsterdam. He said nothing about exactly where he planned to land in the U.K. Neither of them was certain whether they'd be flying home from Amsterdam or from somewhere else. It didn't matter. The crew were busy enough bringing the ship safely through days of sheeting rain and angry sea as they traversed the Bay of Biscay and the English Channel. David had caught cold before joining the crew. With the lousy weather and his stopped-up nose, he grew eager to get this trip over with.

The evening of October 2nd, David woke up suddenly when the boat lurched onto a sandbar in the mouth of the Thames. It was the second time this had happened. The first time they ran aground, he'd been at the wheel and had been able to get it dislodged. Now he heard Keith and Tom talking about what to do. Then he heard Keith shouting into the radio phone that *The Robert Gordon* needed help from the Coast Guard.

The boat seemed especially heavy to David, which Keith said was because it had a lead bottom. David, Niko, and Sally stumbled out of their cabins to see what was happening, but, within a half-hour's time, the boat had unstuck herself, and Keith was back on the phone telling the Coast Guard there was no longer a need for help. David, Niko, and Sally returned to their cabins and sleep.

As he fell back asleep David had the thought, which seemed brilliant and memorable at the time, that the irregularity of when one slept while at sea—depending on when during the day and night you were on watch duty— might explain why trips at sea seem to go on forever, like you are living in another, timeless dimension.

Chapter 17

It was dark on October 3rd when Keith steered *The Robert Gordon* into the River Crouch and upstream to a place in the middle of the river where he lay down anchor. The air was brisk with the chill of early October and he could see his breath. At least it was not raining. He pulled on his waterproof parka, lugged the rubber dinghy to the starboard side of the boat and dropped it into the river, holding tightly to the rope that moored it to *The Robert Gordon*. He could do this without anyone to assist him. Indeed, he'd done it many times in his several years of occasional delivery work, taking yachts from one place to another. He climbed over the side and lowered himself into the dinghy, then paddled toward the shore. No need to disturb the neighbors by running the engine.

Ashore, he walked to the small wooden building where an agent usually sat to take information about arrivals and collect the fees for mooring. There was no agent present. Not surprising at this time of night. But there was a phone box. He carefully extracted the folded paper on which he had written Brian's coded information, the number he was to phone in Chelmsford. He dialed, rang twice and clicked off, the signal that they had arrived. Then he trudged back to the dinghy, rowed back to *The Robert Gordon*, climbed aboard, and pulled the dinghy up after him.

Tomorrow night they would unload farther upstream at North Fambridge. There transport should be waiting to take the cargo off their hands. Then he would be free of the apprehension that had troubled his sleep since picking up the cargo. Previous times when he had ferried yachts his biggest concern had been the boredom, not enough to do. Boredom had not been a problem on this trip. Since Niko and he had talked before they picked up the cargo, his anxiety had been constant. His sleep was sporadic and his stomach acidic.

A black-hooded man appeared regularly in his dreams leaning toward him, face to face, threatening. Tomorrow he hoped all that would end. They would deliver the cannabis resin and sail for Amsterdam. He would pay the crew, leave the boat, and come home to Janet and Teddy. His face involuntarily settled into a smile imagining their reunion.

The next day they all slept in. There was nothing that needed attention, and a long sleep was important for the physically demanding work ahead of them once it became dark, hauling the drugs out of the storage areas, carrying them up from the hold, transporting them to shore, and loading the parcels into the vans.

About seven in the evening Keith awoke to the smell of hot oil. Sally was preparing fish and chips, a meal to symbolize Home for four of them. Bless her. After they had all gathered in the saloon and eaten their only meal of the day, Keith took Tom aside and told him they'd be moving a bit up the river and then off-loading the cargo. The crew seemed energized. Laughter wafted up from galley where the young'uns, Sally and David, were cleaning up. He liked them both, solid and caring people afflicted with the same yearning to see a larger world that had afflicted him in his younger days. They'd get over it, like he had. He hoped their path would be less choppy than his had been, hoped, too, that they would find someone who loved them like Janet loved him. He felt emotion rising from somewhere inside. *Never expected that! Guess it shows how much I want to be home with my woman and my son*, he concluded.

Chapter 18

On the third of October Janet returned from school and set about cooking Keith's favorite meal—lamb stew, spinach salad sprinkled with orange slices and pine nuts, and trifle with custard for dessert. She was expecting him home from his big trip the following day and thought she'd have everything prepared in advance as a special homecoming for her man. She'd turned on the heat for the first time this autumn, there being a bit of a bite to the early October air.

Teddy was upstairs in his room. She could hear his favorite show, *The Fraggles*, about little creatures who lived under a lighthouse. She turned on the small screen TV that was in the kitchen of their cozy cottage to catch up on the news while she sliced vegetables for the stew.

She was glad Keith would be home tomorrow. It had been a long three months with infrequent radio calls that frustrated them both. He would start to talk and in the silence that followed she would respond but learn too late that her voice was being broadcast over his. Neither of them could make much sense of the conversation, so they'd developed a once a week short-hand—Keith would say "I'm well" and wait, then she would reply, "We're well, too." Their respective "Love you" overlaid each other, a metaphor she found quite nice. That was it.

Keith's friend Archie had phoned her early this morning before she'd left for school to say he should be home tomorrow. She'd had her hair cut after school before picking up Teddy and was quite pleased with the result.

Finished preparing the stew, she set it in the slow cooker and made up toasted cheese sandwiches for herself and Teddy, serving them flanked with carrot sticks and a bit of lettuce with salad cream on top. Thankfully, her boy liked his vegetables.

After supper she read to him and heard about his day before bundling him into the tub for a bath and then to bed. He'd been sleeping in her bed while Daddy was gone, but that would end tomorrow, she told him as she tucked him in. Daddy was coming home! Her announcement halted their normal good-night routine, as he wanted to make a sign to surprise Daddy. She brought the colored paper and crayons to the bed to place limits on this extension of his routine, and Teddy colored a sign for the front door that said WELCOME HOME, except that all of his E's were backwards. Then he was asleep.

Janet turned out the lights downstairs and put on her pajamas. She climbed into bed with a stack of papers from her class to mark. They'd done well on the review of their elementary math facts, and she drew happy faces on virtually every student's paper. She was feeling weary and had to force herself to stay awake till she finished them all.

Chapter 19

They moved the boat to a neglected area of the river where only the backsides of abandoned factories were visible from the water. There was a small beach littered with trash on their starboard side. Keith recognized the place and the cement ramp that eased into the river to enable the launching and beaching of boats. Yes, this was the spot.

He lowered the anchor and, with Tom assisting him, lowered the dinghy, tying it securely to the starboard railing. He could hear music now, coming from the saloon, and laughter. The kids were enjoying themselves. Good. That would keep them busy and below deck while he, Tom, and Niko brought up the cargo and loaded it into the dinghy. He didn't want David and Sally involved. He climbed down the hatch and pushed open the door to the saloon.

"We need to be working in the prow so we'll have that hatch open. It would help to have you stay here with the door closed, till we're done. Okay, mates?" Keith wanted to be sure David and Sally heard him. "Could you turn down the volume, please? We don't want to disturb the neighbors." He wanted to avoid noise that would draw attention to their presence. They paid him no attention, so he turned down the radio and repeated his request. "Keep the radio turned low so neighbors won't complain about us, and please stay in the galley," he said.

Half-attentive, David and Sally nodded. From the level of liquid in the two-liter whiskey bottle, Keith knew they'd been drinking. Better that way. Keep them out of the way and in their cups.

It was past midnight. Niko was in the forward part of the hold that Tom had unlocked. He was prying the nails out the doorways to each storage compartment so they could open the doors and remove the rubber sheeting that Tom had installed. Keith told Niko to pass the parcels up through the hatch. Keith and Tom would load them on the dinghy. They worked at it for probably half an hour before Keith called a halt. He and Tom would take the dinghy to the shore and return to make another trip.

Niko walked into the saloon for a drink and a rest. He was sweaty from exertion and didn't say much, just rested with his feet up while he swigged water. He noticed a trash bag near the galley door. It was full of empty liters of coke and potato crisp bags. There was a nearly empty bottle of Jack Daniels on the counter. For a moment he felt angry with these carefree twenty-somethings who had nothing to do but party, oblivious to the dangerous activity the rest of the crew was engaged in. The music playing on Sally's cassette player made his head hurt. He was tired of being a foreigner among these Brits. He wanted to speak his own language and eat his own food. He wanted to see his family. He regretted signing on to this trip.

These thoughts collided in his head as he sat there in the galley watching David and Sally. How could they take life so lightly? Sally approached him and tried to pull him to his feet to dance with her. His scowl put her off and she dropped his hand and turned to David instead. Lost in his regrets, he didn't hear Keith call to him from the deck to get back to work until Keith called a second time. Muscles sore and feeling irritable, Niko left the galley, pulling the door shut forcefully.

More hefting and carrying parcels from the compartments to the hatch. More lifting them and passing them up to Tom on the deck above him. There were so many parcels. Some wrapped in plastic and others in burlap. He wondered how much cannabis they had taken on.

When the dinghy was loaded, Keith told Niko to continue bringing the cargo up on deck while he and Tom delivered the first load by dinghy to those waiting on shore. Niko heard the soft puttering of the dinghy's engine as it moved toward the beach, which was invisible now in the thick cloud cover.

He returned to the hold. His back hurt. It was hard work lifting the parcels and carrying them up the ladder to the deck. Also, the smell of cannabis was affecting him. It was easier when Keith and Tom were on deck to receive them. Still he kept at it.

A small point of light twice flickered and went out. Keith steered the dinghy toward it and, when the dinghy's bottom ran onto the sand, he and Tom leapt out and labored to haul it ashore.

Three vans were lined up on the stony shore facing away from the river. As a sliver of moon emerged from the cloud cover he saw their open backs and the pitch-black caves of their interiors. Two men wearing black hoodie jackets stood at the back of the vans. A third sat in the cab of his van smoking. They did not help unload the parcels from the dinghy, but they did lift them from the beach, where Keith and Tom placed them, and stow them inside the vans. They worked rapidly.

When there were no more parcels to load, the men in black got into the drivers' seats. Apparently they were going to wait there for Keith and Tom to return with the next load. Keith involuntarily shivered watching them, his mind recalling the other set of anonymous men in black off the coast of Tripoli. Strange similarity. Creepy.

"Come on," he muttered to Tom, "We've at least one more load to fetch."

The two men pushed the dinghy off the sandbar and into the river. Keith chided himself for wearing his yellow wetsuit. It was really the best thing to wear for such an operation, but in that moment his gaudy yellow trousers and coat must make him fully visible to anyone happening to pass by. Shite!

Tom was grumbling softly to himself. "Why wouldn't those bloody fuckers help us?

"Quiet!" Keith whispered, as he put the engine in gear. The dinghy moved at a leisurely pace through the water toward *The Robert Gordon*, barely slicing the surface of the River Crouch. That was some relief.

Chapter 20

In the saloon David told Sally he'd split in two if he didn't pee right now. Laughing, he went into the toilet and sat down. He and Sally had had a fun time listening to music, singing along, even dancing. They were both damn happy to be back home in Great Britain, God's country. Or is it the Queen's? he wondered, his brain muddy with booze. Either way was good.

His head was spinning. It was colder in here than in the saloon. He thought maybe he should go find his sandals. Something weird about the head tonight. There were shadows circling above him like neon yellow gulls, so bright that they showed through the vents of the head. *What the fuck?*

Suddenly, he heard a voice barking authoritatively from a loudspeaker. "This is the Police. We have you surrounded. Come out with your hands up immediately. We caution you that we are armed and will not hesitate to shoot if you do not comply."

David zipped his shorts and rushed back to the saloon. Niko had gone up on deck when Keith called him to get back to work, but Sally still sat at the table singing along with the Bee Gees, painfully off-key.

"Something's wrong." He told her. He was having trouble finding his words. "Police telling us to come up on deck with our hands up."

Half-drunk, Sally got to her feet swaying a bit and giggling. She moved toward him, her face looking like a cartoon, jaw slack, mouth open in an O, forehead crowned with waves of wrinkles from the unfamiliar high arch of her brows. He opened the door to the stairs and pulled her behind him. Now he could hear the voice blaring instructions like Big Brother. In his inebriated state, he found it funny, and he, too, began to chuckle as he pulled himself up the stairs to the deck, Sally followed behind him.

The chilly air of the autumn night nearly knocked him over, and he wished for his jacket. It was too late to go back. Hands up, they stood side by side, illuminated by circling searchlights from a helicopter flying low over *The Robert Gordon.*

"What's going on?" Sally asked him.

Keith, Tom and Niko were nowhere to be seen. The deck was strewn with parcels. Their white plastic covering shone in the light from the helicopter. *What the fuck?*

"WALK TO STARBOARD AND LOWER YOURSELVES INTO THE POLICE BOAT YOU SEE THERE." The voice overpowered them, so loud David thought it might be raising the dead. That thought, too, amused him. Sodium searchlights roamed the river and slashed across his face and Sally's, making bars of ugly yellow, the color of gorse. He could actually *feel* his irises contract. It was an unpleasant feeling, and he blinked rapidly.

Squinting against the search beams he could see uniformed police, their guns pointed at him, standing before them, calling them forward. The officers trussed his and Sally's hands behind them and assisted them to crawl over the railing and clamber into the police boat. Again, he noticed white mounds on the foredeck of *The Robert Gordon* as he went over the railing. They looked like piles of snow in the eerie yellow light. He wondered what they were.

When the police boat reached the shore, the officers ordered them out. David stepped onto the wet sand and cringed at the cold, his toes curling protectively inward. Then he and Sally were ordered into separate police cars. Before they pulled off, David asked the policeman who was in driver's seat why he was being arrested. The officer waved him off. "Man, you stink of alcohol. Sit back in your seat so I don't have to smell you."

"I can't, sir. My hands are cuffed behind me. Why are you arresting me?" he repeated.

"For smuggling tons of illegal drugs into the U.K.! If I were you, I'd get a good lawyer as soon as you can."

Sitting there in the rear seat of the police car in the early morning of October 4, 1984, David could not tell if it was fear or the autumn cold that froze him. This was to be their last stop. He was coming home after three years. They were celebrating…not going to jail! His homecoming had become a sodden, scary mess that his liquor-saturated brain could not process.

Chapter 21

In the wee hours of October 4th, 1984, the Chelmsford police took into custody the five crew members from *The Robert Gordon*—Keith Brown, Tom Hill, Niko Karras, Sally Eliades and David Bennie—and three other men, Terrence Gale, John Benton and Geoff Knowles. Gale, Benton and Knowles had arrived at the beach at North Fambridge with Ford vans. Knowles and Benton had tried to drive the vans toward the concrete ramp that led up to the highway but had been stopped by the police. Gale was arrested as he waited on the sand for the dinghy's second delivery of the packages of cannabis resin.

It was two a.m. when the Chelmsford police, aided by Customs and Export personnel, booked into the local jail the seven men and one woman they had apprehended in North Fambridge and began interviewing them. Chelmsford police handled the questioning, two officers meeting with each of the people arrested, one writing out the proceedings and, at the end, presenting the prisoner with the text for him, or her, to sign, then taking them back to their cells. Their interrogations went on throughout the night and well into the morning.

Terrence Gale, who drove one of the vans, told them he had worked with Keith Brown in Keith's car dealership during the previous year. When arrested he had in his possession a coastal navigation map of the Essex rivers and bank account numbers for Mr. Keith Brown, in Palma, Majorca, and for Ms. Janet Morris, Keith's partner, in Essex. He was also carrying a lot of cash, 24,000 pounds, and a receipt for that money from Midland Bank, Romford. He explained that he was arranging car sales through Keith in Palma and that Janet occasionally called him to ask for money when Keith was away and she was short. Gale told the police he ran a salvage business in Brentwood, Essex, Central Salvage Agency Ltd. on Solid Lane, Ashwells Road.

When the police questioned him about a Brian Baker, Terrence Gale said he was Brian Baker's partner in the motor trade a year ago and continued to do occasional driving for Mr. Baker and Georgina Graves, who owned the motor company. He acknowledged he'd recently driven Georgina to Heathrow to catch her plane for a holiday break, though he didn't know where she was going. He claimed not to know the drivers of the other vans, John Benton or Geoff Knowles, although Knowles's phone number was in his pants pocket when he was arrested.

In short, Terrence Gale's statements to the police were evasive. He was not particularly cooperative.

Van driver John Benton was downright uncooperative, refusing to reply to any of the questions asked him. Only later that day, after several interrogation sessions, did he acknowledge knowing Geoff Knowles. In a moment of candor that appeared to surprise Benton himself he said in a rush, "Knowles has nothing to do with this. We're friends and work together in the building trade. I asked Geoff to go with me to pick up some fertilizer. That's all. I hired two vehicles for the job." Then he reset his face to hard, cold and veiled and his silence returned. He refused even to give his address and middle name.

Geoff Knowles was another story.

Knowles said he was a painter and decorator and had known John Benton for ten years or more, doing jobs for him frequently. Thursday past Benton had called to ask him to pick up some supplies. "Said he'd bring a van around on Sunday and leave it outside my house since I said I'd be visiting my mother with the family. When I got home the van was there. The keys were on the floor when I opened the front door to my home. He probably put them through the letter slot. He'd said we would meet at the roundabout at Fambridge at 7:30 last night, so I was there on time. But Benton wasn't. Another man in a van approached me and asked where Benton was. I said I was waiting for him. The man tried to phone Benton and then said to follow him, so I did." Knowles's voice was hoarse and he spoke rapidly.

"We drove down to the jetty. It was a dark night but the jetty in North Fambridge still shone with white plastic-wrapped packages two men were unloading from a dinghy that was loaded to the gills with more packages. I was expecting fertilizer or sacks of lime like I usually picked up for Benton. The man and I stacked the parcels in our vans. I was puzzling about what was happening when Benton drove up and started loading parcels into his van too. I was scared that it was drugs and yelled at him, 'What sort of mess have you got me into?' He told me to take the van, which was full by this time, back to my house and he'd collect it later. I started to drive away when the police raced down the ramp to the beach and blocked my van, telling me I was under arrest. I've never done anything illegal before. I thought I was picking up cement or lime or something." Knowles was having a hard time getting his words out.

The officer asked how much money Benton promised him for this job.

"He didn't promise me anything. I feel so stupid. How can I have been such a fool? I'd feel better if he had promised me a load of money." Knowles's voice cracked and lost volume. If Knowles was faking his devastation, he should be an actor, the officer conducting the interview told his boss. Knowles' next comment was barely audible: "If I'd taken money, at least I'd have a reason for being in jail!"

Knowles was too shaken to say more, so they escorted him back to his cell.

Chapter 22

K eith felt like a sledgehammer was pounding against his skull. While the polite Customs Official fired questions, Keith tried to think one step ahead, to consider the consequences before answering, but the effect was all wrong. In trying to protect Teddy and Janet, he was sinking deeper into quicksand. His answers veered this way and that so that it was clear to the officer--and to Keith himself--that he was grasping at straws, frail inventions that were not hanging together with any coherence.

He told the officer he was divorced, that, yes, he'd left England six or seven months ago, that he didn't know anyone named Brian Baker, that he hadn't seen his ex-girlfriend Janet Morris for nearly a year. Lies. When his responses to the incessant questions exposed something he'd said as an outright lie, he backed up and tried to maneuver his way out of the confusion. He was conscious of sweat sliding down his forehead, making its way around his left eyebrow and resting momentarily on his cheekbone before dropping onto the table, onto his primly folded hands. Even his hands, fingers laced together, looked all wrong. Finally, he shut up.

"I don't want to answer anything else. I want a solicitor," he told the officer, rubbing his burning eyes to avoid meeting the judging look on the other man's face. They passed him the transcript of his answers for him to review and sign, which he did. His heart felt like a massive boulder in his chest. He couldn't remember actually feeling his heart before, except when he'd run races in school.

They brought him aspirin and a glass of water. They called Mr. Twitchen, who he told them was his solicitor. It must have been 4 a.m. when Twitchen arrived, face flushed and eyes bloodshot from being woken in the middle of the night and driving to Essex. Then the questioning resumed. The look Twitchen threw Keith told him, if he had any doubt, that he was in deep trouble.

Twitchen advised him to tell the truth but to decline to comment when the truth would affect others involved. In the small interrogation room with dawn advancing through the venetian blinds and laying down stripes of yellow light across the table, Keith's fear overpowered his awareness of his headache. His hands lay on the table, the fingers of his right hand tapping a tattoo, now softly and slowly, now rapidly. The officer revisited his earlier questions and Keith revised his answers. Except when they concerned Janet.

This time he acknowledged picking up Sally in Rhodes and leaving her there while they went to Tripoli to pick up their cargo. She knew nothing of this, he insisted, nor did the young man, David Bennie. He felt good saying this. It was one thing he didn't need to consider before speaking, one true thing that restored a shred of his self-respect.

Yes, he knew Brian Baker, had met him in Majorca, Palma, and it was Brian who had asked him to skipper the yacht *The Robert Gordon*. He'd met Brian Baker first when he sold Brian a car. He knew most of his co-defendants through the motor trade.

Georgina Graves? She was Brian's boss, or secretary, and girlfriend? He'd never been clear about their relationship. Terrence Gale? He ran a car hire shop. Nikolaos Karras? They'd met in Rhodes soon after Keith had hired Tom Hill to fix up his boat. Niko was a trawler. Both men assisted in readying the boat for sailing the distance.

Who owned the boat? Who proposed the drug operation? Keith insisted he did not know. There was a name on the boat's papers, but he had never met the man it belonged to. Only Brian.

"When you sailed up the River Crouch and dropped anchor, you came ashore. For what purpose?"

"I came to get permission from the marina to put the boat into a slip there. I'd come here before and knew they worked irregular hours, and I'd need to get permission to tie up before the weekend."

"What else did you do on shore?"

"I went to the phone box and made a call."

"To whom?"

"I don't know. I was given a number to call when we arrived. No name. I was to call and say I was at NF and then ring off and destroy the paper with the phone number. That's what I did."

Keith could hear the dull staccato thumping of his right heel against the floor.

"Did you know what cargo you were carrying?"

"I knew it was weed." His foot went silent now and he wondered if the officer could smell his fear.

"For the record, how much did you expect to be paid for delivering your cargo?"

"Fifty thousand pounds."

"And the others in the crew?"

"Like I said, David and Sally not much--just the regular rate for crew."

"Nikolaos Karras and Tom Hill?"

Keith's eyes involuntarily cut sideways to his solicitor, then back to the officer. "I don't want to say anything more," he said.

Sally Eliades was shaken. She told the officers she had signed on in Rhodes to cook for the crew of *The Robert Gordon* because her rent contract was up on the bar she'd been trying without success to run. She'd never sailed before and wanted to try it before returning to England to visit her mother. She hoped the five to six weeks experience on *The Robert Gordon* would enable her to get a job on another yacht and visit the Caribbean, something she really wanted to do.

Keith took her on there in Rhodes, although later he told her to say she joined them in Palma. He said he was a car salesman who sailed yachts for a hobby. He was nice enough, never inappropriate, but always seemed nervous. He treated her well and promised to pay her five hundred pounds a month when they arrived in Amsterdam and provide her with a ticket to London, where her mum lived. She had never been certain where they were to land, and it didn't matter to her as long as she was paid and had the ticket home. She insisted she knew nothing of any drugs being on board. She smelled nothing and, as someone who had smoked cannabis, would have been able to identify the smell. Several times during her interview she stated emphatically, "It matters a great deal to me that you know I am not lying."

Tom Hill's interview produced nothing. He simply replied, "No comment," to every question.

Niko Karras was clearly terrified. His fear caused him to lose confidence in speaking English. Frequently he told the officers he didn't understand their questions. The most they learned from him was that he'd been hired in Rhodes to bring a cargo to the U.K. and that he worked as a trawler, his father's trade, in Rhodes. He said not to call his family. They would be very upset and he didn't want to alarm them. He said nothing about his mates on the crew.

David was questioned for an hour. Somewhere in that hour an officer asked if he wanted to call anyone and informed him of his right to counsel. He asked for counsel and in the second interrogation session, later in the morning, was provided with an attorney whose specialty was divorce law.

David Bennie was still inebriated from the liquor he and Sally had consumed. He told the police he was hired on in Gibraltar. He said the first time he realized they were transporting drugs was when he came up on deck in response to the police command and saw Niko standing with his hands up amidst hundreds of parcels. Even then he wasn't certain what was in the parcels. His mind just made an accurate guess. When one of the officers pushed him to confess that he had certainly smelled the cannabis, he denied it, insisting he was suffering from a head cold during the whole trip.

He was a soft-spoken young man and at times the officer had to ask him to repeat his responses. He seemed confused, which might have been the alcohol. He asked if they could spare a coat or cardigan, he was cold. They found a cardigan, extra large and smelling of old sweat, but he pulled it on and giggled to see the sleeves hanging to his knees.

When finally they allowed him to call home, Mam told him Customs and Excise officers had broken into their home and rifled it, looking for anything to incriminate him, she supposed. Being Customs and Excise men, they needed no warrant.

After questioning him again, the police brought him a cup of coffee upon his request and then retired him to a jail cell he shared with Niko. He was grateful for the blanket they provided. He tucked his icy feet under his knees and wrapped himself like a burrito in the blanket. His last thought before falling asleep was, *Is it possible to die of frostbite?* The thought remained with him all night.

Chapter 23

B rian Baker had received a call the evening of October 2nd telling him to meet Georgina in the park at ten p.m. They had agreed to talk about "the project" only in the park near her apartment in case their phone conversations were being monitored. She was already there when he arrived, tall and striking and, most importantly under the circumstances, very organized. She told him that *The Robert Gordon* had stuck on a sandbar and had radioed for help. They had agreed that he would leave the U.K. at the first sign of any potential problem to protect himself. The call to the coast guard might have endangered the mission.

She passed him an envelope with cash in Cypriot pounds and a one-way ticket from Manchester to Nicosia, flying from Stansfield airfield the next morning—she thought it best to avoid Heathrow. He wondered if she could tell that her news shook him. They didn't talk long.

Brian felt a rush of gratitude for her efficiency as he slipped into his car to drive home and pack a small roller bag. He wrote a note for his mother saying he was going on a business trip and unsure when he'd return. His hand holding the pen trembled a bit, which was worrisome.

He was up at dawn after a restless night and on his way to the airport in a cab. He swallowed frequently; his saliva was working overtime. He was trying to find the right balance between appearing confident and inconspicuous.

By late afternoon he was in his mother's natal country. There his dual citizenship should protect him, should *The Robert Gordon*'s problems be more serious than a sandbar.

Sipping thick, aromatic coffee on the balcony of his hotel two days later, the headlines confirmed his decision to flee the U.K.: SIX TONNES CANNABIS RESIN SEIZED IN LARGEST DRUG BUST IN BRITAIN'S HISTORY; EIGHT ARRESTED.

His coffee sloshed over the brim of the cup and scalded his forefinger. He set it down and strode to the toilet to run cold water over his burned digit. He wanted to talk to Archie and to Georgina. Damn Terrence Gale! Archie said Gale would be so careful, hiring people with no priors and no knowledge of the operation, setting up impressive firewalls and coded messages to keep the operation secret. But the paper said Customs had locked down the entire village of North Fambridge, used 30 agents, helicopters, and divers to make the raid, and arrested Terrence Gale along with seven others. Something in the backgrounds of the people Gale hired must have attracted Customs' attention.

In the past year Brian had learned a lot from Archie about how to operate beneath the radar of the law. At least he thought he had learned a lot. *What went wrong?*

He turned off the cold water and returned to the balcony. He sat in the white wicker chair in his hotel-provided white terrycloth robe, legs askew, soaking up the morning sun. His eyes behind his designer sunglasses followed the progress of a sailboat tacking its way across the bay. He reviewed his actions during the past year. *What had he done that might make him vulnerable?*

He had hired Keith and Niko. Archie had one of his contacts supply Keith with 19,000 pounds to buy and refurbish *The Robert Gordon*. Archie had deposited 100,000 pounds in a bank account in Amsterdam for Keith to use to pay the crew. He had used a fake name and ID on the account and Terrence Gale was to give Keith both the ID and the name he was to use to access the account when Terrence received the cargo. Keith would not have received his instructions for accessing that account before he was arrested. Brian doubted he could be traced to that account or to what the press were calling Operation Bishop.

Of course, he had met with Archie and separately with Gale on several occasions to solidify arrangements for storing the cannabis at the Bentley Golf Club once it arrived in Essex. *Certainly Archie will keep me out of this?* But what about Gale? Gale was bent, which made him useful. If Gale named

Brian, Archie would make him pay. Archie knew things about Terrence Gale and Gale knew Archie knew. He wondered if Gale would rat on Archie. Did Terrence even know of Archie's involvement? Terrence and Archie had been friends growing up, but Archie had insisted on anonymity in this operation, so Gale should not know Archie was involved.

Archie! Squirrelly man, Archie. Smart and clever. Protected himself nicely. With the arrests taking place in North Fambridge, there would be nothing contraband for the police to discover at the Club, nothing to incriminate either Archie or Brian. But Brian might be vulnerable because of those bloody meetings with Keith and Gale. Of course, he'd never explicitly discussed with Keith the yacht's cargo.

God, he was grateful that Georgina had arranged for him to leave the U.K. two days before the cargo arrived there. Against Archie's advice, he'd taken her with him to Palma. Now, she had facilitated his departure from Britain. Were he ever ready to limit his lust and settle down, the statuesque blonde would be a likely candidate. Was Georgina safe? he wondered momentarily before returning to his first priority, himself.

Someone knocked on the door to his room, a brief, soft, obsequious knock with just the right amount of deferential assertion. "Message for you, Sir."

He opened the door to a young man with dark Cypriot good looks wearing the livery of the hotel staff and holding in his white-gloved hand an ivory envelope. Brian gathered some coins from the dresser to tip him and exchanged them for the envelope, thanking the young man before closing the door behind him. Then he opened the envelope. Printed in child-like letters and centered on a sheet of vellum were the words, "WELCOME TO YOUR NEW LIFE." Enfolded within the vellum was a United States passport. He opened it and found his face staring back at him under a different name. There was also a credit card issued to the same name by BCCI bank. Archie was taking care of him as he'd promised.

Archie had told him the U.S. Drug Enforcement Authority had a station here in Cyprus. He'd said it casually, a throw-away comment, but when Georgina brought him the ticket to Nicosia, Brian had remembered. It shouldn't surprise him that Archie had friends here in Nicosia, and probably among the U.S. anti-drug agents. Archie always had a knack for maintaining good relations on both sides of the street.

He wished Archie had provided clearer instructions. Was this envelope instructing him to assume this new identity temporarily, until the drug bust blew over, or from this day forward?

He crumpled the paper that had enclosed the passport and tossed it in the wastebasket. He put the passport in his breast pocket. He would wait a few days and then find a way to call home from an obscure location. By then his Mum would probably have had a visit from the coppers and might have news. But the phones might be unsafe.

Georgina was to arrive in Monaco today. She would fly here to Nicosia two days hence. For now, there was nothing to do but wait. He poured himself a scotch and, when his glass was empty, he put on his swim trunks and took the elevator to the Olympic sized pool on the top floor where he swam probably sixty laps. His mind was too busy to keep a proper count.

His muscles ached when he pulled himself out of the pool and fell back on the sun-warmed concrete. A heaviness of heart pulled at him, a dawning consciousness that things would not be the same ever again. He stood and moved toward a chaise lounge, lowering himself wearily onto its cushions, grateful to see a waiter moving his way. The next two days might last a long time. Everything was so unclear. He ordered another scotch, then made it a double. Brian was unwittingly about to enter the world CIA director William Casey had built.

Chapter 24

Three years ago, when he'd moved into his office at CIA headquarters in the Virginia countryside just outside Washington, D.C., Bill Casey had lost no time re-establishing multiple covert operations. The Contra guerrilla army in Central America had been his favorite. But once Congress cut off funding to overthrow the Nicaraguan government, he had to be especially creative to stay one step ahead of congressional oversight and keep his guerrillas supplied. He'd begun assembling third parties, governments and individuals, to step in where Congress feared to go.

Casey loved the clever ways his predecessors at the CIA had tried to get rid of that S.O.B. Fidel Castro. Their methods of assassination had even included exploding cigars! Don't get him started on the limits Congress placed on the Agency in the Seventies. Banning assassinations of foreign leaders! Ruining creative ways to bury leftist governments! Just thinking about the stupidity of these limitations set his hearing aids buzzing!

This situation in Nicaragua was all the fault of those ungrateful young people who called themselves Sandinistas. They'd overthrown Nicaragua's long-time dictator, Anastasio Somoza, in July 1979. Somoza had been reliably anti-communist, pro-capitalist, and pro-United States. Not so the Sandinistas who replaced him. They claimed to be non-aligned—as did Egypt and Syria, India and even Cuba—but clearly their hero was Fidel Castro, who'd been thumbing his nose at the United States for a quarter of a century.

William Casey had no tolerance for young bloods who rejected U.S. government direction. To Casey nonaligned autonomy was a joke in a world dominated by the struggle between Good and Evil, the West versus the East, Capitalism versus Communism. No country, no person could be non-aligned. It was a binary universe. You are either with us or against us.

When Cuba dispatched boat loads of Cuban doctors, arms and supplies to Nicaragua to aid the Sandinista revolution--"like they were making a God damned mission trip," one of Casey's buddies commented—Casey considered sending in a covert assassination team to Nicaragua, despite the fact that Congress had banned assassinating foreign leaders. But the Sandinistas had rendered assassination an ineffective strategy by governing through nine men, each ostensibly with equal power to lead their new revolutionary government. They called it their "Directorate." Kill one or two and others would step in. Like a damn hornets' nest—or a hydra-headed monster. And they had the gall to include professors and popular priests in their Directorate. Who'd have thought those damned revolutionaries would be good at public relations. But their love affair with Fidel Castro? Well, that was just plain stupid.

Bill Casey was a serious Catholic. He had gone to Catholic schools—Fordham University and St. John's—and he considered himself deeply religious. When Jesuit priests and Maryknoll nuns began defending the Sandinista revolution and argued that its goal was to overturn the violence and oppression of the Somoza regime, Casey became nearly apoplectic. These Catholic orders said Somoza had bled the poor and served the interests of the rich! It made Casey sick to his stomach thinking about what was happening to his Church. As he'd told President Reagan, radical priests were perverting the Church with their "liberation theology" and their insistence that Jesus advocated a "preferential option for the poor." *What a load of communist bullshit*! Casey ranted to any and all who would listen, his gruff voice growing even more garbled and his face flushed as he paced his office. Of course Christians are to help the poor, he sputtered. That's why the U.S. government had sent millions of dollars to Somoza after a devastating earthquake destroyed much of the capital city of Managua.

Nuns and priests from his beloved Catholic church continued testifying before Congress and meeting individually with Members of Congress, urging them to *send aid to the Sandinista government and to end any and all aid to Casey's Contra guerrillas.* It was infuriating how his church had been hoodwinked by the liberal media's version of reality.

For much of the twentieth century U.S. troops had entered Nicaragua to "correct" its government. But the Sandinistas declared that those days were over. No more foreign intervention in their country, especially not by the powerful North American superpower.

The Sandinistas dismissed the United States. They'd raised their middle fingers to the colossus of the north. Neither President Reagan nor Bill Casey would tolerate that. Casey's CIA would "correct" Nicaragua's young revolutionaries.

Casey's Contras were operating from two countries in Central America, Honduras and Costa Rica. Recruiting the Miskito Afro-Indians of the region to join the Contra army was a major coup for Casey.

Casey had been a writer of bestselling manuals and an entrepreneur. He was convinced that a propaganda campaign could be waged successfully to mobilize the American public to support the Administration's anti-communist causes. Americans in the aggregate were uninformed about the rest of the world. They had short attention spans and could be easily turned by repeated messaging through organized educational campaigns. Hell, a lot of churches were conducting such campaigns to build sympathy for the Sandinistas. The U.S. government just had to take it a step farther and use its resources to counter this liberal perversion of Christianity.

The State Department prepared and distributed glossy educational pamphlets on what they called the communist campaign to take control of Central America. Educational forums to teach the public the truth of Nicaragua and solicit their support were regularly held in Washington for specific sectors of the public--the media, clergy, and corporate leaders. The American public must be persuaded that the Contra cause was a Good Guy-Bad Guy fight.

Chapter 25

D espite the U.S. government's costly public relations campaign, by 1984, most Americans opposed overthrowing the Sandinista government.

While Casey fumed, a homegrown army besieged Congress, church people and human rights activists who multiplied across the U.S. They organized fact-finding trips to Nicaragua and harbored Central American refugees in their homes, synagogues, and churches. Offering "sanctuary," they called it. They held prayer vigils on the steps of the U.S. Capitol carrying white crosses, each bearing the name of a person killed by the Contras. Some prayed inside the Capitol and were carted off to jail when they refused police orders to desist. They attracted lots of media coverage.

Some Republicans stopped supporting the Contra war and spoke out. Senator John Danforth, a Republican from Missouri and an Episcopal priest, urged his Senate colleagues to oppose all aid for the Contras. He had interviewed Contras in Honduras, he told them, and was convinced that they did not oppose the Sandinistas. They were simply peasant farmers who needed money to feed their families. They joined the Contra army because it paid them. A few other Republicans in Congress said the U.S. had no business trying to overthrow a government that was holding elections, as Nicaragua was doing.

The army of church and human rights activists prevailed. Congress passed a second Boland Amendment to the appropriations bill, banning any U.S. aid to the Contras, to begin October 1, 1984. The law read: *"[N]o funds... may be obligated or expended for the purpose or which would have the effect of supporting directly or indirectly, military or paramilitary operations in Nicaragua by any nation, group, organization, movement or individual."*

Casey was prepared. Months earlier he had devised another way to aid the Contras. He called on his buddies in the private sector to help. People not in government and foreign governments would locate, pay for, and deliver money and weapons to the Contra guerrillas. The U.S. President's top advisors and the President himself agreed that they would not abandon the Contras. Privatization was at the heart of capitalism after all.

Casey set up a secret network of his wealthy friends, who he affectionately called his "Hardy Boys." One was Bob Anderson, who had extensive experience in government. He had been Secretary of the Navy, Deputy Secretary of Defense, and Secretary of the Treasury in the Eisenhower Administration. An oil and gas businessman with an offshore bank, Anderson had left government service after the disastrous Bay of Pigs invasion of Cuba in 1961.

John Shaheen was a veteran of the predecessor agency to the CIA, the Office of Strategic Services. He was an old friend of Casey and, like Anderson, an oil man and a major donor to the Republican Party.

Max Hugel was a self-made multi-millionaire businessman, a major contributor to Ronald Reagan's campaign for the presidency. He was an orphan from Brooklyn whose speech defied the rules of English grammar, an ultimate outsider among the elite professionals of the CIA. Casey disregarded those professionals and made Hugel director of the CIA Office of Clandestine Activities.

Hugel had close relations with Israel's intelligence service, the Mossad. In his six months at the CIA, before he was investigated for stock fraud and forced to resign, Hugel established a network of private companies that would front CIA activities and protect the Agency from Congressional oversight.

To be a Hardy Boy required absolute commitment to stopping the spread of communism. Members of Casey's private network were multimillionaires or billionaires with considerable knowledge of money laundering and thick checkbooks, a prerequisite so they could make hefty personal contributions to the cause. All of them had high level contacts with foreign governments and leaders of international businesses, who they could tap to fund this operation.

Some of Casey's Hardy Boys were not U.S. citizens, like Palestine-born Bruce Rappaport, whose international banking connections and ties to Israel were important to this campaign. He would control the bank accounts used to receive and distribute the tens of millions of dollars that Casey's friends raised for the Contras.

Casey selected the National Security Council's Colonel Oliver North to manage his Contra supply operation, which he called "the Enterprise." Casey argued that he was not breaking the law because the National Security Council advised the president on national security concerns—the *NSC wasn't charged with conducting foreign policy--so, technically, the ban did not extend to NSC staff.*

The Enterprise worked through strange bedfellows—the governments of Israel and Pakistan, Saudi Arabia and South Africa, and international businesses. It was unknown to the House and Senate Intelligence committees. Congress had forbidden the Reagan Administration from conducting foreign policy as it believed it should. Well, Congress did not need to know everything. Massage the law. Bend it. When you can't get around it legally, break it by using people outside government to achieve your ends. They were acting on behalf of the President of the United States through back channels and so-called black organizations.

At the center, Casey was never sure how much President Reagan really understood of what they were doing. Casey tended to mumble when he spoke, and Reagan was deaf in one ear. When Reagan didn't understand Casey, rather than asking Casey to repeat himself, the President generally just nodded, which Casey and the others in Reagan's cabinet took to mean assent.

The funds for the Contras went into dozens of secret accounts set up through the Bank of Credit and Commerce International (BCCI), an organization run by a close advisor to Pakistan's President, General Zia.

BCCI had branches across the Middle East and around the globe in a total of seventy-eight countries. Its investors included the intelligence chiefs of Saudi Arabia, Pakistan, and the United States. The Contras in Honduras and Costa Rica and the PLO in Syria, Lebanon, and Jordan put their funds in BCCI. So did drug cartels and syndicates of organized crime. BCCI funded wars, laundered money for terrorist groups and intelligence agencies, and funneled weapons to governments that the West officially labeled "terrorist," including Iran. BCCI engaged in covertly funding the production and distribution of illegal drugs. It funded Pakistan's Khan Research Laboratories, which assisted Pakistan's nuclear weapons program. BCCI also funded an international Islamist army based in Afghanistan, which would by 1988 call itself Al Qaeda.

William Casey had his eye on Operation Bishop as the crew of *The Robert Gordon* made their way to jail in England. It was part of his larger plan to carry out his and his President's foreign policy.

Chapter 26

Janet woke up earlier than usual. Keith would be home today! She smiled to herself.

The phone was ringing, and she hurried to answer it before it woke Teddy. The voice sounded like Archie's, although the speaker did not identify himself. "There's been a bit of a problem. Don't talk to anyone till we sort out how to handle this. Understand? Everything as usual, normal routines. I'll get back to you later."

When the voice rang off and she set the phone in its cradle, her hand was shaking. Back in her bed she reached for the radio and tuned in to the BBC, volume so low she could barely hear it.

"Last night Customs and Excise Officials seized a large amount of cannabis resin being off-loaded in North Fambridge on the River Crouch in Essex. Eight people were arrested, including the drivers of hired vans that were transporting the off-loaded illegal drugs. Also arrested were the crew aboard the yacht that was carrying the drugs. Police Captain Alexander will hold a press conference this morning at ten where additional information will be provided. That's all for now."

CANNABIS RESIN? *What could that have to do with Keith and his furniture shipment?* She sat against her bed pillows trying to think clearly. Archie said there was a problem. He said to talk to no one. God, what would she have to say to anyone? Keith was bringing back exotic inlaid wood boxes and small tables. There couldn't be any connection to the news story… Except that Keith expected to bring his boat up the River Crouch.

Teddy was waking up, rubbing his eyes, and she could feel something warm beside her in the bed. "Mummy, I weed." His voice was quiet and he didn't look at her, obviously embarrassed. She got up and walked him to the toilet, took off his wet jammies, still warm with urine, and placed them in the shower stall. She turned on the tap and corrected the mix of hot and cold water. Then she washed Teddy down, letting the soapy water that bounced off his taut little boy body wash the jammies. Absentmindedly she murmured something encouraging to Teddy, like, "It's all right, Teddy. Don't fret about it." She was talking to herself more than to her son.

Photos from the police file-

INDEX TO PHOTOGRAPHS

SUBJECT: Seizure of Cannabis resin

1. Cannabis from the boat 'TS Robert Gordon'
2. Cannabis from the hire van NMK 100X
3. Cannabis in the inflatable dinghy

Part 3 - Prison

Chapter 27

After they were arraigned in court in Chelmsford on Monday, all seven men and Sally, the only woman, were dispatched to London. Sally was taken to Wormwood Prison for Women and the rest to Brixton.

Brixton Prison housed its inmates in double or triple cells, so Keith, Tom and Niko were assigned to one cell and Terrence, John, and Geoff to another. That left David, who was put into a cell with a man who joked with him that their cell was reserved for smugglers. He told David with pride that he was a diamond smuggler.

Janet succeeded in getting Teddy and herself off to school on the morning of October 5th and managed somehow to get through the first hours of the day. She assigned her class a silent reading project to coincide with the Police Captain's press conference and furtively inserted her earphones and turned her transistor radio to the BBC to listen while the children read. What she heard lent little to her knowledge base—a yacht had been captured while unloading illegal cannabis near North Fambridge. All involved would be taken to Brixton Prison in London later today, one woman and seven men, the names not yet released. The boat had come from the Mediterranean and its cargo was estimated to be 46,000 kilos—101,417 pounds weight--of cannabis with a street value of ten and a half million pounds Sterling. It was the most valuable illegal drug cargo in Britain's history. Indeed, the quantity was so massive that it would fill the well of the court, according to the testimony of one of the Customs officials.

When she heard that last bit Janet's hand involuntarily jerked, overturning her cup of tea. She watched vacantly as the rusty brown water spread across the papers stacked on her desk to be returned to the children.

"Are you all right, Ms. Morris?" a child on the front row asked. She couldn't speak, she just nodded with an artificial smile exposing her irregular teeth, which she rarely showed. The children noticed her smile and became anxious. Ms. Morris was a very nice lady, but they knew she always kept her smile in check. One child brought her a pile of paper towels to sop up the spilt tea.

The day went downhill from then on, all of them on edge and the children, uncertain why, acting out from anxiety.

When she left school and brought Teddy home at the end of the day, she could smell the acrid odor of something burning as soon as she opened the door. Damn. She'd left the burner on low under the remains of their porridge. The pan was scorched past all relief. She aired out the house and, when they could stand being inside without gagging, she served them both a dish of Keith's favorite lamb stew, while the Fraggle puppets cavorted across the screen making Teddy chuckle.

Just then the doorbell rang. She opened the door to find two uniformed policemen. The older one was tapping a small spiral notebook with his ball point pen.

"Miss Janet Morris?"

"Yes."

"I'm Constable Jeffers. May I come in, please?" He stepped inside the doorway without waiting for her answer, motioning his assistant to join him. The no-name assistant had a pen and a larger pad of paper on which began to write. "I believe a Mr. Keith Brown resides at this address, is that correct?"

She nodded, paralyzed with fear. All those films where the uniformed officer comes to tell the next of kin that their loved one was killed in war kept circling her brain. "Is Keith safe?" She did not recognize her own voice, it was so faint and frail.

"Yes, ma'am. Her Majesty's finest is taking care of him at Brixton Prison."

She reached behind her for the arm of the loveseat and lowered herself onto it. Teddy was holding onto her right pant leg.

"Do you know why he is in prison, ma'am?" The officer's furrowed brows reprimanded her as effectively as if he had said, "It's always the fault of the woman." The officer looked down at Teddy and suggested he go watch television. He said it with such authority that the child released his mother's slacks and exited the room immediately, sitting on the rocking chair from where he could keep her in sight. Teddy's eyes moved back and forth from the TV to Janet as though he was watching a tennis match.

Janet was remembering the man on the phone—Archie?--telling her to say nothing to anyone. But this was a copper! She decided that she was safe if she stuck to what she knew, which, apparently, was nothing. A slender stream of anger at Keith began to work its way into her brain and she banished it as best she could for the moment.

"Are you familiar with *The Robert Gordon*?"

"I believe Keith sold his original boat and purchased *The Robert Gordon*, but I've never been on that boat."

"Were you expecting Keith Brown to return home today?"

"I didn't really know when he'd be home."

"What was he doing away from home, in your opinion?"

"He was bringing a cargo of inlaid wood furnishings back to England for a distributor."

"Who was the distributor?"

"I never knew his name."

"Does Mr. Brown use illegal drugs?"

"No, sir, not as I am aware. We have a young child, and I'd not allow that. I'm a teacher."

"So we understand. Did you know who was working with Mr. Brown during this trip?"

"No, sir. I know most of the men he works with at the car hire and at the car repair shop. They go out for a pint together some Friday evenings and I go along when I can get my mum to care for Teddy. Different ones of them bring their girlfriends. But I don't know who was working the boat with him."

"Was he in charge of the boat?"

Janet paused, distressed, not knowing what to say. Finally, she said, "I don't know, sir. I am totally in a muddle knowing nothing about all this except that I've heard some awful stuff on the news and you are here, which is scaring me. I was just looking forward to my man coming home." Her eyes blurred with tears that she brushed away with the back of her right hand. "What is he charged with? What happens now? Can I go see Keith? What is going to happen to him? What do you want from me?" Her questions rushed out of her like a rogue car on the underground as her panic took over. She knew she was losing control and could do nothing to stop it.

"If I was you, I'd get Mr. Brown a good lawyer, a criminal lawyer. The court will appoint him one, but one you hire will probably serve you better, though I shouldn't be telling you that. He should be able to have visitors, fifteen minutes a day, once he's been formally charged before the court, which happens Monday. Yes, get a lawyer. There are services you can call that can recommend good ones. And you might start assembling bail money, though the charges are so serious, they may not allow bail. You've been helpful, ma'am. We'll be leaving you and your son alone now. Thank you for your time."

Both men stood, touched their caps, and departed, closing the door firmly behind them. She could hear the guttural grinding of an ignition looking for a spark and then the sound of an engine growing softer as they drove away.

Why hadn't Archie phoned? Keith had said his friend Archie would keep her informed. *Was the man on the phone Archie?*

She spooned Teddy a bowl of ice cream topping it with animal crackers. Then she dished herself a bowl. They ate in silence. She suggested they play Chutes and Ladders and set up the game. Teddy had to remind her each time it was her turn, so it wasn't much fun for either of them. Her legs and arms ached from having been tensed so tightly in her effort to avoid a meltdown. Together she and her son went upstairs and crawled into the bed that was still unmade since morning. The wet spot on the sheet was dry now and barely visible, and she had no energy for changing the sheets. She snuggled Teddy to her and covered them with the duvet. She remembered looking at the green digits on the clock most hours of that night, waiting futilely for the phone to ring.

Chapter 28

The Operation Bishop team assembled for its third meeting in the basement of the grey stone warehouse used by Customs and Excise, in Chelsea. As usual, the CIA man skipped the pleasantries and took control. By now the others had come to expect this. He plunged ahead speaking rapid-fire.

"Congratulations are in order. We have collaborated effectively and caught those smuggling drugs to England from Lebanon. Well done. Seven men and one woman are in prison. Their trials will begin once we are assured our assets are safely relocated."

"What has happened to the contraband cargo, if I may ask?" the American Embassy official asked.

It was a question the others were thinking.

The Chelmsford Chief Inspector looked uncomfortable. "We were tracking a Jamaican Yardie gang that we believed were to receive the drugs that night, but they scattered when we arrived and the fellow leading them went completely off our radar. I've heard he is back in Jamaica and unlikely to return to the U.K., though he made a bloody fortune here pushing drugs the past three years. We have stored the cargo in a warehouse. We've not yet decided how to dispose of it."

The MI-6 man was smiling at his CIA colleague. "Tell him what your American police departments do with contraband you seize."

"We have a program in the U.S. called Civil Asset Forfeiture that allows police to seize money or cargo, even when the person is not arrested, and to sell what is seized, the funds going to support the local police who stopped the suspect and apprehended the contraband. It's been a pilot program, but Congress is currently considering legislation to allow the right of forfeiture in drug crimes to extend to any property used to facilitate the crime—vehicles, property intended to be used as storage, you name it. U.S. police departments like civil asset forfeiture, especially in times like these of economic downturn."

"What do you do with the confiscated drugs?"

"I can't tell you that, but you can use your imagination."

Around the room the men to whom this was an unheard of exercise of government power tried to reassemble their faces and disguise their shock.

"You can be assured, gentlemen, that the millions of pounds Operation Bishop 'liberated' in the form of cannabis resin will be used to support the foreign policy our two governments share." The CIA man looked quite smug.

The Customs and Excise man and the Chelmsford police commander left the building together. They had grown to like each other as they worked on Operation Bishop. The C&E official smiled ironically at the police captain. He chose his words carefully. "The older I get the more respect I have for Lewis Carroll. It is hard to tell those assigned to enforce the law from those who break it. Those who protect our people from organized crime become the organizers. Nothing is as we're taught, like Alice discovered in Wonderland."

"Maybe we should name our next operation 'Wonderland'?"

"I shouldn't be surprised if it's been done."

The two parted in the parking lot after shaking hands.

"For God and Country?"

"For God and Country and Cash!"

Chapter 29

Georgina arrived in Nicosia on the 5th of October. They met at a no-frills hotel where Archie had told Georgina they should stay to be less conspicuous. Brian regretted leaving the luxurious hotel that had been his refuge for three days. No Olympic-sized swimming pool here. They had gone to their room and begun to unpack. Brian's expectations for their reunion were disappointed. Both of them were feeling anxious.

As Georgina shook out the outfit she had folded in tissue paper and placed on top of the rest of her clothes, she heard a soft swish. A thin blue airletter addressed simply "BB" had fallen from the tissue paper and lay on the carpet beside her foot. Surprised, she reached down, picked it up, puzzled over how it got into her luggage, and passed it to Brian.

Brian slit the sealed edges of the airletter with his pocketknife and unfolded it. Inside, letters cut from a newspaper walked a jagged path across the page. They spelled out two partial sentences: "8 10 at noon Pazema Taverna, Argos. Ask for Andreas Vasileiou." Brian knew immediately that this note was what Archie had told him to look for. The last time they met, Archie had said if anything went wrong, he would receive instructions and should do as directed. "8 10" must mean October 8, in three days. Unclear where Argos was, Brian unfolded the road map of Cyprus he'd purchased at the airport in Nicosia. His eyes scanned it searching for Argos. He vaguely recalled his grandfather talking about Mount Olympus, part of the Troodos Mountains that stretch in a crescent along the west of Cyprus, from the island's center to the south. He found Nicosia and Mount Olympus. Nearby was a small dot marked Argos.

What was in Argos, he wondered. And who was Andreas Vasileiou?

For the next three days those questions festered while he and Georgina visited sites in Nicosia, each of them carrying the new passports Archie had provided to them. They practiced referring to each other by their new names. The fourth day he paid their bill with Cypriot cash and hailed a taxi. Argos was a forty-five-minute drive from Nicosia.

Georgina slept most of the way while Brian stared unseeing out the window as the landscape changed to mountains growing up from the earth in enormous humps, the terrain rugged and bleached with nothing but scrub vegetation and occasional stunted trees.

The amount of uncertainty he was experiencing made him uneasy, even fearful. He still carried three passports, although Archie had told him if the operation went wrong, he should destroy his British and Cypriot passports and assume the new identity Archie would provide. At the time it seemed Archie was merely being thorough, planning for every contingency. Now Brian wondered how Archie had been so prepared for the Customs and Excise people to have apprehended *The Robert Gordon* and its cargo. He guessed he would never see a penny from his investment.

The taxi pulled up in front of a sprawling restaurant. It looked especially large since Argos was a town with fewer than a thousand people. A broad flagstone terrace faced the mountains. Grape vines sprawled across a skeleton roof that shaded the terrace. In the shade created by the grape vines, rows of long tables stood in orderly formation. Perhaps festive tourists filled them at other times, but today, as it was well past two and low-season, the restaurant's tables were mostly empty, just a few pensioners and elderly tourists prolonging their good meal with another glass of Commandaria wine while they watched the sun play hide and seek on the mountainside. There was just enough space between the rows of tables for the male waiters to make their way carrying round silver trays loaded with food.

Brian paid the driver and carried their luggage inside, mustering his rudimentary Greek from childhood to ask if he could leave their cases in the office while they ate. He thought he understood the smile on the young waiter's face more than the words he uttered and decided the smile was a Yes.

Georgina and he seated themselves at a table with no other customers in ear shot and looked out across the valley at the Troodos Mountains. They could see the tallest peak, Mount Olympus, snow-topped despite the warm autumn day. Around them the other diners chatted and poured themselves more wine. Had he not been anxious about what came next, he would have simply enjoyed the surroundings. His anxiety always rooted in his stomach, which growled and cramped, causing him to order less than he would normally, despite the attractive meze plates and platters of pork and sausages that he saw the waiters deliver to other diners.

A portly middle-aged man approached wearing an apron and carrying a tablet. When he stopped behind Georgina, facing Brian, Brian trotted out his childhood Greek once again. "Signomi, poo eenay Andreas Vasileiou?" The man's face muscles tightened. Brian thought he detected surprise in his eyes.

"Ne. Kala…." The man handed him a menu. Brian thought he was saying, Yes.

Having exhausted his Greek and feeling totally lost, he eyed Georgina and passed her the menu. She ordered moussaka and salad in what sounded to him like perfect Greek. Bless the woman! His stomach relaxed. Not to be outdone by her, he pointed at an item and nodded to the waiter whose thick eyebrows arched dramatically. He also ordered coffee because he recognized the word, "café."

When the waiter left them, Georgina was smiling broadly at him. "I didn't expect you would order sheftalia," she said.

"Why?" he asked, feeling defensive.

"Because it is a kind of sausage encased in the membrane that surrounds the stomach of a lamb and you usually stay away from sweet breads and tripe and other exotic innards."

Brian stumbled from the table, his stomach flip-flopping, and hurried into the restaurant to find the toilet. When he returned, he saw Georgina motioning the waiter to give the sheftalia to her.

It was three o'clock when they finished their meal. They went inside to pay, and Brian did not see their luggage. His heart began to race. Their waiter motioned him to a room in the rear, through a curtain of hanging beads that shimmered and chimed as he pushed them aside. An older man directed him to sit. In English as labored as Brian's Greek he instructed Brian. "We drive you to airfield. You fly small plane to Tel Aviv and from there to ..." Brian was not sure he understood this part. It sounded like Costa Rica but could have been Cote d'Ivoire or something else entirely. God, he hated feeling so vulnerable. He was placing their lives in the hands of these strangers and had no alternative. He nodded. Then he pulled out his British, U.S., and Cypriot passports, the one from being born in Cyprus, the British dual citizenship one, and the American one with the different name Archie had provided. "Which one?" he asked.

The man reached for them, opened all three, then passed back the one with the new name. "No this one," he said about the British passport, brushing his hands together like wiping off something gritty. "No this one," he repeated holding up Brian's dual citizenship Cypriot passport and making the same gesture. Still holding both of Brian's original passports he turned and walked back into the kitchen calling to someone. The teenaged boy who Brian had met when he brought in their suitcases emerged from the kitchen, picked up their bags, and pushed through the curtain of beads and out the side door of the Pazema Taverna. He walked quickly and they hurried after him. He loaded their luggage into the boot of a recent model white Ford sedan and opened the back door, motioning for them to get in, which they did. Then he got in the driver's seat and they took off, the tires spitting dust as the Ford devoured the empty mountain road. Brian realized with chagrin that the man had not returned his legitimate passports.

The airport had no concrete runway, only a level area with dual use—as pasture for several dozen goats and as a bumpy runway that crossed the pasture and appeared to have been mostly cleared of rocks. Paired tracks ran like furrows toward the end of the field and disappeared in a steep, tree-covered ravine. Two single engine six-seaters faced away from the mountains. Like the van they were white and wore no markings that Brian could see.

The boy had said nothing during their twenty-two-mile drive. Neither had Georgina or Brian. Brian was struck by how young the boy looked. It dismayed him to realize that they, who in their early thirties thought of themselves as young, must seem old to the boy. Old and without an identity. His usual confidence that he could charm his way out of any situation felt shaky. He was apprehensive, depleted and lost. He had control over nothing, not even his name. He pulled out his new U.S. passport and obsessively studied the name under his photo.

The boy moved quickly exiting the car. He lifted their bags from the boot and carried them to the nearer plane, calling them to follow. Then he grinned, briefly, shook their hands, and skedaddled back to the car, which spat gravel as it accelerated and vanished down the curl of road.

Chapter 30

Janet was awakened by an indeterminate sound coming from the front of the house. In her current state of distress she was sleeping fitfully. She'd gone into London yesterday to see Keith at Brixton Prison and been granted only fifteen minutes to speak to him, sitting across from him at a long table with a board barrier to prevent any physical contact. Guards stood at either end of the table to monitor their contact. Half the time she'd spent crying. Not so that others would notice, no sobs or ragged breaths, just wet tracks winding down her cheeks and drops falling off her chin into her lap, slow and steady. It was the expression on Keith's face and his silence that set her off. He was truly frightened, panicked, even.

She'd never known Keith to be at a loss for words. He was cheerful, loquacious, an arm around your back, hand clasping your shoulder kind of man, always taking charge with bluff good humor. But not yesterday. And his fear was contagious. She could not stop it from showing.

They'd exchanged very little information sitting there across from each other. Neither of them seemed to know anything. He told her he was worried about two of the crew, the two youngest, Sally and David. They were innocent and terrified. Sally, the cook, was held in the women's prison where she had no opportunity to talk with the rest of them, unlike here in the men's prison where they had an hour a day out of their cells and where he shared a cell with Tom and could converse, although Tom was habitually silent. They'd moved Niko into another cell, maybe because he was a foreigner? He wasn't sure.

Keith didn't know if Sally had any family to turn to for support.

David? Well, they'd taken him on in Gibraltar, the last leg of the trip, and the young hippie was a salt of the earth kind of kid, totally oblivious to the nature of their cargo. Here Keith blushed as he realized that Janet had also been oblivious.

"If my friends contact you, ask if they can help these kids." They seemed to be what worried him most, next to Teddy and her.

"What about you? Should I be contacting anyone, a solicitor? Or your family?" As long as they'd been together Janet had never met Keith's Mum. His Dad hadn't been part of his life since he was three. Each year she would offer to invite his Mum for Boxing Day or Guy Fawkes Day—one of the less intimate holidays--but Keith would brush her suggestions away, "She'll be too mashed to remember to come and I really don't want Teddy around her. He doesn't need to see his granny pissed and tiddly. I know the woman. That's the only way he would see her." Surely there was someone she could call?

"My brother John was in Aberdeen last I heard. Don't know how to reach him. I'm counting on Archie to know how to handle this....I'm right sorry to have brought you into this mess...."

There'd been time for little more than that brief exchange, except for him to inquire about Teddy. When he said his son's name, his voice grew gravelly.

"My Dad was a royal mess, in trouble with the law and on the run till he ran so far I never saw him again. I been so determined to not follow either of 'em, but look at me now!" That was when he broke down, just before the prison officer tapped Janet on the shoulder to tell her that their visit was over.

Seeing Keith like that at Brixton Prison had made it more real that their lives were crumbling around them. Now she stretched out on their bed, legs tensed and straight, every muscle tight, listening for the sound that had awakened her to recur. It didn't.

In a few moments she sat up, willing herself to get up and go to the front door. There underneath the mail slot she found two folded pieces of paper. On one a message had been typed, no salutation, no signature: "PUT THIS IN THE CAR HIRE FILE. TALK TO NO ONE. YOU KNOW NOTHING."

The other paper was an invoice for the rental of two vans dated 3 October 1984. The party hiring the vans was a Mr. Geoff Johnson, the address somewhere in Inverness.

When Keith had left to pick up the yacht and begin what she'd thought would be his first import trip, she'd taken over managing the businesses, since she was out of school for the long summer holiday and Mum was willing to continue caring for Teddy during the weekdays. But she'd turned that responsibility over to Keith's mate Jack when her autumn school term began. It was Jack who would have let the vans and Jack whom she would ordinarily consult about adding an invoice to the files. But the message was clear, TALK TO NO ONE. That would include Jack.

She returned to bed, the two papers folded together and tucked into the pocket of her coat. She lay there wide awake until she heard Teddy stirring. Then she got up and dressed, made breakfast for the two of them, and bundled Teddy into the car for a ride to the car hire shop where she nonchalantly entered the office--Jack was not there—and inserted the invoice into the file according to date. She noticed there was no other invoice for van hires for that date. With Teddy in tow she exited the shop, tossing friendly greetings to the men who worked there, communicating that there was nothing amiss with a merry confidence she had to summon up, acting like she had nothing to worry about. She got to her car before any of them could question her about when Keith would be returning.

Chapter 31

Before October 4, Janet had loved the freedom of her life with Keith. She loved teaching six-year-olds to read and write and do sums. She loved being Mum to four-year-old Teddy. Most of all she loved living together as a family with Keith and Teddy and being with a man who supported her making her own choices for her life.

There was no question it was still stressful when they were with her parents. The first time she brought Keith home and made it clear to her parents that they'd be sharing her bedroom, she thought her Dad would have a heart attack—red face, the pulse point on right side of his forehead pumping rapidly, and a scowl on his face like the Rapture had come and left him behind. Fortunately, Mum and Dad confined expressions of disapproval to body language and heartfelt sighs, at least that time, although after she and Keith said good night and went to bed, she overheard bits of her parents' conversation about the immoral activity taking place in their sanctified home.

When she discovered she was pregnant and decided not to marry Keith, their disapproval and her accompanying stress magnified exponentially. Her father no longer restrained himself, roaring about what was happening to this world and how could she bring a child into a pagan home. Impatient with their hypocrisy Keith had reminded her irate father that he'd got Janet's unmarried mum pregnant at sixteen! By contrast, Keith and Janet were both well past a quarter century and presumably wiser and better prepared to decide how to handle an unplanned pregnancy. Keith's audacity—and the truth of his observation—had positively ignited Janet's dad. Janet and her mum each had grabbed hold of her man and held on tight to keep them from battering each other.

Janet was raised in the Plymouth Brethren Church and her parents were both staunch believers in its conservative ways. As a child she attended church several times a week: Thursday evenings for Bible study and a midweek worship in addition to three-hour services on Sunday mornings. She'd been a star Christian, according to the Plymouth Brethren. She knew her Bible well enough to win awards in the Youth for Christ open air meetings, and proudly recited the answers to the central questions of faith, citing the Biblical texts that proved them Truth.

Question: Who will be saved? Answer: "Everyone who shall call on the name of the Lord shall be saved." (Romans 10: 13)

Question: What is faith? Answer: "Faith is the substantiating of things hoped for, the conviction of things not seen."(Hebrews 11: 1)

Question: What happens after we die? Answer: "When a believer in the Lord Jesus dies, they are immediately in His presence—'today shalt thou be with me in paradise.'" (Luke 23: 43)

Question: Will Jesus come again? Answer: "When Jesus comes again, the dead in Christ will be raised first and the living who remain faithful to Christ shall be caught up together with them in the clouds ...and 'thus we shall be always with the Lord.'" (1st Thessalonians 4: 17)

Once she became an adult she no longer found meaning in the stringent Dos and Don'ts of the Plymouth Brethren Church--that women must cover their heads, that you must not eat with a person not part of your religious fellowship, that you should not vote. But that didn't mean she had abandoned her faith. Some things persist when you leave the church you are raised in. In Janet's case, what remained was the sense that there is a Holy dimension in life, the belief that God is Love, and a moral plumb line that guided her behavior toward generosity, charity, and forgiveness.

Gradually Mum had come around in the years Janet and Keith had been together. Even Dad grudgingly observed that Keith was a good man and treated his only daughter well, for a person living in sin.

She found herself thinking back on the path her family had followed to reach accommodation with her and Keith. She knew they continued to feel profound regret that their daughter and her man would be separated from them in the life after death, but for the present they recognized that their differences were immutable. Accept them or face the future alienated from their daughter and their grandson. For the present things were smooth...*but they didn't know the present, not the present as of the fourth of October!* Even Janet didn't know the full story. But she knew enough to feel distraught.

Thank God she hadn't married Keith, or she would be fully liable financially for this crazy venture that was likely to take his life savings and the businesses, as well as years of his life. *How could he have been so stupid?*

She had never tried drugs, not even at her most rebellious, but only a fool would think he could import a large shipment of illegal drugs under the watchful eye of the combined drug enforcement and customs agencies of a dozen nations collaborating in a multinational war against drugs. CCT surveillance cameras had been monitoring Trafalgar Square, London's rail stations and parts of the underground for a decade. Anyone who worked the docks or fished had stories of the Black Gang, customs men dressed in black carrying massive toolboxes, who inspected every boat that arrived in Britain, taking them apart expeditiously looking for illegal cargo. Nothing got past them. *What had Keith been thinking?*

The papers were full of the story of the crew of *The Robert Gordon* off-loading millions of pounds worth of cannabis resin on the shore of the River Crouch in North Fambridge, and other men loading it into rented vans. Customs apprehended all of them before the vans reached their destination, whatever that destination was. The papers named Keith as the captain, charged with masterminding the whole crazy operation. Thank God, her parents kept to themselves and others in their Plymouth Brethren congregation. Thank God, their belief that they must keep separate from those they considered non-believers and from the material world included not watching television or reading newspapers. But they were bound to find out eventually. It was terrible carrying the little bit of knowledge she had about the situation by herself, without support, but for now she would try to keep her parents out of it.

The police had been around to interview her twice. They'd asked about the trip to Rhodes, about Brian and his girlfriend, and about Keith, of course. She would not lie to them. Fortunately, she knew so little and was so infuriated with Keith for getting into this nefarious business that they seemed to believe her when she said she'd thought this was a trial run importing inlaid wooden tables and small items of furniture. They never asked about Archie. Since she didn't know Archie's surname or Brian's either, she rationalized that she would not bring either of them up, as she wouldn't be much help to them. When they left the house the second time, she watched the two officers walking back to their car in conversation, shaking their heads. She could see their profiles through the glass of the front door. She thought they were commiserating with her, feeling sorry that the poor girl was duped by her boyfriend.

At school no one spoke of her situation. The other teachers continued to be friendly, even a bit more helpful than usual. They avoided conversation about the story that the press was chasing like a dog with a rabbit. Today when she entered the lunchroom the buzz of conversation suddenly quieted, and she was certain they had been speculating about her situation. She sat in a vacant chair next to the kindly older woman whose classroom was beside hers and asked about her grandchildren. She suspected her behavior succeeded in altering the course of the group's conversation.

Now she sat at her kitchen table, both hands gripping her teacup like it was a lifeline. She assessed her situation. There had been no word from Archie. She was still completely in the dark. She had no one she could talk to.

She alternated between longing for Keith's strong arms to encircle her and wanting to slap him silly. She had not gone to see him in the past two weeks. When her anger at him was boiling over, like now, she didn't trust herself to see him. She knew he needed her support, but he'd been daft to take on serious illegal activity like this and endanger all three of them, absolutely daft! He'd written her that bail was denied and that they'd be appearing before the magistrate in the second week in November. She hoped to summon more self-control by then. She wanted to be in the courtroom for that proceeding.

Every day she visited a different chemist and bought up copies of all the papers that carried the story. After putting Teddy to bed each night she slogged through them, making notes in a small black spiral notebook when she found something new to her, something that might be useful. So far she'd learned that the eight arrested were three men who were on shore and four who were on *The Robert Gordon*, plus the woman who was the cook. All the stories named Keith as the captain. She read nothing that mentioned an Archie and the photo in the *Telegraph* of the man named Tom Hill looked nothing like the Brian they'd traveled to Rhodes with. The reporters focused on the amount of cannabis resin brought in by these men and seized by Customs, calling it the largest drug bust in Britain's history. One story quoted an unnamed Customs officer who said they'd been watching some of these men for nine months. Could Keith have been involved for that long?

Friday her Mum picked up Teddy, and Janet gave herself a treat, stopping on her way home from school for a sausage roll and a coffee above a chemist's she had not yet visited to purchase the daily papers. Afterward she pulled up in front of their house, surprised to see several other cars parked along their usually quiet and empty street. She slid out of the car carrying her newspapers and the deep canvas bag in which she kept her students' papers. A young man stood on the step, his finger on her doorbell. Her stomach knotted seeing him there, and she debated returning to the car and driving away, but he saw her first.

"Janet Morris? Would you have a minute to talk with me about Keith Brown?" He flashed a badge identifying him as a reporter with one of the tabloids, and that movement brought a cameraman out of one of the cars parked in front of her home. She felt herself go cold and paralyzed, like a deer in the headlights.

"I don't have anything to say to you." Her voice was nearly inaudible.

"You're keeping up with the press coverage, I see." The young man gestured to the stack of newspapers under her arm. It seemed to her he was sneering.

"I really know nothing about all this. I am totally in the dark. Now if you will excuse me, I must start supper." She moved past him and inserted her key in the lock, hands shaking. She had to get rid of these press people before Mum arrived with Teddy.

She was aware of flashes that illuminated her back as she stood in the doorway with its shiny brass numeral. Instinctively she kept her head lowered as she turned the key, pushed open the door, and closed it firmly behind her.

She heard the reporter's voice calling to her from outside. "We'll be seeing you in court, then."

Chapter 32

To say Sally was terrified would be an understatement. Humiliated also. She had taken this job to see the world. All she saw now was the inside of Wormwood Women's Prison from this small cell that she shared with a stranger she was wary of.

She lay on the top bunk trying to think through her situation. The police had interviewed her mum and Brenda, her sister. So they told Sally in her last interrogation session. According to the police, Brenda said Sally had told her when she called from Rhodes that she'd landed a job where she'd be earning 500 pounds a week, not a month. *Of course that sounded dodgy.* Brenda got the amount dead wrong. Brenda was eighteen and a right frivolous bird, concerned only with boys and make-up.

The last time Sally had seen Brenda, before she had moved to Rhodes, Brenda had chewed her up for leaving, jealous that her older sister was seeing the world while Brenda was left back home with the parents. Brenda always was the spoiled one. The pretty one. Full of herself. It was probably not deliberate, her telling the police that, probably a matter of being ditsy and not hearing correctly, but Brenda's statement to the police was the main evidence against Sally, other than the circumstance of her being on *The Robert Gordon* for the whole of the trip from Rhodes to the U.K.

Did Brenda realize she'd set her sister up? She hadn't come to the prison to visit Sally. Probably she never would. That was Brenda, not a thought for anyone but herself.

Mum had come to see her once. She said she couldn't afford to take off work to make the trip—which required an hour by coach each way. Sally knew Mum would be embarrassed and ashamed that Sally was here. She'd also be worried that Alfred would be upset with her for allowing Sally to go to Rhodes in the first place. Alfred was Mum's "husband." Not that Mum could have stopped her. Sally was of age. And she had wanted adventure and had the courage—yes, courage—to seek it. How many other twenty-one-year-olds would leave their country for another and take on starting a business abroad?

When she came to Wormwood to see Sally, Mum was still agitated that she'd chosen to go to Rhodes, where Sally's father came from. All the time growing up Mum's face flushed on the rare occasions when Sally asked about her father. Never said much other than that she'd met him in a pub and that he came from a good family in Rhodes. *If Mum had provided more information about him, I would probably have gone somewhere other than Rhodes and never been involved with this fiasco.*

Funny how Mum kept his name, Eliades. Uncommon name in the U.K. and now, with the story of the drug bust screaming from the tabloids, that name put Mum in an unwelcome spotlight. Sally hadn't thought much about that before, but now she wondered why Mum hadn't taken back her maiden name when they divorced. Had she still had feelings for him, maybe?

Her father had left when Sally was three. The only things she remembered of him were his smiling brown eyes and his head of thick dark hair that he was always pushing back with his right hand…And she remembered him lifting her high in the air when she was a wee one. Weird what you remember.

If she was completely honest with herself, her decision to go to Rhodes in 1982 had been based on wanting to look him up. No luck there. She couldn't even find grandparents, although, knowing nothing more than his name, that wasn't surprising. Apparently, he hadn't gone back to Rhodes. He might still be in London reading about her in the papers. Maybe he was thinking to himself, Good thing I left that lot.

Mum had never married Alfred, who came along when Sally was four and became her "dad." He'd treated her well enough, no differently than her half-sister, his biological daughter, Brenda. Probably that was because

Alfred spent his life in the military. He took seriously his obligation to be responsible and loyal. That was part of the army's code of behavior. She sensed he never understood her wanderlust and eagerness to try new things, which was a mite odd since he was the only one in the household who had lived outside the U.K.

Thank God, Alfred was off in the Falklands with the British occupation army for his final tour of duty before retirement. Of course, he wouldn't say "British occupation army." Alfred--as patriotic as they come. What kept running across her mind was how horrified he'd be at what she'd gotten herself into, *a drug smuggling scandal!* She doubted Mum had even told him. Limit who knows the family shame. That might explain why Granny and Granddad hadn't been in touch.

Sally leaned back on the top bunk staring vacantly out the barred window at the swiftly moving clouds. Grey like everything else, inside and out: Grey stone walls, grey smoke and damp air, grey wool blanket on the dingy grey sheets. At least the jumpsuits she and the other inmates wore provided some color.

The one thing that saved her in this situation was her curiosity. Most days she consoled herself with the thought that she was having yet another adventure--like leaving home for Rhodes, taking advantage of her dual citizenship, and running a bar there despite her meager knowledge of Greek and total lack of experience managing a business. Some might say she was naïve, but she preferred to think of it as being willing to try new things. Sounded better than naïve.

She'd taken the cook job on *The Robert Gordon* to get experience that would, she hoped, allow her to be hired on to a boat traveling to the Caribbean. It hadn't worked out well, but who's to say something useful wouldn't come from this experience once she got out. Maybe she'd write a book or television show about being imprisoned for drug smuggling!

She wondered where her curiosity came from. Of course, both of her parents must have been somewhat curious and adventuresome or Mum would never have married her father at nineteen, and he would never have left Greece for the U.K.

Her mind's ambling came to an abrupt stop as the seriousness of her situation began to sink in. *It's possible I could sit in prison for a decade or more if they conclude I was in on the smuggling.* The prosecutor seemed convinced that both she and David knew about the cannabis, would have smelled it with so much of it on board.

From his appearance she doubted the prosecutor had ever smoked weed recreationally. Definitely not part of the popular youth culture where smoking weed was a nightly normal. He probably never spent time at sea either, especially during a wet, chilly September when everyone on board is ill with flu or colds and congested. Barely able to breathe, much less smell anything. Why was it so hard to imagine that she and David hadn't a clue about the drugs?

It irritated her that the older generation had never tried weed but made it into some monstrous powerful substance taking over the world of the young—like demon alcohol in her grandparents' generation, she guessed. She could think of no one among her age mates who hadn't smoked weed. Frankly, it never did much for her, a slight lift of the spirits when her period took her down, but nothing more. She heard her voice speak the question out loud: *So why am I sitting here in prison despite all of the crew testifying I knew nothing about the cargo?* And she suspected she knew the answer: Because the prosecutor had missed out on using weed and was jealous.

Jealousy taking her down, Brenda's and the prosecutor's. It was just not fair. She wasn't a jealous person, being mostly content with who she was. Self-reliant. Competent. And curious. Traits she always thought were good. And here she sat in Wormwood Prison totally stuck and without a clue. *God, what can I do?*

She had no money for bail and neither did Mum. Could she make it through a decade spending the best years of her life in prison? She turned over and buried her face in her pillow, trying to swallow the terror and the tears that she could no longer restrain.

"You all right, lovey?" It was her cellmate. Moira had climbed out of the bottom bunk and stood next to the bed, one hand reaching out tentatively toward Sally. When Sally lifted her head, damp strings of hair sticking to her cheeks, the kindness in the woman's eyes surprised and moved her.

"You'll be all right, duckie. We all feel blue at times, especially at first. But once you know how long you'll be here, you'll find the time passes more quickly. I'd not lie to you about that. We've all been through it. And you can make some good friends in this place, though it sounds daft to say so. Here…" Moira dug in her pocket and pulled out a sweet wrapped in paper. She untwisted both ends and passed it to Sally. "At least in here it matters naught if your mascara runs!" She grinned and winked.

Sally savored the Werther caramel as it melted in her mouth. "Thank you," she said to Moira. "I've not had one of these since I was in Rhodes." The taste, combined with Moira's kindness, triggered more tears.

"Go ahead now, love. Cry it out. Then, if you want, you can talk about it. That's one thing we've got plenty of—time to listen."

Chapter 33

Niko had been asleep when metallic grating of the key in the lock pulled him to full alertness. He had been moved to a single cell the week previous, no explanation given. The older guard approached him followed by another man, their faces grave. The guard had been kind to Niko these two months. Nice man. The other man Niko had never seen before.

"This is Mr. Stephanopoulous, from your embassy." The guard nodded toward the smartly dressed man behind him. "He has news for you, son. I'll leave you now." He retraced his steps to the corridor and locked the cell.

Mr. Stephanopoulous looked uncomfortable as he pulled the lone white plastic chair in the cell toward the bed and placed it closer to, but still some distance from, Niko. He lowered his large body onto its molded plastic seat, his brow furrowed. Niko felt sorry for the man. He wondered if the man's size caused him anxiety each time he sat on unfamiliar chairs. The chair did not break, although its legs protested audibly, skidding wider than their usual alignment on the concrete floor. Niko sat on the edge of the bed.

Mr. Stephanopoulous cleared his throat and reached into the breast pocket of his expensive suitcoat. He extracted a thickness of folded paper. "Your mother sent this to our embassy for you." He spoke the Greek of the educated, and his eyes did not meet Niko's.

His mother. Niko felt fear working in his bowels. Why would his mother send him a letter through the embassy instead of directly to Brixton Prison? What would bring an official of the embassy here to his cell? Mr. Stephanopoulous extended his hand holding the papers out to Niko who had to stretch to reach them.

"Why?" Niko's voice was soft and uncertain.

"Just read it."

His mother had written weekly since she'd been notified of his incarceration. The familiar, careful way she shaped her letters, her beautiful penmanship touched him. In here it was the little things that constricted his throat and threatened to crack the veneer of his self-control. He struggled now to hide his emotions as he read her words.

My dearest son, Niko,

I wish I could be with you to bring you this news. We would hold each other close and our shared tears would help us wade through the waters of grief. Your papa suffered another heart attack November 24 from which his poor, overworked heart could not recover.

You know how much he loved you, how proud he always was of you, regardless of this current trouble. When your sister and I told him what had happened with you, he wept, not from disappointment, Niko, but from fear for your welfare. He wanted to take your place. He experienced prison when he fought with the guerrillas in Cyprus. He knew how prison changes a man. His worst fear was that they would deport you and you would have to serve years in prison here. He said you must serve whatever sentence they give you in Britain instead of here in Greece. [She had underlined this sentence twice for emphasis.] He knew how bad our prisons are, the lack of medical care, the crowding.

Please, son, do whatever you can to prevent deportation. I am sad writing this, because if you were here, your brother and sister and I could come to visit you. Your father was working very hard to save money to come to Britain to see you. I think he knew he did not have much time left in this world.

Do not despair, Niko. You will come through this difficult time. Do not worry about me. Your brother and sister are watching over me and I am well. We will all be reunited, Niko.

I will keep writing to you. I carry you in my heart, my beloved son.
Mama

Mr. Stephanopoulous waited for Niko to recover his composure before speaking. "Your mother has been most persistent, coming to the office of Prime Minister Papandreou to beseech him to help you." He smiled. Then his face took on a disapproving look, and he shook his head. "You know that your government cannot smile on drug smuggling. The most we can do for you is to encourage the British government to hold you here until your sentence is served and only then to deport you. We will do what we can because of your mother's tireless intervention." He smiled again. "I wish I had a mama like yours." He finally made eye contact with Niko and the expression on his face turned grave.

"There is a more serious problem. As we researched your case, we found that you had not applied for Greek citizenship when you relocated to Rhodes. As you are aware from your passport, you are a citizen of Lebanon. Unlike the rest of your family, you do not hold dual citizenship. This makes your situation more problematic, Mr. Karras, as I am sure you can appreciate."

Niko was stunned. "But I was seventeen when we moved from Lebanon so my status should have been determined by my parents' status. My parents have dual citizenship, Lebanese and Greek. I've been using my Lebanese passport, but I was certain that I had dual citizenship like the rest of my family. Mama was holding all of our Greek passports." *How could it be? I've lived in Greece nearly half my life.*

"Because they were refugees, your parents were required to live in Greece for five years before applying for Greek citizenship. By that time you were twenty-two. Our citizenship law reads"--He fumbled in the breast pocket of his suit jacket, pulled out several additional folded papers, and located the passage he needed to read. "'The children of aliens of Greek ethnic origin, who acquire Greek Citizenship…become Greek citizens at the same time their parents acquire Greek citizenship *provided that at the time of their parents' petition to the Secretary General of the Prefecture they are minors.'* You were no longer a minor. You might apply for citizenship now, but the law disqualifies those who apply if they have been convicted of crimes involving trade and trafficking of narcotics. I am afraid the government of Greece cannot help you, Mr. Karras, other than sending your solicitor a letter to the court explaining your peculiar and difficult circumstances, which we will, of course, do."

Mr. Stephanopoulous stood and turned toward the door out of the cell, then turned back to offer his hand to Niko. "Good luck, son," he said before stepping to the door and calling the guard to let him out. He looked relieved to have finished this visit.

"Thank you for coming." Niko mumbled. Mr. Stephanopoulous may not have heard him. He was already disappearing down the corridor and out of the prison, and he didn't look back.

Niko lay down on his cot facing the icy window wall. Why hadn't he thought about taking his Greek passport? Then he would have learned before leaving on this trip that he had none. Perhaps he wouldn't have agreed to join the crew of *The Robert Gordon* had he known.

He told himself to think about the dilemma of his citizenship later. Now he must grieve for Papa.

His heart seemed to have broken open inside his chest, spilling pain and misery through his body. Papa was his compass, his mentor. How could he face this desperate situation without Papa's guidance?

Lying on the cot, his head cradled in his hands, he left this place. He was at sea again, but Papa was not there. The sea was tearing at the sides of his boat, battering and hammering. He was lost in the worst storm of his life. It would not stop and fighting it left him too weak to control his boat. He could not navigate his way through these terrifying waters without Papa to guide him. The raging sea and the black sky would surely pull him under. A wail pushed up from his gut, Papa!

The sound startled him and pulled him back to his bed. He must not show weakness. This was prison, and he was a foreigner with no one but himself to rely on. He must restrain Grief, not let it overwhelm him. Huddled there on the bed he began counting the seconds between his breaths, forcing his body to submit. *One...two...three... Papa, oh, Papa. His chest heaved. One...two...three...four... Papa... (Deep breath)...One...two...three...four... five...*

In the afternoon the prisoners were allowed out of their cells for "association" or exercise in the courtyard where they could absorb what little sunshine there was in London in late November. It felt like months since he'd been outside, though it had only been yesterday. He wanted to smash the schedule, to stop the daily round of activity—cell time, meal, cell time, meal, cell time, association or exercise, cell time, meal, cell time. He wanted it all disrupted. How could anything go on the same in a world without Papa?

In the yard he saw David Bennie, Tom Hill, and Keith Brown. He avoided them.

"You all right? You look like paste, man." Keith's tone sounded concerned, and he draped his thick right arm over Niko's shoulder. Keith was a short man who carried himself like a large man, taking up a lot of space and attracting attention. He took care of his team like the star fullback he had been in his youth. "Looks like a black dog's come on you...You know, depression."

Niko didn't respond.

"Rumor has it David will be in court later this week requesting bail. The bloody trial should have begun by now, but my lady says she's heard they may wait till April or even later. Bloody solicitors don't seem to know what they're doing. Delay, delay.... You feeling poorly?"

Keith was still their skipper and the others closed ranks around him. Their backs made a wall against the frigid wind. They watched the one-sided conversation between Keith and Niko.

Niko decided not to tell them about Papa's death or the deportation threat. On *The Robert Gordon* he'd felt like an outsider, especially after they took on the drugs. Once he'd expressed his reservations about what they were doing, Keith had begun to talk more with Tom, the two of them joking and carrying on like they hadn't a care in the world. But he had read their hilarity as a front to cover their anxiety. He wasn't sure he trusted any of them, other than Sally, and he didn't want their pity. At Brixton he was even more the outsider, the foreigner who would definitely be deported in the end and likely be treated differently by the court, once the case went to trial. He was truly isolated.

"A bit sick this morning," he replied, not making eye contact with Keith or the others.

The prisoners began sauntering toward the door heading back to their cells. Some days were too miserably cold to remain outdoors. Keith passed Niko his half-smoked cigarette and vaguely patted his shoulder. David and Tom made no attempt to connect with him. He recognized on their faces the same distant look of most of the men in the prison yard.

Chapter 34

When they were arrested on October 4th, the police interviewing David had cautioned him that if he admitted his guilt, he would get a lighter sentence. Otherwise, he was facing five to six years in prison. After that conversation he had begun to prepare himself for the worst. He wouldn't admit to something he hadn't knowingly done. The likely consequence? He'd be spending his middle twenties locked up. He told himself there was nothing he could do to change his circumstances--other than try to get released on bail. He had no money so had to accept legal aid—a court appointed solicitor.

The solicitor appointed by the court was a divorce lawyer named Mr. Ramett. He was squat, plump and balding. His suit jacket was missing the middle button and the greying edges of his shirt, poking out of the sleeves, were noticeably frayed. He must suffer from some chronic ailment, for he twitched every few moments and blinked rapidly when he couldn't find the word he was looking for. David could hear what Mam would say: "Poor man can't help it." But this "poor man" would be in front of the court representing David, and his presentation would determine David's future! David was certain Ramett would make a sorry first impression. God help him with Ramett representing him. Yet the man was his only hope for getting out of Brixton.

David tried to be as helpful as he could in the brief fifteen minutes allotted for his meeting with his solicitor. After their meeting David ruminated obsessively on the hopelessness of his situation.

The one encouraging thing Ramett told David was that he would be a good candidate for bail, having no prior offenses and having joined the crew after the cargo had been picked up from Lebanon's waters. But the first time David was delivered to the court for a bail hearing, Ramett didn't show up.

The second time, Ramett was present but had apparently caught a cold. His nasal voice and his pauses to loudly blow his nose into a large, much used handkerchief—combined with his awkward waddle when he approached the bench--told David before the judge spoke that bail would not be granted. Blimey! he thought, I am in trouble.

Later that day he learned that Geoff Knowles, the builder who had driven one of the vans to the jetty in North Fambridge and loaded bags of cannabis resin into the van, had been granted bail. His family had offered nearly half a million pounds to guarantee that he would not run. The fact that he also had a wife and two kids dependent on his earnings may have contributed to the judge's decision.

The law allowed three appearances before the court to request bail. David's third and final attempt came December 17, a week before Christmas. Mam and Dad had mortgaged their small house and another couple, friends of David, had done the same to raise the funds for his bail. Somehow they assembled 30,000 pounds which, with Aunt Peggy's contribution of 10,000 and 5,000 from his friend, Karen Crombie, who worked in the Home Office, together made 45,000 pounds. None of them could afford this, least of all Dad and Mam, who would not be able to retire if they had to continue making mortgage payments. Nonetheless, all of them were there in person to assure the court that they would guarantee David would not flee if released on bail. Their generosity moved David. Those scarce funds represented such an abundance of love. Surely the court would let him have bail.

Ramett's argument meandered. Awkwardly he shuffled his unbound paperwork looking for something. Papers spilled out of a tired black folder and skittered across the table, some landing with a swish at his feet. "I'm sorry, your Honor, but my specialty is divorce law," he muttered from down on his knees scooping up the recalcitrant papers. David thought he heard Mam and Aunt Peggy sigh. He felt his hope deflating. His family had come through so sacrificially to help him, but he felt certain their sacrifice would not overcome Ramett's incompetence.

Bail was denied on the grounds that David was a flight risk. How could he possibly flee, when his family would lose all the money they'd mustered for his bail? He didn't even have a passport. His was in the possession of the court! Both the judge and the prosecutor were men of means. They probably would have no problem coming up with hundreds of thousands of pounds. How could they understand what David's family had gone through to raise this money?

As he was led from the court to the caged van that transported him back to Brixton, David made eye contact with Mam, trying to reassure her that he would be all right. Her face looked like it was carved from stone and her eyes called down the wrath of God on Mr. Ramett, the prosecutor, and the judge.

That night in their cell his cellmate asked how it had gone. David recounted what had happened, striding back and forth across the narrow width of their cell and mimicking Mr. Ramett's presentation. He was a natural comic, and his cellmate guffawed watching him. David finished his account of the devastating day and sat down on the edge of his bed.

His cellmate pulled the plastic chair closer to David. "Listen, mate, I've an idea that might be worth something to you. My solicitor and I met today, and he asked about you and your case. Said he'd read about it in the papers. A high profile case, says he. Said he'd be interested in representing you, should you want him, but that he can't ask you directly as that would be soliciting and solicitors can't solicit." He waited for David to join him chuckling at this and when David remained silent, he continued. "Said his firm doesn't take legal aid cases normally but, this being such a big case, he'd make an exception. You would have to write the court and explain your reason for being dissatisfied with Ramett and request Mr. Bernard Carnell take your case instead. If you're interested, he'll pass me a copy of the skeleton letter they use for this when next we meet. Then you fill in your reasons and pass it back to him to submit. I figure having a solicitor of his standing might help you."

David wasted no time thinking it over. Don't look a gift horse in the mouth and all that. He filled out the form and submitted it. But with the holidays, he heard nothing from Mr. Carnell.

At Christmas David's Mam brought a basket of goodies to the prison for her weekly visit. Dad and Trisha, his sister, were with her. The guards sampled the biscuits and fruitcake before they'd let her carry them in. It was one of the perks of the job. The week previous he'd learned that his final bail request had been turned down. Trish was in a twit about it. "Mam and Dad mortgaged the house and the Watsons mortgaged theirs as well to put together the bail. And Aunt Peggy is culling her savings to match what we've raised. You'd think 45,000 pounds would be enough for them to let you out, knowing you'd be staying with us in Corby." She was angry.

Several people in the visiting room turned to stare at Trisha hearing the sharp edge and volume of her voice. "Hush, now, or they'll throw us all out," Mam cautioned her.

David liked that Trish was angry. He was, too. "They say I'm a flight risk! As though I've any funds with which to fly!" Despite the seriousness of the situation they all laughed, settling back into their default teasing that was how they showed their love for one another.

"Are they giving you enough to eat, son?" Mam was herself so tiny you'd think a good wind would knock her over. David resembled her in his small, lean frame. She reached over and ruffled his hair.

"Watch it, now, Mam. This is prison. You know what they say happens to men who are momma's boys in prison." He was teasing but she pulled her hand away so swiftly they all laughed again, this time a bit nervously, and David could see in her eyes that he'd made a joke about one of her worst fears. "It's all right, Mam. No one is bothering me."

Dad was looking around the room, his eyes lingering on any of the larger prisoners and sending them looks that might kill if Dad wasn't himself a small man.

161

The fifteen minutes passed all too soon. At the end Mam whispered in David's ear that they weren't putting the Christmas tree up until he was released, whenever that would be. His eyes smarted at their caring. Being in prison for something you hadn't done was crap, but being in prison was also a way to learn how much your family loved you.

Chapter 35

At Wormwood, Sally also had visitors that day, her mum and Brenda. "Alfred phoned from the Falklands and I told him about your situation," Mum told her. Finally, Sally thought, and prepared herself for rejection. "He says to stay strong and that he knows you'd not be involved in any drug smuggling. Said he'd swim all the way back to London to stop them from holding his innocent girl."

Sally had not cried since that afternoon with Moira but now her tears were uncontrollable. Alfred had surprised them all. "Dad" had come through, maybe more than her blood kin.

Janet dressed Teddy in a red-and-green tartan jacket and dark green wool slacks she'd found at the charity shop. Discovering the Christmasy outfit in Teddy's size among the mark-downs had brought a rare, genuine smile to her face. She fussed over her own appearance, wanting to look pretty for her man. Teddy kept asking her to hurry so they wouldn't be late to see Daddy.

The visiting room was crowded with Christmas visitors. She noticed David Bennie sitting across from his family on her right. While she was waiting for Keith, she scanned the room for the other two, Tom and Niko. She thought she would recognize them from all the photos in the newspapers, but she didn't see either of them. She startled when Keith's large hands squeezed her shoulder from behind and she turned to embrace him—discreetly. That was all that they allowed at Brixton. Teddy was jumping up and down, his mouth running with things he'd been saving to tell his Dad. Observing them, she momentarily sloughed off all worry and fear. No matter how foolish his judgment, she still loved this man. She knew this more strongly than ever watching him relate to Teddy, listening attentively to the child, his eyes like a camera taking in Teddy's animation and delight. She knew he was storing these images in his memory to get him through the months ahead.

When Teddy ran out of words, she asked about Niko and Tom. Keith told her Niko seemed withdrawn and depressed. One of the guards had told Keith that Niko's father had died recently, and that Niko was taking it hard.

"Poor man! Far from home, no one to visit him, and losing his father." She saw that Teddy was listening closely.

"How did he lose his father?" the child asked and they both smiled at the literalism of children.

"He was an old man and he died," Keith told Teddy, who began to cry at the thought of fathers dying.

"It's all right, Teddy, your father is not going to die for a very long time," Janet reassured him.

"I don't want you to die before you come home," Teddy said, eyes intent, face serious. Janet had to get up and walk away for a moment. When she came back, Keith was holding Teddy close, patting his back and speaking softly to him.

The moment passed and Teddy slid down and ran to join some other children around the bin of toys some charity had provided for visitors' children.

"They denied David bail again."

"At least it isn't in the papers much now," Janet was determined to rescue the visit from the sadness she knew they both were feeling. "Is Tom okay?"

"Tom is Tom. No friends to speak of. No family. A loner who seems to not be bothered by anything. Probably has more people literally close to him here than ever in his life, what with daily association times and sharing a cell. The man's truly a recluse. I guess that's why he loves the sea life... Have you heard anything from Archie?"

Janet set her jaw and her mouth made a tight straight line. "Don't mention Archie to me. He set you all up and is nowhere to be found. Probably off somewhere enjoying the good life while the rest of you rot in this place." She had never spoken so bitterly before, but he understood her anger. She was right. What he obsessed about most was whether Archie had deliberately set him up, set all of them up, and whether he ought to tell the police about Archie. In this brief moment of privacy he asked her what she thought he should do.

"If he did set you up to fail, he is powerfully connected. Who knows how he would retaliate?" Janet's eyes were on Teddy who was building Legos with a girl about his size. "I did tell you that someone paid off the car dealership, didn't I? I figure it must be him who did that. We're not in the poorhouse, anyway, and I've kept my job."

If Archie paid off what Keith owed on the dealership, then he was living up to his promise to protect them, at least in part. "Maybe I'll talk with my solicitor about Archie, get his advice?"

"Or maybe not?" Janet's eyes were wary and fearful.

Chapter 36

Niko sat on the floor leaning against his cot. The older guard who'd always treated him kindly had come by last night with a bag of sweets and a jigsaw puzzle, "My Missus thought you might enjoy this." Niko had worked on the puzzle for more than an hour and located most of the straight edge pieces, fitting them together to build the frame for the rest. The lid of the puzzle box showed a sunlit scene of the eastern Mediterranean, perhaps Greece or Cyprus—turquoise sea and pastel houses walking up the hill behind the sea, baskets of bright colored dahlias and crimson geraniums decorating terraces. Sunflowers framed the stone road that wound uphill. Such a kind thing for "the Missus" and her man to do for him, giving him this little bit of Home.

The chaplain also had come by yesterday and brought him a copy of the Bible in Greek. Although it wasn't yet the Orthodox Christmas, Niko had been reading the stories in Matthew and Luke, grateful for the feel of the words in his mouth, his words, his language.

The past month he had written to his mother and she to him almost every day. Somehow he'd felt different the past few weeks. *It's almost like I'm seeing the world through Papa's eyes as well as my own*, he'd written her. There was comfort in that. When she wrote back, Mama's tone was almost joyful. Of course, she was grieving, she wrote, but knowing he felt Papa's presence with him was the greatest gift she could hope for.

Mama had begun writing long narratives about her past, telling him stories about her life in Cyprus before she met Papa and their life together during the civil war. She wrote that the war replayed in Beirut and forced them to flee a second time, this time from Beirut to Rhodes. He had not thought of his parents as refugees before.

If Niko had not been in prison, he would probably not have read all of Mama's letters--too time consuming for a young man working on the boats. But in prison he had nothing but time, so he read and reread each letter and found that Mama's stories helped the days pass more quickly. They connected him with Home and Family. She should put her stories in a book, he thought. Maybe he could help her. It might be something to occupy him while he was here.

Chapter 37

Hogmanay—December 31 through January 2--was the lowest time for David. For Scots, Hogmanay—New Year's--is the major celebration of the year. Christmas wasn't a public holiday in Scotland until 1958, and Boxing Day, December 26, not until 1974. Scots traditionally threw everything into their Hogmanay—torch-light parades through the streets, men in kilts carrying balls of fire enclosed in wire frames that they threw into the sea, young men jumping into the icy water after the fireballs. Though the Bennies lived in England now, Hogmanay remained the day when they celebrated their Scottish identity with their whole heart. Of course, David's siblings Raymond, Anne and Trisha—would never miss coming home for Hogmanay.

Mam would be cleaning the house thoroughly on December 30 and preparing an evening meal of traditional foods—haggis, tatties and neeps, steak pie, Clootie Dumpling, and a special cake into which a variety of small treasures were baked—omens for the new year for whoever found one in their portion. The person receiving the coin was destined to receive money in the new year; the one receiving the tiny plastic baby, to welcome a new wee one, etc. Every family watched for the first person to enter their house after midnight, hoping it would be a man bearing gifts of food, a harbinger of a good year to come. He remembered the year his sister Anne, her hair newly blonde, had come home at two a.m. Blonde women taking "the first step" into a house on New Year's Eve brought misfortune, so Mam and Dad had barred the door to her. They'd had a good laugh over that. They insisted Anne find someone with dark hair to enter before her. Only then did they let his sister in.

Sitting in Brixton Prison during Hogmanay 1985, David's happy memories of Hogmanay only darkened his blues.

In mid-January it was bitter cold outside, but in his cell, David was perspiring. The decrepit heating system of the prison pumped hot air into the cells on cold nights like these. Stifling it was, so much so that he had opened the cell's one barred window hoping that cold air from the world outside Brixton would battle with the heat inside and reach a truce that would make the night bearable.

Because Brixton was a temporary holding facility for people who had not yet been tried, men entered and left with no pattern or predictability. His new roommate was a junkie who said nothing, just sat on the plastic chair holding the box that contained his things. The gaunt man rocked back and forth, hugging the box to his chest, his eyes downcast and unfocused. David tried to get him to eat supper, but the man was unresponsive. Unresponsive also when the hot drinks, tea or hot chocolate, were brought around at eight in the evening. The man's silent, rocking, unresponsive presence provoked David. It was eerie for him to be here-but-not-here on this peculiar hot and cold night. Feeling spooked, David retreated to his bed and tried to sleep. His cell was so overheated that he lay on top of his blanket, covered only with the sheet.

Something awakened him hours later. He heard eerie sounds, a wordless mess of guttural noises interrupted regularly by gasps. Still half-asleep and disoriented, he gradually became aware that something was weighing heavily on his body. He touched his left arm. Cold. His cheeks. Cold. He licked his lips. Cold. He thought he must be dead. The moonless night had sucked everything warm and pulsing out of him and left only this shell of a young man's lean body weighted and immobile. He was not yet twenty-two, too young to die, but in this darkness that obscured even the hand he held in front of his eyes, there was nothing but cold and stillness.

He felt something crawling across the back of his hand and lay there as if turned to stone, petrified and comatose. He felt slithering things inching across his thighs and into the valley between his legs. His hands crept to the edges of the space where he lay. On his right side he felt the cement wall, rough and icy. On his left, nothing, an abyss. He was in a pit, the Pit from which no one ever escapes, and snow was filling it up, suffocating him.

He lay there unmoving for some time, attempting to communicate with Mam and Dad and Trisha and Ann and Raymond. He tried to send some current of love and gratitude to them in these last moments of his life. He felt so very cold. He noticed that his body had begun trembling uncontrollably. He concentrated all his energy and kicked the heavy weight off his legs. His kicks set in motion a whirlwind that drifted down onto his face and into his open mouth.

For what seemed a very long time he waited to see what would come next. When the window over his bed brightened just a little and let in a haze of compromised pre-dawn light, he saw that what covered him was snow. An overnight blizzard had blown through his open window and over his body and bed. A blanket of snow lay across the sheet and over his pillow, his face, his hair.

He forced himself to stir, easing his stiff and frigid legs from under the wet sheet and over the edge of his bed, testing them tentatively against the ground, his feet surprisingly cold on the cement floor. Warm feet were one of his blessings, his Mam had told him. Snow slid off the sheet and puddled on the floor. He could not stop shaking. He reached for the navy and white striped denim shirt and brown denim trousers that comprised his prison clothing and, with great effort, pulled them on. He topped the shirt with the prison's regulation brown sweater and sat there on the edge of his wet bed, rubbing his feet vigorously, trying to restore some feeling to them. Left foot, then right, then left again. When the guard announced toilet time, he was still sitting there in a nearly catatonic state rubbing each foot in turn.

From the fog inside him words slid about trying to find coherence. As he returned from the allotted five minutes of toilet time, his words found each other. I must get out of here, they said.

Several weeks later David lay on the narrow cot in the narrow room while cloud shadows moved across his body. It was February and it was raining, tiny needles of rain so close together that the sky looked like a thick soup. He could hear the rain needles hitting the window high above his bed, the rain coming on nearly horizontal. He pulled the stained woolen blanket around him from each side of the bed, too weary to get up and get under it. Where the edges joined, they made a jagged seam from his neck to his knees from which his bare feet stuck out, surprisingly warm for the chill dankness of this place.

Under the mattress he kept sheets of toilet roll on which he'd marked off each day as soon as he woke up using the nail of his forefinger to scratch lines into the tissue. It was one of his prison rituals. He engraved four lines, then a diagonal; four lines then a diagonal--four weeks on each sheet, four sheets so far. He'd been here since October, and was half into his fourth month, the 100th day, to be precise. He never told anyone about his sheets of toilet roll and his morning ritual. They'd probably think he'd gone over the edge. The sameness of life inside could drive a person daft.

The hum of rain made it worse. It jumbled his thinking, although "thinking" was probably too grand a word for the random roving of his mind in this deadly dull void that was his temporary home.

His cellmate had left weeks ago after that terrifying snowy night. He didn't know where they had taken him. To the hospital? Rehab? The morgue?

On rainy days they weren't let out in the yard. Instead, for an hour their cell doors would be opened so they could converse with the other inmates, a diversion he appreciated. He didn't interact much, but just listening to the conversations of others kept him sane. Before his incarceration lying about with nothing to do had seemed a luxury. Now he found such prolonged, enforced inactivity crazy making.

Mam and Trish had come down to see him yesterday for the allowed fifteen minutes in the visiting room. Mam said she'd keep coming each weekend.

Dad no longer came. David remembered his face at Christmas, the first and only time he had accompanied Mam to the prison. His eyes in his flushed face had roamed the visiting room, avoiding David's. David had felt a spasm of regret so fierce it nearly felled him, imagining the shame Dad must feel to see his son, his youngest child, imprisoned here.

Mam handled the situation differently. She seemed taller, her tiny, trim body tight as a spring and the fierce look in her blue eyes enough to terrify Satan. No one would malign her son without hearing from her verbally or, more likely, visually. Her eyes fired at the guards like machine guns, although David knew another part of Mam wanted to get to know each one of them, learn their wives and children's names and from where they came to London. She was that sort of woman, full of caring for anyone and defiantly protective of those she loved. In another time he would have teased her about this inconsistency, but not now. Teasing and joking, the currency of their family life, had nearly dried up in these months.

The whole damn system stank. Mam could come to see him but only for fifteen minutes each visit, even though it took her three hours to travel each way for those fifteen minutes—fifty-five minutes on two buses to get to the nearest train station, one-and-a-half hours on the train to London, twenty minutes on the underground, and, finally, a third bus from the tube stop to Brixton. It was especially mad in the winter--a cold weekly journey that required taking a full day off work! Still she came.

At first he'd felt full of regret for ever seeking the job on *The Robert Gordon*, but as time passed, anger replaced regret, anger and fear. *Why were they holding him here when all the other crewmen had said David knew nothing of the cannabis resin stashed in the forward section of the yacht?* Keith had told him that the area of the yacht walled off, rubber sealed, and locked had contained the illegal drugs--but David only learned this after they were in prison. He was innocent, at least of the grand scheme. Of course, he smoked pot on occasion. Of course, they all drank. He'd been drinking whiskey with Sally in the saloon and listening to music when the customs officials had called over loudspeakers for them to surrender, to come up with their hands raised.

Obsessively he reviewed the nine days he had spent aboard *The Robert Gordon*, seeking anything he might have overlooked. Their case against him seemed to rest on the smell of the cannabis that prosecutors insisted he would have noticed. Well, he never had noticed, maybe because the smell of cannabis had been part of his recreational life since he was sixteen, a full six years ago. What teenager in the 1980s didn't recognize the smell of weed as part of his natural habitat? They had all smoked weed aboard the boat, though the prosecutor didn't know that.

What a joke this whole war on drugs was. He was sitting in prison charged with importing drugs, yet here at Brixton Prison you could easily secure those same drugs to smoke in the prison! Damn!

He'd taken the job on *The Robert Gordon* because the one he had wasn't paying him, despite his months at sea. Now he would never be paid for any of his work on *The Robert Gordon* either, no pay for tending the engine of *The Robert Gordon*, for taking his turns at watch, or for helping navigate the sorry boat from Gibraltar through the Bay of Biscay while it suffered one technical malfunction after another.

He needed a cigarette or forty of them. He needed to get out of this stinking place, back to the fresh air of Scotland, back to the sea. He was wasting away here, depressed and bored, bankrupting his family, and lacking any idea what to do.

With these happy thoughts he turned his body to face the wall, curled up like a child, and let himself drift off to sleep.

He awakened to the sound of silence, unusual in Brixton Prison in the middle of London. Outside his window a sea of fog, grey, ominous, opaque and impenetrable, covered everything. It slithered into every crevasse of the prison yard and the city beyond it like a rank three-day-old gravy. The only sound was the soft hiss of tires against the wet road that followed the Thames just across from the prison. A fragment of memory quickened his breathing, a scene from an old sci-fi film of the end of the world and slime crawling insistently and silently over a major city. Was it New York?

The sodium street lamps dispersed a jaundiced half-light over London that the fog overwhelmed. It must be several hours after midnight. He held up his right arm, eyes straining to make out his fingers. They were there, a reassuring thought, and he stretched out on the cot, looking up, intent on identifying whatever he could see in the dark of his cell. There wasn't much to see. Only the sallow toilet and washstand facing him and the plastic chair.

Terror surprised him. It lodged in his throat and tasted of bile. They might put him away for decades, the way they were treating his case, lumping him with the others who had acknowledged they knew they were smuggling Lebanese Gold. His life was ruined at twenty-one. Whenever he emerged from prison—if he emerged—with a felony conviction he'd never find work, certainly not as a skilled mechanic, the work he'd trained for at school.

He rolled onto his stomach, his face pushed into the thin pillow. He heard a human sound, ragged and wretched, someone sobbing and trying hard to stop. He recognized the sound of his own voice. His new cellmate murmured something in his sleep and David quickly sat up, swinging his feet to the floor. As a small man, thin and graceful like his mother, he knew that he must not let down his defenses in here. He'd been warned of that by the crewmen arrested with him. Silencing his despair gave him something to work at.

In the morning when the guard came by, he asked if he could have paper and a pencil. He had been a draftsman and had dabbled at painting before leaving Britain. Perhaps he could make the time pass by drawing pictures. To his surprise, the guard reappeared an hour later with a tablet and a pencil. David began to draw the world of Brixton Prison. It was his salvation.

Chapter 38

Prison life was regulated to the max. Even bodily functions were allocated to specific times. Regularity took on a whole new meaning in prison. Wake up and empty your slop bucket, brush your teeth and use the toilet in five minutes, (cell unlocked); enter the landing to pick up your tray and walk along the food line to collect your breakfast, returning to your cell to eat, (cell locked); pass your dirty plate to the matron and sit or pace for four hours, (cell unlocked); enter the landing to collect your lunch, returning to your cell to eat, (cell locked); pass your dirty plate to the matron, wait an hour, and mingle on the landing or outside in the yard with the other prisoners for an hour of "association time" (cell unlocked); return to your cell until tea time (cell locked); receive your plate of supper passed to you in your cell and, at seven, hold your cup through the bars to receive your hot drink.

Occasionally he bumped into the other crew arrested with him. Several times Keith approached him and apologized for getting David into this mess. Occasionally Keith would pass on a bit of news he'd heard about their case.

Mam kept up her weekly visits, bless her, sometimes accompanied by one of his sisters, Anne or Trish. Meanwhile, David kept filling his tablet with drawings.

The letter telling him he'd been reassigned to Mr. Bernard Carnell arrived February 8th telling him to prepare for a conference with Carnell in a few days.

Carnell looked like a headmaster at some posh private school—actually, Carnell looked like how David imagined a headmaster would look, never having seen a headmaster in the flesh. He was probably in his late forties or early fifties, carefully trimmed black beard, intense eyes, serious expression, obviously very intelligent. And precise. He interrupted David's narrative frequently to clarify the exact meaning of each thing David said. Already David felt better. Better yet when Carnell told him they would attempt to appear before the judge in chambers to request bail, although such meetings were not free when you'd used up your three chances. Not to worry, Carnell would use some of the money David's mam had raised.

By the end of February, David had celebrated his twenty-second birthday, Christmas, and Hogmanay in prison. Still there was no word when they would go to trial. Carnell succeeded in arranging for them to meet with the judge in chambers to argue that David should be released on bail and to persuade the court that he would not flee. The meeting in chambers was brief. Carnell made a concise and persuasive statement to the judge. David would live with his parents in Corby and report each evening at seven to his assigned officer. Traveling by bus and rail to and from London to check in would eat up most of each day, so he would not be able to work, even if someone was willing to hire him. It would be David, not Mam, making this six-hour commute, but he would be out of this place.

After five months of incarceration, on his fourth request--and after Carnell paid the court from David's parents' savings for the privilege of this meeting--the judge granted David's release on bail under these conditions. It took the judge only a few minutes to decide.

There was much rejoicing at the Bennie home the next day when David arrived home. True to her promise Mam had put up a scrawny Christmas tree, the haphazard placement of its ornaments revealing how little notice they'd had that he'd be coming home. Brother Ray and sister Anne and her kids joined them for a festive dinner that night, and David moved back into the bed he had used for most of his childhood. For the next three and a half months the little house held four of them—David, Trish, Mam and Dad. Each morning he left on the bus to make the three-hour trip to London to check in with his officer followed by the three-hour return. It was definitely better than Brixton.

Chapter 39

Each of the defendants had their own barrister. Sally, on her dad Alfred's advice, was represented by a man with a reputation for winning difficult criminal cases. The downside was that he was involved in another major case that seemed to drag on and on. Because of that case, Sally would remain in prison for at least four additional months before her barrister could free his calendar and argue her case.

Niko had discovered a way to survive incarceration. He'd begun to assemble his mother's letters into a kind of book. He'd never liked history in school, but now the history his mother was writing felt relevant and important. It helped him understand his family and the choices they had made that affected his life.

The one person at Brixton he spoke to was the friendly older guard. Niko sometimes asked him questions about what was happening in the news. Seeing his interest, the guard brought him day-old newspapers from the guard's lounge to help him keep up with the world beyond Brixton and Britain. The tabloids weren't much help, but occasionally there was a copy of The Guardian or The Independent. Gradually, with the aid of a couple of books the guard found for him, he began piecing together bits of the history his family had lived.

Niko learned that his mother's father had fought with the British Army during World War II. After the war, as the British Empire was breaking up, his father had joined Cypriots who wanted independence from Britain and fought against the British. His mother's family had continued working for Brian Baker's family. That Niko's father had fought against the British was an inconvenient truth Niko hoped would not be brought up at his trial.

It seemed from what he was reading that the years since World War II had been dominated by communists and anti-communists fighting each other around the world, including in Greece, where his family had moved after he finished secondary school. Maybe in Lebanon, too?

Trying to understand what was going on in Lebanon stretched his mind. It was confusing. The press reported there were eighteen different ethnic and religious groups, most of them with their own armies. When they won independence from France, they all were forced to share power. But sometimes that "covenantal agreement" broke down, especially when other countries got involved.

For the past decade the various groups of Muslims and Christians had been fighting each other and fighting their invading neighbors, Israel, an ally of the United States and Britain, and Syria, an ally of the Soviet Union. So was the fighting in Lebanon part of the Cold War?

He read an article that said the United States was providing $150 million in military aid to Lebanon's Army and that Lebanon's Army was cooperating with Israel. As best he could sort it out, the Americans were working with Israel and Lebanon's Christian president to fight the Soviets, who were funding and arming Syria and the Palestinian refugee groups in Lebanon. It seemed that each superpower had clients. Was that how the Cold War worked—the two superpowers fighting each other through their clients in other nations?

His growing interest in this history helped take Niko's mind outside these walls. It made life at Brixton easier.

Niko remembered three years ago on his sister's birthday when Papa had interrupted their celebrating to tell the family that Israeli troops were surrounding Beirut and in the streets of Muslim West Beirut. He'd looked upset. Papa had read aloud to them a press report that Lebanese Christians slaughtered hundreds of Palestinian refugees in the Sabra and Shatila refugee camps within the area that Israel occupied. After that, many foreigners were kidnapped, and truck bombs destroyed the U.S. Embassy. Troops from the U.S., France, and Italy also came to Lebanon.

Niko had tried to tell Keith a little of this history when they were in the waters off Tripoli waiting for the delivery of the cannabis resin. *How was this history connected to those men in black who boarded their boat?*

Some British newspapers he read claimed that the Bekaa Valley of Lebanon produced most of the drugs entering Britain, and that Lebanese and Palestinian Muslims, aided by the Syrians, controlled the production and distribution of Lebanon's drugs. The cannabis carried by *The Robert Gordon* probably originated in the Bekaa Valley. *So who had they been trading with?*

Palestinians had fled to Lebanon after Israel claimed their land for its new nation in 1948. Twenty-five thousand more Palestinians fled to Lebanon when Israel seized more territory in 1967. Many Lebanese blamed Palestinians for the fighting devastating their country. Lebanon had expelled the major Palestinian organization two years ago. If you paid any attention to the news, you knew the Palestinian groups were considered terrorists by the governments of the U.S. and U.K.

Suddenly Niko put down his reading material. *Could the suppliers of our cargo have been Palestinian terrorists? Could we be charged as terrorists?* The thought appalled him. He sank back on his bed, his eyes closed, and tried to reconstruct his memories from the night they picked up the drugs.

He remembered hearing the leader of the smugglers say something to one of his men in Arabic. Niko hadn't understood him. Arabic is Lebanon's official language, spoken by Christians and Muslims, Palestinians and Syrians. Speaking Arabic would not identify the men who supplied the drugs as Palestinian. His head ached trying to sort it all out. His own Arabic was not good enough to distinguish differences in pronunciation that distinguished the groups. Even if he could identify the accent of the suppliers, why should the British court believe him? He was a stateless person caught bringing illegal drugs into Britain. It would be easy for them to assume the suppliers were Palestinians and charge the crew with trading with terrorists.

All he knew was that Brian Baker had gotten him into this. Brian Baker, the son of the family his mother and grandparents worked for in Cyprus before he was born. Brian Baker, who made him promise to never mention his name to anyone. Brian Baker, who was not in prison with the rest of them and who seemed to have escaped any charges.

In his weak moments Niko considered telling the authorities that Brian had recruited him to make this trip. But he had given his word to keep Brian out of it, and giving your word was a serious commitment. That had been drilled into him as a child by his father and his grandfather.

Niko had kept his promise. He had not named Brian and he would not.

He wondered if Keith had told the police that Brian Baker had hired him to skipper *The Robert Gordon*? If he had, *why hadn't the police arrested Brian Baker?*

Chapter 40

E very week letters arrived from Niko's mother. Stories poured out about his father during their years in Cyprus and about Niko's father's family, whom Niko never knew. She wrote of her joy when her husband arrived in Beirut on January 6th, 1960. He had waited until the state of emergency was lifted and dates set for the new independence constitution to go into effect and for elections to be held. Then he could not wait any longer.

Mama wrote about seeing him in the crowd exiting the ferry, handsome and powerfully built, his eyes wet as he swept her into his arms. She remembered the Christmas lights and the sound of carols coming from the churches of Beirut as her father drove them to the house they shared on the east side of the city. Every able-bodied Christian in the country was in church for the Orthodox Christmas eve.

She described entering the house where she and the children had built a crèche, a cave of *paper mache* that they had painted. For the previous two weeks they had sprouted grain by sprinkling it on damp sheep's wool to use for the cave floor. Niko's sister's Barbie and Ken dolls posed in the front of the cave, dressed in caftans, hijabs and keffiyehs that Niko's grandma, Yaya, had sewn. Wooden sheep and donkeys were arranged around them.

Yaya had twisted a small piece of white cloth to form a tiny swaddled baby and wired it to Barbie's right arm. The arm was unbendable, so Mary appeared to be about to drop the baby. Mama wrote that they laughed and laughed at what a careless mother their Mary was. She said she would never forget that Papa entered the room and went down on his knees before the crèche, praying his gratitude for being safely home with his family.

Her words brought the scene to life so vividly that Niko seemed to remember it, although he would have only been two. Still he seemed to see his father kneeling and silent before their crèche. He remembered him walking on his knees toward Niko, arms out, and cradling him very gently. He remembered how safe he had felt in the arms of this stranger they called Baba.

In one letter she wrote her memories of Lebanon in the 1960s. What good years those had been, the country thriving, the family together. Weekends they'd go to the beach. Niko remembered watching women in bikinis strut down to the water, lifting each leg gracefully and replacing it carefully so they would not cast sand onto well-oiled sunbathers, bending to splash themselves with seawater, turning, their sunglasses hiding their eyes as they surveyed the other sun worshippers who were watching them. Then the women, fleshy in all the right places, would move back to their chairs, breasts undulating. How old must he have been when he first noticed these sunbathers? Maybe eight?

Her letters triggered his own memories of school plays and soccer games and of Papa taking him out on his boat to fish or to explore the coastal inlets.

Mama enclosed pictures of beaches with five-star hotels rising twelve stories into the air and streets full of people and cars. The faded photos left him nostalgic for the city that was his home until he was seventeen. He couldn't tell from those pictures who was Muslim and who was Christian.

An especially long letter arrived this week. Mama wrote how their peaceful life had unraveled. It began in the late 1960s.

When you were nine, a Palestinian group attacked an Israeli plane in Athens, and Israel attacked the Beirut airport, destroying thirteen of our planes. Then Israel attacked Egypt, Syria and Jordan in the Six Day War of June 1967 and seized territory much larger than Israel itself—the Golan Heights from Syria, the Sinai Peninsula and Gaza from Egypt, and the West Bank and East Jerusalem from Jordan. The Israelis said this was retaliation for attacks by the Palestinians, who had armed themselves in 1964 and made rocket attacks on Israel from southern Lebanon. When I look back, the Six Day War and the PLO moving to Beirut seem to have been the beginning of the disastrous changes in Lebanon.

In 1972, the PLO murdered eleven Israeli athletes at the Munich Olympics. Israel retaliated by smuggling its commandos into Beirut led by Ehud Barak. Everyone remembers this because some of the Israeli commandos, including Barak, disguised themselves as women. Agents of Israel's Mossad intelligence service drove them to different parts of Beirut where their targets were located. There they assassinated three PLO leaders. The Israeli secret service set off a massive quantity of explosives and brought down a building on a crowded street in Central Beirut, where one branch of the PLO had its headquarters. That was the end of Lebanon's days as 'the jewel of the Mediterranean.' Virtually all of Lebanon's religious and ethnic groups were pulled into civil war, Mama wrote.

It surprised Niko how important it seemed for her to tell him this. She had been living in Beirut in the midst of it, desperate to keep her family safe. He supposed it was similar to his situation now. When your future is in jeopardy, you work hard to learn as much as you can to understand what you are up against.

Mama's handwriting changed as she wrote about the 1970s. Whole sentences would be struck through and carefully rewritten. She added a parenthetical note apologizing for her sloppy writing. Her memories were racing her fingers, she wrote, and it was important that this was legible so Niko could read it.

We got along well before—with each group allotted some political power—but once the Israelis, the Syrians and the PLO were all fighting inside Lebanon with different groups of Lebanese allied with each of them, it was chaos--too many weapons in everybody's hands.

Niko was twelve when the Seventies began and totally absorbed in the physical changes taking place in his body. He was the baby of the family, allowed to hang out with his buddies and play football. Living in Christian East Beirut, life went on more or less normally. He was protected from politics, oblivious.

There were two specific memories Mama's letter brought back to him. The first was seeing a weeping man on television carrying a limp child in his arms out of a collapsed building. Niko had never seen a dead child before or a man crying. The second was taking his grandparents and their belongings to the airport the Saturday following his graduation from secondary school and that evening learning they all were leaving Lebanon and moving to Rhodes, Greece. He had assumed his grandparents were going on holiday. But when Papa gathered them for a family meeting, he told them the whole family would follow Mama's parents to Greece. Papa would join them after he sold his business. He kept patting Mama's hand and saying it would be okay.

Several months later Papa joined them, and Niko remembered being surprised how much older Papa looked. Creases like valleys crossed his forehead and his shoulders were rounded. Mama's letter all these years later explained those changes in Papa.

We got out just in time, Niko. Papa saw terrible things. Lebanese Muslims hid locked in their homes in West Beirut, terrified and hungry, while foreigners—Syrians, Palestinians, and Israelis—fought in their streets and buildings shattered like glass under bombardment. The American ambassador and his deputy were abducted and murdered, their corpses left on the beach. Syrian tanks rolled west across the Bekaa Valley over the mountains into Beirut. Nearly 60,000 Israeli and Syrian soldiers occupied Lebanon. It was the first time an Arab nation was occupying another Arab nation's capital. Parliament was reduced to a heap of rubble and the roads were clogged with Lebanese refugees. In the end Papa had to abandon the business and our home and flee with only what he could carry.

When he finished reading Mama's long letter, Niko felt exhausted. He laid this letter with the others and secured them with a flimsy rubber band. When he glanced in the metal mirror of the prison lavatory, the face he saw looked startlingly like Papa's.

Part 4 - The Trial

Chapter 41

It was early June, 1985, when the trial of those charged with smuggling cannabis resin from Lebanon to London began. The courtroom in the Crown Court seemed dark with its rich paneling of English Oak. Its large lead-paned windows, set high up on the wall, admitted a greyish light when the weather was soggy as it was for much of June.

Barristers, who would do the advocating for seven of the eight defendants, sat before the judge, looking a bit incongruous in their formal black gowns and Eighteenth-Century white wigs that sat precariously atop their heads. Female barristers with slippery hair had to secure them with hairpins. Behind the barristers sat the solicitors who had done the research on each of the defendants' involvement. Solicitors wore suits and ties, pantsuits if they were women, but were spared the wigs and gowns.

High benches rose behind the barristers and solicitors. That was where those on trial sat.

The five-person crew of *The Robert Gordon*--Keith Brown, Tom Hill, Nikolaos Karras, Sally Eliades, and David Bennie--sat together filling a row. Behind them sat the three men accused of accepting the cannabis resin for distribution—Terrence Gale, John Benton, and Geoff Knowles--flanked by guards on either side. On the floor level sat observers, including family members. Among them were Keith's partner Janet Morris, David's Mam and sister Trisha, and Geoff Knowles's wife and parents.

Although there were eight defendants, there were only seven barristers, Sally's barrister being too busy with the Brink's-Mat robbery case, one of the most celebrated cases in London's history and the largest gold heist ever in Britain. In that case gold, diamonds and jewelry valued at twenty-six million pounds had been stolen from a Heathrow warehouse in November 1983. Her barrister would represent her after his work on that case concluded. Although she would be forced to remain in prison extra months until her barrister was free to argue her case, by law she had the right to be present while her mates were tried, to hear what witnesses said, and to be called as a witness herself.

Day one of the trial was memorable, not in the details but in establishing a pattern that would quickly become familiar and mundane, the way learning to ride a bike or drive a car requires careful attention at the start but, once mastered, needs little forethought or concentration.

The procedural back and forth was enough to put one to sleep. By day two, despite the serious consequences riding on each small decision, David found his ability to focus diminishing. In the aggregate the minutiae of decisions were terribly important, but mentally wading through that minutiae and trying to listen carefully caused his eyelids to lower involuntarily. He tried to focus on Mam and his sister. Mam was scribbling fiercely, making extensive notes on the trial. Trisha's color told him when he needed to pay closer attention. Her face went red and a fierce scowl took it over when the prosecutor said anything that besmirched her baby brother. He could see Mam reach across and squeeze Trisha's forearm to restrain her from speaking out and disrupting the proceedings. When the prosecutor in his opening arguments implied that David Bennie had to be lying when he swore that he didn't smell cannabis with 43 thousand kilos of the drug on board, Trisha stood and stomped out of the room. David thought he saw four rosy finger marks on her arm from Mam's attempts to restrain her.

It spooked David to be back in prison. The judge had ordered his reincarceration for the duration of the trial, and his solicitor suggested they comply without complaint. Living with his parents while he was on parole required too many hours of travel time to and from the court. Residing at the prison would make it easier for his legal staff to confer with him, and he would save money if he let Her Majesty's prisons pay his keep for the month or so the trial would consume. Better not to challenge the judge at this point.

Returning to the prison was definitely a downer. He tried to think of it as merely saving time and money he would otherwise have to spend commuting, but it felt like a giant step backward. The possibility that he could be in prison for five more years haunted him.

The trial commenced with the Customs and Excise officers called to the witness stand. They told of meetings between various defendants spaced over nine months, the period they had been watching the movements of Keith Brown, Terrence Gale, John Benton and Brian Baker, who seemed to have disappeared. They told of Keith and Brian traveling to Palma to take *The Sallykins* for a trial run to check the route Keith and his crew would take to collect the drugs.

Keith was shocked to learn from their testimony that right from the start he'd been under surveillance.

They said *The Robert Gordon* stopped in several ports including Gibraltar as it made its way from the eastern Mediterranean to Spain, through the Bay of Biscay, along the English Channel, around the south of England, and into the mouth of the River Crouch. David hadn't realized the boat had made so many stops carrying its contraband cargo. He wondered how Keith had managed to keep Customs and Excise in each of those places from boarding the yacht to have a look. He still wasn't seeing the larger trap they had been caught in.

Several agents described meetings they had observed between Terrence Gale and Brian Baker at several scummy pubs and at the posh Bentley Golf Club. A Chelmsford police officer recounted watching Keith coming ashore October 4th to make a phone call from the phone box at the pub in North Fambridge and then seeing him return to the boat to load the dinghy. The officer saw Keith and Tom Hill bring the dinghy to the jetty where Terrence, Geoff, and John moved the mound of white plastic- and burlap-wrapped packages now known to contain cannabis resin into the vans.

Keith and Janet exchanged looks when Brian Baker was mentioned. His name was in the court record so why wasn't he here with the rest of them on trial?

For David, who had joined the crew after the cannabis resin had been brought aboard, hearing his mates testify under oath how they had sailed to the Lebanon coast and picked up the drugs was most interesting. It was the first time he was hearing a full accounting of the circumstances that had led to their imprisonment. During the one hour a day their cells were opened to let them mill about and socialize or go out in the yard, they had exchanged information about their case, but there had never been time for a detailed recounting of their whole experience from late July to the fourth of October. He guessed from Sally's face, her eyes intent and her mouth open, that she also found this part of the trial fascinating.

When Keith responded emphatically to a question from his barrister with, "Neither David nor Sally were with us when we picked up the cannabis resin and neither of them knew anything about the drugs on board," Sally had reached across and squeezed David's hand.

One after the other they were called up and questioned. The prosecutor was good at his job, and Terrence Gale and John Bridges, for different reasons, made the prosecutor's job easier. Terrence was a smart dresser with a Rolex watch and expensive shirts. He was a big man, 6'3" or so, who carried himself with an aura of self-importance. Like you'd expect of a drug lord, David thought. Dark brown hair, dark eyes, arrogant. David, watching the judge, was certain the judge did not like Terrence. Terrence's answers wavered like a drunk staggering down a street. No, he didn't rent the vans. He had driven to the jetty to make a social visit to his old mate Keith. John Benton and Geoff Knowles did odd jobs for him, nothing more. Then he'd reverse himself. For a person who looked so confident, he made a lot of obvious mistakes. It did not take the prosecutor long to get him to correct his testimony and acknowledge that he had secured the vans, did know he was bringing illegal drugs into the U.K., and had been part of the planning of Operation Bishop for much of the past year. One thing Terrence remained mute about: Brian Baker. Strangely, no questions were asked of any of the defendants about the elusive Brian Baker.

When Benton took the stand, rather than lying he refused to respond to most of the questions asked him. When he did reply, he was sullen, monosyllabic and uncooperative, avoiding eye contact with his interrogator, the judge, and his own barrister. Didn't he realize that such behavior would cost him? Benton seemed to be trying to protect Terrence Gale, although Gale did not return the favor.

David had watched the two men during his four months in prison with them and had concluded that Benton was in awe of Gale. Short, stocky and usually silent, Benton followed Gale like a lap dog. In court he came across as a want-to-be gangster, behaving the way he'd seen gangsters behave in television crime shows. David wondered what was going on beneath his surface toughness.

The third person in the triumvirate accused of accepting the drugs with a plan to distribute them was Geoff Knowles. Knowles said he'd been asked to do a favor for Benton and drive a van to the North Fambridge jetty to pick up some building supplies. Knowles said he had done similar deliveries for Benton in the past. It had seemed a bit strange to him that Benton instructed him to use a van that Benton left parked outside Knowles's home rather than his own truck. But he'd agreed to take the job because he needed some extra money, although Benton had said nothing about how much he'd be paid. He had assumed they were hauling bags of cement but, when he saw the packages piled on the jetty, he suspected they were illegal drugs. He said he felt "utterly stupid" when he discovered what they were really doing and didn't know how to get out of this nightmare.

At that point Knowles broke down in tears, sobbing. Between sobs he said that he was a family man who worked hard at his job in construction and had two small boys and a wife to take care of. He had no criminal record and was ashamed and very, very sorry he was not smart enough to realize what Benton was inviting him to do. Benton looked daggers at Knowles.

The court apparently accepted his story since they had granted him bail and let him out on parole barely a week after he'd entered Brixton Prison. The man's remorse was impressive. He appeared to be a not-very-bright nice guy helping a friend who didn't deserve it.

The crew were up next, Tom Hill and Keith looked like brothers with their blonde hair, greying beards, ruddy faces, and squat, muscular bodies. Beside them Niko looked like a Greek god, lean and handsome with dark, brooding eyes in a movie star face. It struck David that most of them who were crew were on the short side. Was that a requirement for working in the low-ceilinged quarters of a yacht, he wondered?

Within twenty-four hours after their arrests Tom and Keith had abandoned the lies they had told in their first depositions. Each acknowledged that they knew what they were packing into the forward compartments of *The Robert Gordon*. But Keith continued to insist that he did not know who provided the money to purchase *The Robert Gordon* once it was clear that his boat, *Sallykins*, was inadequate for the job. He also said he had not been paid for the smuggling job.

Tom Hill came across as an unfortunate man from the wrong side of the tracks who adapted well to that environment. He had a history of petty theft and, after leaving the U.K., had worked in various Mediterranean ports delivering boats without asking questions.

When Tom was on the stand, his barrister showed him some bank deposit slips and transaction records and asked him to verify that the bank account belonged to him. Tom seemed genuinely perplexed as he scrutinized the papers. "I can't seem to make it out," he said. David heard Niko mutter under his breath, "He doesn't read."

In the end Tom, like Keith, acknowledged that he knew he was breaking the law by smuggling illegal drugs into Britain. It seemed both of them would definitely be found guilty and sentenced to five to ten years in prison.

The third week of the trial Niko was called to the stand and interrogated. His face was unnaturally pale. His barrister explained to the judge that Niko was a citizen of Lebanon who had lived the past ten years in Greece. While in Brixton Prison, Niko and his family learned that Niko had never applied for Greek citizenship. He had assumed that he would receive it as part of his family's refugee status. As a foreigner in Britain, if found guilty of a crime, he would be deported to his country of origin. But life in Lebanon at this time was terribly violent, and his family, who were Greek citizens, begged the court not to deport him. To be deported to and imprisoned in Lebanon would surely be a death sentence.

His barrister was passionate. "There is barely a functioning government in Lebanon now," the barrister stated. "Mr. Karras has acknowledged his guilt and misjudgment in participating in this operation. He besieges the court not to deport him but to allow him to remain in the United Kingdom to serve whatever sentence he receives."

The prosecutor was on his feet to protest that the barrister's comments were irrelevant for the immediate matter before the court. His argument was inappropriate while the court was hearing evidence against the men accused. The judge agreed, overruling Niko's barrister and proceeding with the prosecution's questioning of the accused.

David could see that Niko was terrified that he would be deported. Now he understood why. As the questions resumed about how Niko had become involved and what he knew, David found his mind fixed on Niko's plight. He hadn't much liked Niko on the boat. Niko had seemed proud, especially when David heard him talking with Sally about his brother who ran an exclusive night club in Marbella on the coast of Spain. Hearing him testify gave David a different sense of the man.

Niko stated that he had been uncomfortable when the black boat had pulled alongside *The Robert Gordon* and the men in black came aboard with such a huge quantity of drugs. He said he had proposed to Keith that they throw the drugs over the side before returning to Rhodes.

The judge interrupted Niko. "If you were so uncomfortable, why didn't you leave *The Robert Gordon* while you were in Rhodes or Gibraltar or others of the ports where you stopped for repairs or to take on fuel?"

"I had no money and was far from home. I thought I would complete my obligation to Keith, and then buy a ticket back to Rhodes as soon as I could."

The judge looked unhappy with his answer. The prosecutor, on the other hand, was gloating. The case against Niko was getting stronger by the moment.

"Did you say the men who delivered the drugs were part of the PLO?" the prosecutor asked, standing very close to Niko. "The PLO is a proscribed organization. Any dealings with them that would increase their ability to do their work of terrorism would be an added violation of British law." The prosecutor paused over-long to let the implication of his words sink into the consciousness of all in the room.

"Yes, I suspected they might be PLO." Niko's voice was low and hard to hear. No one moved in the two rows of accused seated in the high seats above their barristers.

"Why did you think it was the PLO supplying you with the drugs?"

"Because I know they--and the Syrians—are in the Bekaa Valley where most of Lebanon's drugs are grown. And because I understand Arabic and could make out at least some of what they were saying."

"What were they saying?" the prosecutor asked.

"I need time to remember." Niko's face had gone completely ashen and his anxiety was evident.

The judge's eyes bore into Niko and he said sternly, "Mr. Karras, I would ask that you work very hard at remembering. I call a recess until nine o'clock tomorrow morning." The judge stood and swiftly exited the chamber.

"Why were they being watched all those months, I wonder?" David asked his solicitor, Mr. Carnell, when that day's session ended. Carnell informed him that protracted observation by Customs and Excise was common in Britain. It marked nothing unusual, just what they called "prevention" work that was often coordinated with the secret service and immigration. Customs agents worked undercover. They also utilized people who had retired from Customs to chat up fishermen and dockhands. It was how they learned of unusual activity or unfamiliar people who might be involved in smuggling. There were hundreds of places along the British coast where one might bring in illegal goods. As an island nation, Britain was ripe for smugglers. It always had been.

David remembered when he was a lad his dad had taken them to Banff, on the northeast coast of Scotland, for an outing. Dad had pointed out the enormous stone warehouse facing the harbor and the large Georgian home beside it, built, Dad said, by the region's richest smuggler. Dad said it's a safe bet that most rich men have criminality in their past. Mam had added that every town along the coast of Scotland had pirates' warehouses like this.

In the armored van that carried them back to Brixton, Keith said only four words: "We were set up."

Chapter 42

Niko stretched out on the bed in his cell struggling with what to say to the judge's question about the PLO and what he knew about their involvement in drug smuggling. He knew that there were several armed groups loosely related to the PLO, and that Syria supported the group living in the Bekaa Valley in eastern Lebanon, closer to Syria's border. He was certain the man in charge when they made the transfer of the cannabis had said "soo-ri'-a," the Arabic pronunciation of "Syria" so similar to the English that he had noticed and remembered. He knew Syria received support from the U.S.S.R., which would make it an unfriendly nation as far as the anti-communist Western nations were concerned. If he could not recall more to tell the court, would his troubles multiply?

He lay back on the bed and tried to reconstruct each moment of that terrifying night when *The Robert Gordon* was accosted by the ghostly black ship with fifteen or more heavily armed and unfriendly men dressed in black.

He visualized the tall man with the AK-47, the man who seemed to be their leader, pointing his gun at Keith. He remembered him asking a question that neither Keith, Tom, nor Niko understood. He had repeated the question. Keith had pulled something out of his pocket along with a small piece of paper and passed it to the man, who then turned to his men and in rapid-fire Arabic gave them an order. They had responded by tossing the sacks of cannabis into the hold and onto the deck of *The Robert Gordon*. The man had come close to each of the three of them in turn, his face inches from theirs, as though he was memorizing their faces. Niko remembered knowing that Keith was spooked. He had told Tom and Niko to start loading the sacks into the compartments in the hold that Tom had constructed back in Palma, his voice a bit shaky.

Niko remembered he had descended into the hold, and Tom, standing on the stairs, had passed more parcels down to him from the deck. He had tried to pack them into the compartments as tightly as possible, working faster and faster as more and more sacks thudded onto the deck over his head and down onto the floor of the hold. He had felt like a robot, accelerating his speed. Lift, carry, pitch. Lift, carry, pitch. Tom was no longer passing them to Niko. He was simply throwing them down the hatch onto a pile that grew into a massive mound and filled the open area of the hold. Niko could not keep up. The white plastic and burlap wrapped packets blocked the doors to the compartments that Niko hadn't yet opened.

He remembered feeling he was inside a nightmare and fearing he'd suffocate. Claustrophobia and the scent of hashish muddled his thinking.

The noise on deck had suddenly stopped. He had heard Keith's voice and then the sound of Keith's feet following Tom's through the hatch and down the ladder. They've gone. Keith's shaky voice had said. We've got to get this stuff stowed, NOW. We've got to get out of here! Keith and Tom had pitched in prying open the doors to the compartments, tossing the packages into the compartments, nailing the rubber seals over the doorways, and restoring the hold to "normalcy." Then all three of them, totally spent, had collapsed on the floor of the hold.

He hadn't seen the men in black or their leader again. The only thing he was certain of was that their leader had said "soo-ri'-a," which the prosecutor could interpret as meaning they were part of one of the Palestinian groups that were challenging the PLO for the allegiance of the Palestinians. They were a group that had not been expelled from Lebanon, a group allied with Syria and therefore with the Soviet Union. This trial would not only be a criminal trial about bringing illegal cannabis resin into the U.K. It would be part of the Cold War and the international fight against terrorism.

Chapter 43

The judge retired to his chambers for a cup of tea and a scone. It was a little early for a glass of his favorite single-malt scotch, as he'd adjourned them at two. His secretary buzzed to say someone from Special Branch wanted to see him. News travels fast, he thought to himself as he reluctantly told her to bring him or her in.

As he expected, it was a him. The man strode toward him, nodding once before speaking.

"May I sit down, your Honor?" The judge nodded assent and the man lowered himself into the chair across from his desk. "It's about this case you're hearing. This Mr. Karras is in a bit of a pickle--of his own making, of course, but a pickle that Her Majesty's Secret Service may be able to benefit from."

The judge nodded again and waited for more. He wondered where this conversation was headed.

"In the past five years, international drug trafficking organizations have begun operating on an unprecedented scale, thanks to the availability of money laundering through international banks and, frankly, thanks to corruption within governments on both sides of the Atlantic. For this country the largest supplier of drugs has been Lebanon.

"Both the U.S. and the U.K. are involved in Lebanon providing the Lebanese Armed Forces millions of pounds and dollars in military aid, equipment, weapons, and training. With our help the Lebanese Armed Forces have been fighting Syria and one of the Palestinian groups, the PFLP-GC. The fighting is concentrated in the Bekaa Valley—which is where the cannabis resin smuggled into the U.K. by your defendants originated.

"The U.K. and U.S. both have had troops in Lebanon, too, as part of the Multi-National Force. Her Majesty's Government wants to end Syria's support for the Palestinians. The Syrians are closely tied to the Soviets, and we want them out of Lebanon. You know how the Cold War goes: The ally of my enemy is my enemy. Am I being clear?"

The judge's face betrayed a hint of contempt. Did the man think he went into these cases without preparation? This was a high profile case, although for some reason the government obviously was downplaying it, requesting that it not be held at the Old Bailey where the most celebrated cases were tried. So far the man from Special Branch had not made clear what any of this had to do with his trial. So the judge asked him.

The man from Special Branch replied, "Karras said he thought the people who provided them the cannabis resin were PLO. Her Majesty's government does not want this pursued in open court for reasons of national security."

The judge had not seen this man in his courtroom, and he'd put the court into recess only an hour or so ago. How did this man know what Karras had testified that caused him to bring the court to an abrupt recess? He decided not to ask.

"Karras has acknowledged his guilt and is terrified of being deported to Lebanon." The man from Special Branch stood and walked to the window facing away from the judge who looked sharply at him.

Now the judge had to ask: "And how do you know this?"

"We've monitored Karras's correspondence. We believe he may be willing to help us, if we can prevent him from being deported. To prevent him from being deported, we would need your assistance."

The judge had heard rumors of this kind of intervention from other branches of Her Majesty's Government, but this was the first time he had personally experienced it. He was not pleased.

"I am pledged to uphold the law," he stated as if that ended their conversation. But the Special Branch man was not about to take his hint.

"Your Honor, the young man has no other criminal involvements. He left Lebanon ten years ago and has lived in Greece all that time. He did not realize, nor did his family, that when they applied for Greek citizenship, he would not be granted it along with the rest of them." The agent's words sounded surprisingly compassionate, which made the judge suspicious, suspicious and irritated. He was not used to being propositioned in his chambers by another branch of government.

"What is it you are asking of me?" The veneer of civility that had masked the judge's face was gone now.

"We are asking you to follow normal procedure—give him the minimum sentence for drug smuggling, five years, and instruct that he spent two years of his sentence in the U.K. But instead of deporting him after those two years, grant him a U.K. visa on grounds of 'extraordinary circumstances' and release him on parole to the Special Forces. Of course, none of this would be stated in the record of the proceedings, nothing other than his sentence. The record of this trial will be classified Top Secret, unavailable to the public for the usual 25 years, to be renewed for a total of 80 years. By 2064, all participants including you and me will be more or less out of play, so to speak."

"We have one additional request...that you not allow the questioning to include references to Mr. Brian Baker. I cannot tell you why. Consider it simply a request from the highest levels of Her Majesty's Government. Do you understand?"

"I am not used to taking instructions from the other branches of government, sir. I remind you we are a democracy with power distributed among the branches of government and an independent judiciary." He was frowning and his displeasure was unmistakable. He forced himself to calm down. He must be judicious. "I will not give you an answer today. I need to think about this highly irregular request." He was clearly annoyed.

"Take your time, sir. But please do not reconvene the court before you make your decision." The agent stood, nodded curtly to the judge, turned to the door, and left his chambers. The judge had the distinct impression the man was not accustomed to being denied what he "requested."

The judge did not understand the connection between the requests.

Let Karras off after two years with permission to remain in the U.K. and let Special Branch look after him? Don't allow Brian Baker, the mystery man of this whole case, in his opinion, to be mentioned during the trial? Close the record for eighty years? Trying to puzzle it out made his head hurt. Maybe a scotch was in order.

He called his wife to see what was on for this evening, hoping there was nothing on their calendar. He wanted to do more research into this case, but she informed him that they had a cocktail party, a black-tie affair in honor of the former U.S. Secretary of Defense, Clark Clifford. Damn. He needed time to decide what to do about the Special Branch request. He asked his secretary to notify the prosecution and defense that the court would reconvene late tomorrow, at two. Then he left the office, walking along the Thames to clear his head.

The party that evening was hosted by Lord and Lady Llewellyn in their elegant home in Chelsea. Elaborately dressed couples ascended the steps to the mansion. To the judge they resembled over-groomed poodles at a dog show. Society parties were his least favorite activity.

Scuttering about were young people filling drinks and passing platters of starters. He remembered being one of them, two decades ago. Eager-to-please young waiters, pandering to the wealthy and hoping that good fortune would be contagious. God, he hated these parties even though he'd paid for his law books with what he earned servicing the almighty rich.

Lord Llewellyn was in his element introducing his guests to the American celebrity who the judge would just as soon avoid. His wife, however, kept squeezing his elbow until he gave in and moved into the queue of notables clustered around the tall, white haired Clifford. He was a distinguished looking bloke, and before he knew it, they were in conversation.

Clifford had advised U.S. presidents Kennedy and Truman, according to the invitation. He was in London for a board meeting of the world's largest private bank, the Bank of Credit and Commerce International or BCCI, to whom he was both a client and their lawyer.

Clifford was garrulous and disarmingly open. "I'm BCCI's barrister, as you Brits would say," he told the judge. It seemed Clifford was also president of an American bank that was linked to BCCI. Clifford was full of praise for BCCI, which he boasted had branches in eighty countries and clients that included governments, celebrities, and guerrilla groups, even the PLO. That comment grabbed the judge's attention.

At that moment in their one-way conversation a robust man with an Israeli accent approached Clifford and gave him a bear hug. "So good to see you again, Clark." He was the sort of man the judge avoided at all cost, pushy and pre-emptive, chomping on a large cigar and blowing the smoke without regard for who was in its path. He interrupted the judge's conversation with Clifford and took over the space in front of the American celebrity, expertly elbowing the judge out of his way.

Clifford, at least, had some manners. He introduced the judge to Bruce Rappaport who, he said, divided his time between the islands of Barbados and Antigua and Geneva, Switzerland. "Bruce is the most diversified big businessman I know," Clifford was saying, "Arms, cement, melon farms, oil in Texas and the West Indies, banks, and a major funder of charitable institutions in Israel. Bruce, this is the judge who is trying that drug smuggling case."

The judge had not—would not—mention cases he was trying. Was it his imagination or did a knowing look pass between Rappaport and Clifford?

Rappaport turned to the judge and invited him into their conversation on his own terms. "The fellows involved don't seem very bright. But ten million pounds worth of cannabis resin could build a tidy fortune, eh? Too bad they are such losers." He sent the judge a conspiratorial grin, but the judge had had enough. It was inappropriate for this man to be discussing a case he was in the middle of trying. His disapproval was obvious and Rappaport picked up on it. "Sorry if I offended you, judge. In these days it's the clever entrepreneurs who make the fortunes, not clumsy amateurs, that's all. Wouldn't you agree?"

The judge excused himself and retreated to the farthest corner of the room. Someone else had got there before him and was about to take a seat. A man who looked to be in his sixties, tall and rosy faced, introduced himself. Another American. "I'm John Shaheen, president of the Macmillan Ring-Free Oil Company. I just must sit down. My dogs are killing me." With that Shaheen plopped down into an armchair, stretched out his long legs, and smiled with relief. The judge appreciated his informality. Here was a man who was not putting on airs.

"Mind if I join you?" He settled himself in the chair next to Shaheen, venturing into what he thought would be the least demanding small talk. "What brings you to London?"

"I'm here for a meeting of CSI—the Center for Strategic Investing."

"I've not heard of that organization, sorry."

"It started in Virginia, but we have on the board people with intelligence backgrounds from all across the world who advise us on 'strategic investments.' For example, everyone knows that petrodollars are poor investments right now, but we knew in advance what was happening in the OPEC countries, thanks to our board. That allowed us to shift our money elsewhere ahead of the curve."

"Mr. Clifford touts investing in 'his' BCCI. I've not heard much about BCCI or the Center for Strategic Investing." The judge was out of his depth talking investments, but his earlier conversation with the guest of honor might help him here.

Shaheen was smiling. "BCCI is a very good investment. They have the technology to handle huge transactions within minutes, even seconds, and that changes everything. Imagine it, investors notified by CSI that there is a problem coming in one sector of the world's economy--or an opportunity for rapid profits through investing in a specific product—can in seconds shift billions of dollars away from what is about to lose money and into what makes it, done through BCCI. It is truly incredible."

The judge was intrigued. "Isn't there regulation of such huge flows of capital?"

"No. Thanks to President Reagan and Prime Minister Maggie Thatcher, regulation has become a bad word. Capitalism! It's a lovely thing to watch in action and even lovelier to watch as it fills up your bank accounts! It's no surprise that we're all Republicans and Tories."

"John!" the voice was from a somewhat elderly man who'd approached them looking for a place to sit. "Good to see you!"

"American Cousins" were everywhere. The judge was surrounded by them.

Shaheen introduced the judge to Bob Anderson. He said Anderson was as much a celebrity as the guest of honor—President Eisenhower's Deputy Secretary of Defense, Secretary of the Navy, Secretary of Treasury and economic advisor to Presidents Kennedy and Lyndon B. Johnson. Anderson seemed cordial enough. He pulled up a chair to join them. Across the room the judge saw his wife throw him a look that signaled she was ready to leave, but politeness dictated staying just a bit longer to get acquainted with Anderson, so he waved her off.

"Did I overhear you talking of my two favorite people?" Anderson was smiling broadly.

"Reagan and Thatcher? Yes. So, Bob, something I've always wanted to ask you: How did you manage to work both sides of the aisle, working in Republican and Democratic administrations?" Shaheen was teasing his friend, who took the bait.

Bob Anderson leaned back in his chair, laced his fingers over his chest, and replied with absolute confidence. "Money. It's all about money. Like you, I know the key is to reduce the power of government and make government operate like business, unregulated and unrestrained."

All right, the judge needed to get away from here and home to do more research for his case. "I hope you will excuse me, sirs, but my wife is signaling me that she is ready to go home," he said. "It's been very nice to meet you both." With that the judge stood, shook hands, and left them. He wasn't about to tell them that he was a member of the Labour Party and that he found the policies of Mrs. Thatcher and her American sidekick appalling.

In the car going home he found himself mulling over the idea of an international team of former intelligence officers and international businessmen combining their knowledge of potential trouble spots to identify the most strategic investments ahead of the market's curves, and an international bank with the power to transfer huge sums in seconds to facilitate money making. He wondered if such quick money transfers became invisible to government monitoring agencies because of their speed. Wasn't that money laundering? He wondered what the current most strategic investment was. Probably arms sales. Or could it be drugs?

That thought took him back to the conversation in his chambers that afternoon. He had to make a decision soon.

Chapter 44

The Special Branch officer sat on the edge of his seat, both feet planted staunchly as he made his report to his superior. He was fidgeting and knew that it showed. He hadn't expected intransigence from the judge. What he was proposing--giving a defendant special treatment by granting him a visa--was not unheard of, if it served the larger purposes of Her Majesty's Government. Such a variation in enforcing the law simply had to be done without public knowledge. That could be accomplished by classifying the trial records. The media no longer was devoting columns of space to this case. Reporters were easily diverted to other stories when cases went on this long. With encouragement they would take up other big profile cases and forget about Operation Bishop. Surprisingly, no reporters were questioning why Brian Baker was not on trial. Ah, the fourth estate. Always after the newest story and few of them able to stay focused for long.

He told his supervisor that, if he read the judge correctly, the man was likely to be sympathetic to giving the young man from Greece a break by not deporting him to Lebanon. The next challenge would be to convince the young man that working for Special Forces would be to his and his family's advantage. Ironically, Karras was mostly irrelevant to their interests. They were using his stateless status as a reason for classifying the trial transcripts so that the government's intelligence service's connection to this case would not be discovered, which might well come out if the court pursued Brian Baker's connection to the drug running. For all MI-6 cared, Karras could be shipped back to Lebanon and rot in jail there. But someone higher up had an interest in Karras and had proposed this strategy, which would protect Her Majesty's Government from scrutiny. It was mutually beneficial. The public, generally hostile toward immigrants who were undocumented—would not protest that Karras was getting special treatment instead of being deported if they didn't know about it. Embargoing the trial records would ensure they wouldn't know.

The supervisor reminded him that Maggie Thatcher and Ronnie Reagan were in agreement that their intelligence services needed more human assets. People on the ground working in private businesses or as floating assets had access to important information that high tech satellite monitoring could not provide. It's quite possible that Karras with his Lebanese-Cypriot-Greek background might become a useful asset. That his father had fought with the EOKA against the British would give him added credibility if they decided to use him as an asset.

His supervisor seemed pleased with his report and dismissed him. He walked to his favorite pub for a quick lunch before checking back with the judge. Over a Guinness and shepherd's pie he pondered who had suggested granting special treatment to Karras and then closing access to the trial records? Could it be the person watching out for Baker? Was Baker an asset? Closing the records would certainly protect all of them—MI-5, MI-6, Special Forces, the CIA, the FBI and Drug Enforcement Agency and maybe other government agencies on both sides of the Atlantic. Not a bad tactic to embargo the records and keep them classified. That would prevent some adventurous cub reporter from unearthing the fact that Brian Baker was never charged or tried in this case and keep the press from following the trail to whoever was protecting Baker.

He found it curious that the press had not questioned why Baker was not on trial. When he'd happened on people discussing this case over sandwiches or at the water cooler, the general opinion seemed to be that Baker was probably the mastermind of the operation. But in the press Baker received at most a sentence or two, and no one was speculating in print that he was at the center of *The Robert Gordon*'s drug haul. Perhaps he wasn't.

One never knew who was behind such operations now that the U.S. and U.K. were so closely aligned ideologically and both governments actively using covert operations to attain their foreign policy goals. The Cold War was such a diverting game when played like this.

The judge, however, was a bit of a loose cannon. Labour Party Progressive, even though he tried to hide it. Stubbornly by-the-book. Would he agree to leave Brian Baker out of this trial altogether?

Generally, the operation seemed to have worked out well. They had planned for the drug smugglers to be caught off-loading the cannabis resin, and had engineered sensational press coverage that presented Her Majesty's Customs and Excise men cooperating well with the police and together doing a sterling job combating the heinous import of a massive quantity of illegal drugs. The British people could sleep well, confident that their government was protecting them.

And the revenue that a yacht full of cannabis resin produced once sold to distributors? Involuntarily he shook his head imagining its magnitude. The money paid to the suppliers probably came from different accounts at BCCI. Or maybe the suppliers were paid in-kind with high tech military weapons that the Iranians lusted for. Probably signed, sealed, and delivered even before that yacht entered the River Crouch. Brilliant! Oh, he loved his work.

Chapter 45

The journey that Brian Baker and Georgina took from that obscure airport in Cyprus to Tel Aviv, Israel, and on to San Jose, Costa Rica had been uneventful. Someone had met their plane in San Jose and driven them to their new home, an eight-thousand-acre ranch on the Nicaraguan border owned by a former CIA man, John Floyd Hull. After eight months, by the beginning of the Operation Bishop trial, Brian and Georgina were settled into their new identities and relatively well adapted to life in Costa Rica.

The ranch was a major transit point in the international drug and arms trade. Hull told them he had been retired from the CIA for eight years when Director William Casey had invited him back to handle an operation that provided weapons and supplies to the Contras. Hull accepted the job happily. His ranch was a Central American hub for the international trade in cocaine and weapons. From the ranch, cocaine grown in South America was dispersed to the United States by some of the Contra leaders, and weapons were dispersed to the Contras. *[See Discussion of Sources]*

Of course, Brian and Georgina did not know that when they established residence at the ranch. Hull monitored them at first to make sure they could be trusted. Gradually he brought them into the operation. He put Georgina to work helping him keep the books, if you could call them that. She recorded flights coming and going from the Hull Ranch to an assortment of destinations. Hull used Excel spreadsheets, a new software, to record the weight of cargoes transiting through the ranch, the date each plane arrived with its cargo of arms, the date each delivery was loaded onto a small aircraft and sent off, and the pilots' codenames, the date the planes left the ranch for the U.S., although the cargo was disguised with a codename. Most planes flew north to landing fields outside Miami.

It did not require a lot of brain power to keep these records. Excel performed the math for Hull's monthly reports to Casey. Georgina was a quick learner and welcomed the activity. She liked being of service and was ideologically an agnostic.

The ranch received a parade of transitory visitors bringing in cocaine or arms and then returning to wherever they came from. Nicaragua being on the western border of the ranch, Contra groups occasionally came through on their way somewhere else. Brian got to meet Eden Pastora, the leader of the Costa Rican branch of the Contras. Recently he had a conversation with Brooklyn Rivera, the man who led one branch of the Miskitos, Afro-Indians who had joined the Contras. Hull had seen Brian talking with Rivera and later warned him to be careful how chummy he was with Rivera. Rivera was known to be negotiating with the Sandinistas to get his people the right to return to their land, which made Rivera, formerly an insider, an outsider.

Am I on the outside, too? Brian wondered. He told Georgina he felt like he was on probation, being tested to see if he could be trusted with any sort of work here.

"You are," she replied with a grin.

There really wasn't much for either of them to do. They were learning Spanish as well as learning about the flora and fauna of Central America, especially the birds. John Hull had been a gentleman farmer in Maryland after he retired from the CIA. He'd grown wine grapes and dabbled in experimental agriculture before relocating to Costa Rica and accepting Casey's invitation to work for him. Hull liked teaching Brian and Georgina what he knew, and he knew a lot. He could tell you the name of every bird and even imitate its call. He was, in fact, an interesting and pleasant man. They both liked him.

What Brian didn't like was being in limbo. It was frustrating feeling temporary and unclear about what was expected of him. What was his future? Also frustrating was the absence of news about the trial of the crew of *The Robert Gordon*. Brian wished he knew how the trial was proceeding. He felt responsible for involving Niko and Keith and regretted that they were sitting in Brixton Prison while he was lounging around here in a tropical paradise. That this bothered him surprised him. It was uncharacteristic. Maybe that was the upside of having a new identity; he could reinvent himself. He had a new name, a new backstory, and even thought differently.

In the past month a Marine who worked for the White House had come twice to meet with Hull, Pastora and Rivera. His name was Colonel Oliver North, and, rumor had it, his office was down the hall from President Reagan's. He was tall with an open, boyish face. Georgina called him the "aw-shucks guy."

No one talked about why North was here. He always came and went like a whirlwind and spent his time with the Contra leadership. He appeared to be quite confident--"full of himself," as Brian's mother might say.

Brian had to admit that, if he was honest, this cloak and dagger stuff didn't much interest him. He guessed it must interest Archie, though. Otherwise, he was certain he would be in Brixton Prison with the rest of them, on trial for organizing the biggest drug trafficking operation in British history. He smiled, liking the sound of that. The biggest drug trafficking operation in British history. Of course, it had turned into the biggest drug bust, but he didn't blame Archie for that. Archie had been helping him. In fact, he thanked God for Archie, who, he assumed, must have seen to the intricate preparations that ferreted him and Georgina safely out of the U.K. just as the project blew up. Sometimes he wondered how Archie, as smart as he was, could have believed they could pull off such an operation, all the players being novices. It wasn't like Archie to be naïve. He also wondered how Archie arranged to bring them here to Hull's ranch. Did Archie work for one of the intelligence services? He didn't like the follow up questions that question led to. He was not in a position to do anything other than follow Hull's cues.

Hull had told Brian they were likely to have a visitor at the ranch before Christmas. No details, just "a visitor." Might Archie come to Costa Rica to see them? What had happened to Archie? Archie always landed on his feet, like the cats they had tortured when they were in grammar school. It wouldn't surprise him if Archie showed up here on Hull's ranch. When it came to Archie, nothing would surprise him.

Other than missing contact with his mum, the outcome of what the papers called Operation Bishop was, for Brian, not unpleasant. Having a new name and passport was interesting. Being well provided for and having little work to do—no problem there. It was even possible that, once his trial period here was finished, he and Georgina could meet his Mum in some South American city. Mum would probably have a new passport and identity just for that trip. Maybe they could even go together to Machu Picchu or the Mayan ruins in the Yucatan. Of course, that was contingent on their staying incognito on the ranch until after the trial was over and communicating with no one from their former lives. Hull told them he expected they could eventually leave the ranch and "come out"--live in their new identities elsewhere in the hemisphere. By then they should be speaking Spanish mas o menos fluently.

Hull's ranch lacked little--lots of liquor, smokes, good food--and it looked like a Hollywood set for *The Blue Lagoon*, stunning shades of green with an abundance of huge, primary-colored hibiscus blossoms, sweet scented white frangipani, and bougainvillea that spilled a profusion of assertive pinks and purples all over the compound. But, once his probationary period was up, would he be of use to what the people here called the Agency? At some point he would need to make some money.

He was glad Georgina was with him. Their relationship could predictably have gone sour, just the two of them together every day for so long, but, to his surprise, they had grown more connected. When Brian thought about what she had given up for him, he felt gratitude. Gratitude was an unfamiliar feeling in his former life. Maybe that was another plus of his new identity.

He checked off the calendar each day they were here, waiting for the end of the trial, hoping Archie would find a way to let him know about the trial and what lay ahead for him.

Dad remained a problem. Dad could not know anything. Dad would probably insist that Brian stand trial if he did know. He wondered what Mum had told Dad when the papers at first carried his name and announced his disappearance. Probably he would never see his father again. At least he wouldn't have to see his dad's eyes, unable—or unwilling?--to hide his disappointment in his only son.

Chapter 46

While Keith and his crew sat in the courtroom on trial, the U.S. Congress relaxed its ban of any and all aid being provided to the Contras. Congress voted to allow *humanitarian* aid although it continued to specifically prohibit the Department of Defense and the CIA "or any other agency or entity of the United States involved in intelligence activities" from providing military equipment, training or intelligence to the Contras.

The renewal of some U.S. government aid to the Contras was a major news story. It stirred a hornets' nest among the sizeable and vocal groups of Americans determined to stop the President's wars in Central America. But for the community coming and going to Hull's Costa Rica ranch, it was a cause for celebration.

"House Votes Aid for Contras; Major Victory for Reagan" read Lea Donosky's story in *the Chicago Tribune* on June 13, 1985--$27 million. With the start of the new fiscal year, October 1, 1985, U.S. government funds for humanitarian aid would resume flowing to the Contras.

William Casey saw no reason to dissolve his network of private citizens who engaged in covert activity and arranged the funding of the Contras. The Contras still needed military aid, and Casey's secret Enterprise network was getting it to them. They would continue to keep Congress in the dark.

According to Oliver North, funding for Contra military aid was coming in from seventeen countries, and sales of arms to Iran were netting so much profit that millions of dollars were being diverted to the Contras. Money from the arms sales was routed through private bank accounts. There was no oversight of how those millions were spent. The Enterprise's covert activities were accountable to no entity. The two men handling the money had been personally selected by CIA Director William Casey for this work and reported directly to Oliver North.

Through the Enterprise, the United States sold 1,000 TOW missiles to the Iranians and gave Iran military intelligence. In return for the missiles, Iran was supposed to release the seven Americans it was holding hostage. So far, no hostages had been released.

Twice a week planes owned by the Enterprise and flown by Enterprise pilots landed on the Hull ranch runway that was also owned by the Enterprise. Some planes delivered cocaine that was reloaded into other planes and flown to airfields outside Miami or in southern California. Sales of those drugs in the U.S. and in Europe raised money that was laundered through the largest private international bank in the world—BCCI--using bank accounts in the Caribbean to hide U.S. involvement. It was a massive operation involving Israel, Pakistan, Panama, Switzerland, and Saudi Arabia. The Enterprise made a profit of more than $6 million just from the first sale, money diverted to the Contras and other so-called black ops. It was a most profitable business.

Chapter 47

At one o'clock, an hour before London Crown Court was to reconvene to hear Niko Karras's testimony regarding what he heard the provider of the drugs say, the judge was at his desk in chambers. He had been scrutinizing the law for the previous several hours.

Now he hit the desk in an uncharacteristic show of excitement. "Ah, ha! I've got it!" He read aloud Section 3(5) (a) of the Immigration Act 1971: "A foreign national may be deported if the Secretary of State has decided that deportation would be beneficial to the public good or if a criminal court makes a 'recommendation' that he or she should be as part of its sentence [Section 3(6)]." *The operative word here is 'may'—I have the legal authority to decide not to include deportation in Mr. Karras's sentence, and in this case the Secretary of State does not find that deporting Karras would be beneficial to the public good. Deportation is not required by law.* All right. He buzzed for his secretary and asked that the prosecution and defense barristers see him in chambers.

When they assembled, he told them what he had found to support a decision not to deport Karras. "I realize that we are not yet in the sentencing phase of this trial, but I have called you here because Her Majesty's Government has asked--for national security reasons--that we not pursue questioning Mr. Karras about his overhearing something that made him think they were receiving the drugs from the PFLP-GC, the most extreme group among the Palestinians. I am inclined to respect this request from the Foreign Office, but I wanted to check with both of you before making a decision. What do you say?"

After the prosecution and the defense both said they would not object to dropping any further questioning of Mr. Karras on the PFLP-GC, the judge spoke a final time to them. "We have three members of the crew who have acknowledged in their depositions that they knew they were transporting drugs and two who deny any knowledge of the cargo they were carrying. We have three men accused of loading and transporting the drugs, one of whom protests his innocence and the other two who are pleading not guilty. But there is a missing person in this trial, it seems to me--Mr. Brian Baker. Do either of you plan to introduce evidence implicating Mr. Baker in drug smuggling?"

The prosecutor looked uncomfortable. "Your honor, we have no evidence of Mr. Baker's involvement. The other defendants, the two who we believe met with Mr. Baker, Mr. Karras and Mr. Brown, deny knowledge of him or his involvement. We have nothing to bring to the court on this man, sir."

The defense attorney spoke up next. "Frankly, I suspect Mr. Baker was involved but, like my colleague points out, we have no evidence. The man appears to have disappeared. Without evidence, we cannot charge him with putting undue pressure on the crew or any of the defendants, enticing them to commit this crime."

The judge sighed. His mouth was tight and stern, "Thank you for your time. We will proceed as scheduled at two. I will see you in court shortly."

While they returned to the courtroom, he made a call to the Special Branch agent. He spoke crisply. "I am calling to inform you that I will not be pursuing questioning Mr. Karras about the PLFP-GC and will not be recommending deportation. The law gives me that right. I need not bend it because of heavy handed tactics from people in the Special Branch. Am I being clear?" He clicked off before the agent could reply. The Special Branch request to allow no questions about Brian Baker was irrelevant if there was no evidence that either side could present pointing to Mr. Baker's involvement in drug smuggling. Baker somehow remained squeaky clean

Placing his wig on his head and pushing his arms into the sleeves of his gown, the judge cast a quick glance in the mirror to be sure nothing was askew. Then he entered the courtroom.

Niko had feared that the afternoon's questioning of him would be a disaster because the prosecution would attempt to connect him to the terrorism of the PFLP-GC. To his surprise, the prosecution had no further questions of him. The barrister representing him slipped in some information about his clean record and Christian Orthodox background before being found out of order. Within minutes Niko was dismissed from the witness stand and returned to sit with Keith and Tom, David and Sally.

The following day during visitors' hours Niko's barrister came to see him. "I have some good news for you, Mr. Karras. You have acknowledged your guilt and apologized for your actions and the judge has agreed to not add deportation to your sentence when he announces the sentencing. You will still serve more time in prison, but the months you have been held here in Brixton will be subtracted from your sentence, so you are likely to be released after another year and three months. I am also told that upon your release Special Branch will be supervising you for some time and will employ you in their office as well. I think you've hit the jackpot, Mr. Karras. You will want to let your mother know of this development. I will see you in court on Monday." The barrister shook his hand and departed.

Niko could not believe this news. He had just returned to his cell when he was summoned again to the visitors' room, where a man he did not know told him that there was a condition he must accept in exchange for not being deported. He must agree to work for the Special Branch. He might be sent back to Rhodes or elsewhere in the region, or he might remain in London. Whichever, he would report to the Special Branch and be assigned by them to various jobs. Was he prepared to accept this condition?

"If I am not to be deported, what passport will I have?" he asked his visitor. "A dual passport, a U.K. passport as well as your Lebanese one, to enable you to move about in the region," was the answer. Niko had no idea what working for the Special Branch would entail, but "move about in the region" sounded like he would get home to see his family at some point. And he wouldn't be held in prison in Lebanon or be tried as a terrorist. He accepted the condition. For the first time in eight months, Niko would sleep through a dreamless night.

Chapter 48

Janet arranged to take a discretionary day off work the day she thought Keith would be on the witness stand. She sat alone in the stalls for visitors, shivering, whether from the air conditioning or from fear she couldn't say. There was another possibility. Anger. Over the past six months since Christmas anger at Keith's decision to participate in smuggling drugs had burrowed deeper into her. She felt abused and depressed. His solicitor said ten years was likely, five before he could be paroled for good behavior. The time he'd served would be subtracted from the sentence. At best, if the trial ended at the beginning of July, he could be released on parole October 4, 1989.

By then Teddy would be nine and a half. He would have lived half his life without his dad present. *How could Keith have chosen to take that risk?*

She knew he was sorry, keenly sorry. His letters and his tears told her that. Sometimes she worried whether he could sustain all that time incarcerated, whether the weaker side of him that had been willing to commit such a serious crime would find other distractions in prison. She knew he was smoking again, though he hadn't told her. She could smell it on him when she visited. Nasty smell, like the whole bloody business. Brixton was the remand prison, which she had heard was considerably better than the long-term places they would be sent after sentencing. She knew other habits were available in prison, behaviors to make the time pass. You learned them from your cellmates' extensive experience on the dark side, much worse than cannabis, especially in prisons other than Brixton.

How would he be changed once he was released? Would his outgoing personality and his capacity for caring be eroded by years in prison? Could she ever trust him again? He had willfully ruined their life as a family. How could she forgive that?

Her life was just so lonely. The teachers at her school looked the other way when they saw her, not meeting her eyes, and stumbled expressing the most basic conversational norms like "Hello. How are you?" She had no other social relationships. The men at Keith's car hire business looked at her sympathetically when she went in to go over the books and one or two asked how Keith was holding up, but if she said more than "He's okay" or "It's hard," their eyes shifted away from her and she could tell they were uncomfortable.

Could she live with this isolation for four more years?

When her parents eventually discovered what was going on, Dad suggested she break up with Keith and look for another man, someone stable and conventional (and religious).

She sat in the visitor stalls with a pen and notebook ready in case she heard something important to remember. The prosecutor did not ask Keith about Brian or Archie. Their names had not been mentioned in the trial. The only questions were what Keith and his crew members knew about their mission and their cargo, where the money came from to purchase *The Robert Gordon*, what he himself had known before sailing to the waters off Tripoli, Lebanon, and what was to be done with the drugs once they were off-loaded.

He looked nervous up there responding to their questions. He'd lost a bit of weight in prison, probably two stone, and appeared quite fit. He still had his beard, though it appeared more grey without Teddy to keep the white weeded out. His face was paler, but he looked good. She felt a pang of longing for his strong arms, his mouth… She stopped herself. She needed to listen carefully and in case something was said that might be grounds for an appeal.

Keith spoke haltingly. "Tom and Niko have testified to what they knew, sir. I didn't tell them much, figuring the less they knew the better. David and Sally knew nothing. "Some bloke I never actually met provided me an envelope with the cash to pay for *The Robert Gordon*. I picked it up at a pub at the marina in Palma. I was trading my tired old *Sallykins* for *The Robert Gordon*, trading up for a more seaworthy yacht, you see. I knew we were bringing in illegal drugs, but I never thought it would be such a massive amount. Shocked me to see how much. Shocked me and scared me so I nearly pissed my pants." A rumble of suppressed laughter crossed the courtroom.

Keith's face turned pink and he looked chagrined, worried he'd offended the decorum of the court, Janet guessed. He rushed to add, "I'm sorry, your Honor. That was a bit too much information. I have a way of saying too much—diarrhea of the mouth, my brother used to call it." Then, realizing he'd compounded the problem by referring to more body functions, he shifted in his chair, shaking his head and looking quite pitiful. The judge looked at him sternly and then turned back to his papers. Janet took consolation from the fact that Keith's penitence for his language was quite evident on his face and in his body language. She hoped the judge could feel empathy or had a sense of humor.

"If there are no further questions and you have nothing more you want to add, you may step down, Mr. Brown." Keith stood awkwardly, sending his solicitor an "I'm sorry" look. He nearly fell in his haste to leave the witness box. She hoped his little boy awkwardness along with his language faux pas might make him a more sympathetic figure, a nice ordinary chap caught in something much bigger than his skills and experience could handle. That was the truth as she saw it.

Why were there no follow up questions about the envelope of money left for him by "a bloke I never met"?

When Dad and Mum invited her to bring Teddy and come for tea when she got back from court, she decided to accept. No one else was inviting her out.

She called out Hello as she and Teddy entered the front door of Mum and Dad's small brick home. Teddy ran to the kitchen to hug his granny while Janet paused in the doorway to the parlor, startled to see a forty-something man sitting in the flowered side chair, sipping a lemonade. He looked out of place, but he did not look surprised to see her. He stood and stuck out his right hand.

"You're Janet, right? I'm Julian." The hand he offered her was damp and cold. "Your Dad told me what's happened to you. I'm sorry."

That was at least something. But she didn't know how to respond, so she excused herself and joined Mum and Teddy in the kitchen readying the tea. "You should have told me you'd invited someone else," she whispered to Mum. He must be the man Dad had talked about last week, someone from their church who owned a laundry in an upscale neighborhood in London.

She heard Dad coming down the stairs, entering the parlor, and the two male voices talking. She carried a plate of sandwiches to the dining room table, and Mum called them to come for tea. Mum seated Janet across from Julian.

After Dad's extended blessing of the meal, Julian attempted to talk with Teddy, which was nice enough. Janet noticed that Julian was a fidgeter, constantly rubbing his left thumb against the nail edge of his forefinger like he was sanding it and tapping the heel of his right foot against the floor. The tapping set off her tea, which slid precariously from side to side in her teacup and nearly spilled over the lip.

The conversation was stilted. Dad, Mum, and Julian talked of church and church friends, the weather, and the birdhouse Dad was building. It wasn't until they began clearing the table that Julian spoke directly to Janet. His voice was low and confiding.

"You seem to be a nice person. I'm sorry for you and Teddy that you got involved with that man. I know he led you astray and brought about your Fall. This may be your chance to get back on track, to get right with the Lord. Like your Dad says, God makes us pay when we stray."

The pomposity in his voice and the judgment on his face left Janet livid. How dare this stranger presume to understand her situation! She stood like Lot's wife, looking back at what her life had been when she was confined to her parents' world. This cretin belonged to that world and, no matter how angry she was at Keith, Keith stood head and shoulders above this sanctified excuse for a Christian.

She tried to speak, but her rage overpowered her. "Come Teddy, we're leaving. Come right now." The hard edge to her voice brought Teddy from the kitchen, his face worried. "Now!" She took his hand and made a hasty exit without saying good-by to anyone.

Driving home she thought how little her parents understood her. How could they think she would find this narrow minded, boring man from their church attractive? It washed over her how truly alone she was, and she tried unsuccessfully to staunch her tears and keep her attention on the wet road. To be so profoundly misunderstood, to have her feelings denied and her commitments discounted, to be so abandoned…

Teddy patted her arm. "Are you all right, Mummy?"

"I'm fine," she lied.

As she pulled up in front of their house, Teddy asked why that man kept moving all the time. She mumbled that he was probably nervous. What she really thought was that Julian was probably still a virgin, sheltered from the world by the Plymouth Brethren, and taught to think that his sorry existence was a superior life. Maybe Julian was terrified. Well, she was terrified, terrified of the possibility of a loveless life with someone like Julian who'd she settled for because she had no other options.

I'm not that desperate for a man in my daily life. She spoke the thought aloud and saw Teddy eyeing her in the rearview mirror.

Mum phoned as they were entering the house, her voice artificially bubbly. She apologized for missing their departure and asked what Janet thought of Julian. Janet could not respond. No point in getting into it. She said she had to prepare for school, couldn't talk, and rang off. *Why were her parents incapable of caring about anything other than her coming back to their fucking church?*

After she put Teddy to bed, she sat at the kitchen table and cried. She felt quite desperate. She missed Keith dreadfully. Were he to come home this year, she had no doubt they would pick up again with vigor and mutual love (as well as some very nice snogging and shagging).

She stood and moved to the stove to make some tea. Her mind was working overtime trying to sort it all out. The prospect of ten years apart was what left her in despair. All those years in prison could change him, or her.

What she could not forgive Keith for was not only his decision to smuggle the drugs but also his refusal to mention Brian Baker or Archie when they interrogated him. Those two men got him into this. Why weren't they on trial? Why was he protecting them? If he revealed who got him into this, the court might give him a shorter sentence. When she'd asked him, all he'd said was he'd given them his word, and he was responsible for his decision to get into this mess.

She had heard nothing from Archie. She'd asked the staff at the car hire about Georgina, the blonde woman they'd traveled to Spain with. Georgina had briefly managed the car hire business. But her inquiries about Georgina and her boyfriend, Brian, brought dull looks from the staff and awkward responses. They had not seen her in nearly a year, neither had they seen Brian. Both seemed to have disappeared about the time this whole business came crashing down on them. Was she the only person to think there was something strange about this that needed investigation?

She drank her tea and felt anger elbow in front of her empathy for Keith.

At least she loved her work, which was a good thing. With the car hire shop paid off—maybe by that same person who paid for *The Robert Gordon*?—she could manage the rest of their expenses, as long as she was frugal. Frugality was not hard for her, one good thing from her conservative upbringing.

By the time she climbed the stairs to bed she was thinking that she would do her best to keep Teddy connected with his daddy. She and Teddy would manage.

Chapter 49

S ally sat through the trial feeling invisible. Not only was she the only woman charged with smuggling, she was also not being tried with the others because her barrister was still tied up with his other case. She was there to listen to the others who were called to the witness stand and to give her testimony, which she had done a few weeks ago. The trial seemed almost over and she had to admit she was losing interest, "losing the plot a bit," was her mum's expression when she talked about Granny. Once it was truly over and the sentences read out for the other seven of them, she would remain in limbo for an unpredictable amount of time, still in the women's prison, and still waiting.

She felt a fool. She had planned to make her first trip at sea on *The Robert Gordon* and return to England, see her Mum, Dad, and Brenda, and then, with experience as a crew cook, sign on with another boat that was headed to the Caribbean and see the world. Her plan seemed completely naïve in light of how things had transpired. The best scenario that could come from this mess was her being found innocent and her passport—and her life—restored to her. She still would have lost a year or longer, depending on when her barrister could make time for her defense. *A whole year of her life*. All because she had stupidly misjudged that nice blonde-grey haired man who had offered her a job.

It was hard to be angry at Keith, who presented himself as an average, nice enough bloke, but sometimes, like now, she did feel angry with him. What if she was found guilty? She had known nothing about the cargo. They had all smoked weed on board, so how could she be expected to pick up the smell as something different from the generic aura of marijuana that each of them gave off?

If she was found guilty, she would probably receive a five-year sentence, or more. Subtracting from that the time she'd already spent in prison, nearly four additional years!

She also felt responsible, in a way, for David being here in the dock. If she hadn't encouraged him to ask to join their crew and asked Keith if he wanted to hire on another hand, David would still be aboard that other yacht, unhappy and penniless, yes, but at least not unhappy, penniless and on parole after four months in Brixton. And facing the same possible outcome she did—half a decade in prison.

Today she had chosen to sit at the far end of their row, next to Niko, who had the worst situation of them all, she figured. Sitting next to him put her own troubles in a different perspective.

Her mum and Brenda weren't attending the trial now. They were saving their vacation days for when Sally herself would be tried. But Mum still came to see her every other Saturday.

Last week Sally had found the courage to ask Mum about her biological father. When she was feeling very sorry for herself, she blamed him, because wanting to know about him was why she had left the U.K. and gone to Greece in the first place. He'd been a taboo subject growing up, but last Saturday with Mum and Sally facing each other across the visitors' table, Mum had responded to her questions. What she said surprised Sally.

"He was a lovely man," Mum said, "and he loved you very much. It was just that money was so scarce and--well, it was the Sixties." Mum paused, as though Sally should understand what she meant, but Sally wasn't at all sure what Mum was implying. Afraid to ask, she remained quiet, waiting for Mum to say more.

After an awkward silence, Mum continued. Apparently, Sally's father had taken up with another woman. To be fair, Mum had begun to meet Alfred at the pub by then, "the sexual revolution and all that. Your dad and I just didn't have much in common, other than you. When a friend told him they'd seen me with Alfred, well, that was too much for your father. He was off. Nearly broke my heart, even if I'd brought it on myself." Mum's eyes were far away and clouded over.

"To be completely honest with you, Sally, I half-hoped he'd turn up after reading about you in the papers. Not that I'd leave Alfred to go back to him, but because, well, I guess he'll always be the love of my life, my grand adventure. Taking up with him was not characteristic of me, coming from a family not very tolerant of foreigners and full of mean things to say about them. It was me being brave and daring and following my heart. But it was not to be. I've heard naught from him since this terrible business and, with Alfred back from the Falklands, it's probably best." Mum looked at her hands and shook her head. "If he did get in touch, he'd probably never recognize me now, or he'd think he was lucky to have left me while I still had a stunning smile and a body like Brenda's."

Sally had been so grateful for Mum's honesty that she brushed aside Mum's comment about Brenda's body. Sally knew Brenda was the looker of the family, which she'd always thought accounted for Brenda's brashness. Guess if you're gorgeous you can say what you please and hurt people's feelings?

She hadn't known that Mum had had Alfred in her life while she was married to Sally's dad. Funny, she'd been worried Mum wouldn't approve of her going off on her own to find adventure in Greece. *Sounds like Mum is proud that she did her own seizing of the day in marrying my father*, Sally thought. That surprised her.

When their fifteen-minute visit was over, Sally had hugged Mum and thanked her, feeling emotional but not wanting Mum to know. Mum had held Sally's face with both hands and said quite fiercely, "We're going to be okay with all this. It'll soon be over, and we'll chuckle about this time sitting over a pint after your life rights itself. And it will--right itself, I mean." With that Mum turned and left the visitors' room.

Chapter 50

The prosecutor spent nearly two days attempting to prove that David was fully knowledgeable of what *The Robert Gordon* was carrying in its forward hold. Surely David had smelled the cannabis in his nine days aboard? An expert witness was brought in to testify to how strong the scent of cannabis resin is and the impossibility of living in that small space--a forty-foot yacht--for nine days and without detecting its smell. The suggestion was even made that David had masterminded the entire operation, joining the crew in Gibraltar to directly oversee delivery of the drugs.

David's barrister was Anne Worrall with the Carnell office. Dad called her a terrier, so fiercely did she pull at any and every shred of the prosecution's argument. David had been ill with a head cold most of the trip. She asked him if he had taken any medication while on *The Robert Gordon*. He told the court that Sally had given him Benelyn from the medication box on board, and Keith had asked if he might have bronchitis, it was that bad. "I was serious sick with the flu the day I came on board," David testified.

Worrall asked if it wasn't true that yachting crews routinely smoke marijuana during long days at sea and was that the case aboard *The Robert Gordon*? David answered, "Yes, yes."

"So you are familiar with the smell of cannabis?"

"Yes, Mam. But I don't think it would have penetrated the fog of my stuffy head."

"And as you recovered?"

"I am embarrassed to admit this, but the smell of marijuana is familiar and unremarkable to those who work the yacht delivery trade," David answered. "Also, I did not join the crew until Gibraltar and the hatches to the forward hold were closed the entire trip as the weather was wretched— sheeting down rain and more rain."

Before he stepped down, Barrister Worrall reminded the court that Keith and Tom and Niko had all testified that David knew nothing about the drugs and that nothing in the other defendants' testimony contradicted anything David told the court.

Watching Worrall work, David felt hopeful. The woman was truly effective. When he glanced at Mam, she was smiling in a way he hadn't seen her smile thus far during the trial.

July 2nd, the day before the jury gave its verdicts, a teacher at Janet's school appeared in the doorway of her classroom while Janet was preparing for the children's arrival. She was not someone Janet had ever talked with. Like Janet she avoided the teachers' lunchroom. Janet was not sure she'd ever heard the woman speak, other than a Hello on the rare occasions they'd passed each other in the hallway.

"I'm sorry to disturb you. I'm Diane Jones. I teach grade three in Room 12. Do you have a moment?" The woman stood in the doorway of the classroom smiling tentatively.

"Of course, come in." At this point Janet would have welcomed any human contact that was accompanied by a smile. Her parents had offered to take Teddy while she went to the court, but their offer felt more like wanting to see their grandson than wanting to support their daughter in her most difficult time. Everyone at school greeted her cheerily, but she felt their smiles were fake. None of her colleagues actually talked with her or asked how she was.

The woman pulled the door closed behind her. "I know this must be a terrible week for you."

Janet could feel her tears coming and worked extra hard to keep them in check.

"I thought...Well, I know we don't know each other, but I thought if you were up for it, I could take you for a pint or a cuppa after school. I don't know if it would help to talk or if there's something else I could do that would help, but I imagine you could use a friend right now and, I guess I'm offering myself. I'm sorry it's taken me so long to speak with you."

Janet wavered. These nine months she had been so isolated and alone, except for Teddy, that she wasn't sure she remembered how to behave with anybody older than the six-year-olds in her class. But the woman looked trustworthy, something in her eyes seemed warm and welcoming.

"My sister lives in London with my Mum. I know you don't know them, but they read in the papers that the court will be handing down verdicts tomorrow and sentences likely the day after. They asked me to tell you if you don't want to travel back and forth to London for the court, they'd be happy to have you spend the night at their place. They have a pull-out bed. It's not much, but you wouldn't be alone. Your son would be welcome, too. I know you don't have any reason to trust us. It's probably hard to trust anybody with the press swarming around. Anyway…?"

The children were arriving full of their morning spunk and energy. "Today after school? You think about it. I've got to get to class before mine total the room. I'll check back with you. No pressure. We can do it later if today's too complicated. Chiao!" She turned and hurried down the hallway.

When school was out the woman returned. "Just checking in. Are you up for a pint or a cuppa today or would you rather wait till next week?"

Janet had been going back and forth all day on this. In this moment she made a mental coin toss. "OK," she said. "I'd best not have a pint—have to pick up my son in an hour—but a cuppa would be lovely."

They slid into a booth at the rear of the bakery across from the school. The woman ordered scones and cream with their tea. Janet spoke first, thanking the woman for her offer of friendship. "It has been a lonely time. Everyone seems to avoid talking to me. I feel like I'm wearing a scarlet letter of shame: HER MAN IS A CRIMINAL! Only he's not a bad man. He made a very stupid decision that I don't know if I'll ever be able to forgive him for, but he's still a good man, a really good man in so many ways." Her tears could not be contained. She talked through them and the woman listened as her tea cooled. Janet was grateful the woman didn't urge her to stop crying.

"Tomorrow you learn the verdict?"

"Yes, and it won't be good news. Then the sentence. Probably ten years with credit for time served and good behavior."

The shop girls were watching them. Had they never seen a woman crying?

The woman spoke quietly. "It's all right, they're young. They will have their own time for tears. We all do. They'll learn that tears are one way we get through."

Janet liked Diane's response. "You sound like a voice of experience," she replied.

"Yes, my brother spent several years locked up due to a bad decision. My family stood by him, but friends of ours distanced themselves from us. We can imagine what you've been going through."

They talked for a while, the time passing quickly. Janet was surprised how easy it was to talk with Diane. When her eyes found the clock over the doorway, she startled. "Damn, I must leave to pick up Teddy. I wish we had more time."

"Do you want to spend the night with my mum and sister?"

"No. I'll come home and take the train back in the morning. Please thank them for me for their kind offer. And thank you for the tea and scone. I'll take it with me and share it with Teddy." She stood, wrapped the scone in a paper serviette, and put out her hand. Diane stood also. Instead of shaking Janet's hand, she opened her arms for a hug, and Janet hugged her back gratefully.

"Do you think we could get together again soon? I know you'll need time by yourself the next couple of days, but if you'd be willing, perhaps we could share a pizza or fish and chips some night next week?"

"I would like that," Janet smiled. She dug in her handbag for her notebook and pen so they could exchange phone numbers.

Chapter 51

On Wednesday, July 3, 1985, the eight defendants sat in their balcony all in one row. The judge had called them in to hear the jury's verdict. David could see Mam and his sisters Anne and Trish below in the observers' gallery, Mam with her ever present notepad and pen at the ready. There was no whispering, no glances exchanged among them as the jury filed in. There was no noise at all in Crown Court, other than the shuffling of the jurors' feet and the slight swish of cloth against chair as they took their seats. He looked at their faces, looking for any hint of their conclusions, but found only blank stares. One, the youngest, looked up at them and then away when his eyes met David's. It felt like an eternity before the judge made his remarks. He said that this was the stage for hearing the jury's verdict. Tomorrow he would announce their sentences.

David glanced down the row to his right: Keith's knee was moving up and down involuntarily and his hands were clasped tightly on his lap. Tom, beside him, was as still as a statue. Terrence and John Benton likewise. Geoff Knowles showed the most agitation, pawing at his tie and tapping his right knee in an audible staccato that sounded like a drum brush.

To David's right Niko and Sally looked straight ahead. He was surprised to see Sally holding Niko's hand.

"Have the jury reached their verdicts?" the judge asked.

"Yes, Your Honor," said the head juror, a lean man in glasses, rising from the seat closest to the judge. The man's voice was soft and hard to hear. It struck David for the first time in the whole month of the trial that it must be hard on them, the jurors. None of them looked comfortable or smug, just serious and a bit nervous.

"Will the defendants please rise." It was not a question and all but Sally stood as one.

"In the case of *Regina vs. Keith Brown* what do you find?"

"We find the defendant guilty."

"In the case of *Regina vs. Tom Hill,* what do you find?"

"We find the defendant guilty."

"In the case of *Regina vs. Nikolaos Karras,* what do you find?"

"We find the defendant guilty."

"In the case of *Regina vs. Terrence Gale,* what do you find?"

"We find the defendant guilty."

"In the case of *Regina vs. John Benton,* what do you find?"

"We find the defendant guilty."

"In the case of *Regina vs. Geoff Knowles,* what do you find?"

The jury foreman's voice was crackly as though he was recovering from a cold. He asked if he could have a glass of water and one of the attendants brought one to him. He cleared his throat before saying, "We find the defendant not guilty."

An audible sigh could be heard from the gallery where Geoff's wife and mother sat clinging to each other. Geoff's knees went weak and he had to sit down suddenly. The judge waited for him to regain his composure and stand up again. Then he resumed his questions.

"In the case of *Regina vs. David Bennie*, what do you find?"

"We find the defendant ....." The others in the dock looked at David in disbelief. They thought he said guilty. Below in the gallery David heard his sister Trisha exclaim, "No!" and saw the judge give her a stern look that silenced her. His sister Anne was scribbling on Mam's notepad, and Mam was nodding as she read what Anne had written.

"I remind the jury that we have one additional defendant to try within the next few months. You are under oath not to discuss this case with anyone until the trial of Miss Sally Eliades is completed. Do you understand? The Court will notify you when we go back into session for that trial. Are there any questions?"

David's barrister was on her feet. "May I approach, Your Honor?" The prosecutor and Anne Worrall conferenced before the judge. It seemed to David that everything in the room froze. No one coughed or cleared their throat. No one scratched their head or wiped their eyes. No one moved. All eyes were on the two men and one woman conversing quietly but, in the case of Barrister Worrall, with considerable animation. Then they returned to their seats.

The judge turned to the jury foreman. "It seems there is disagreement about what you said regarding Mr. Bennie, so at the suggestion of Barrister Worrall, I am going to poll the jury just to be certain. As one, those in the room stirred and shifted position. It felt like a brisk wind had blown into the courtroom. Then all grew still again, watching as the judge repeated the question again to each person on the jury.

"In the case of Regina vs. David Bennie, what do you find? And please speak up so we can all hear you."

Each of the twelve jurors arose in turn and responded, some looking directly at the judge, a few looking up to the dock and fixing their eyes on David. Ten not guilty; two guilty. It did not need to be unanimous.

"The jury finds Mr. David Bennie not guilty," the judge stated for the record. "Are there any further questions?" After a brief pause he resumed. "There being none, we stand adjourned. Mr. Knowles and Mr. Bennie, you may collect your belongings and rejoin your families."

John Benton, Terrence Gale, Tom Hill, Niko Karras and Keith Brown filed out of the room, the weight of being found guilty visible in their shoulders and the blank expressions on their faces. Keith turned to cast a devastated look at Janet who was still seated and weeping. Those five defendants had known there was little chance of being found not guilty. Nevertheless, each was stunned. They would return tomorrow to receive their sentences from the judge.

David and Geoff Knowles collected the contents of the boxes each had been provided for their personal belongings. They changed into their own clothing and were ushered to the exit of Crown Court.

Except for the swarms of reporters and television cameras hovering around them impeding their departure from the courthouse, the end of their ordeal was anticlimactic. Especially for David and Geoff, who each went off with their families, disbelief and relief hovering over them like a personal fog. The five men found guilty returned in the caged van to Brixton, and Sally by similar conveyance to Wormwood Prison for Women.

The next day the judge waived deportation for Niko and sentenced him to five years in Her Majesty's prisons with probation available after two years on good behavior. It was a surprising sentence. Niko was a lucky man. Janet wondered why the judge was so generous with him.

Tom and Keith received ten-year sentences, probation available after four years served, subtracting the nine months they had already been in prison. Probation was contingent, of course, on good behavior. Their verdicts had not been a surprise. But the sentences were one year shorter than Janet had expected. *If they behaved themselves, Tom and Keith could be paroled on October 4, 1988.* It was a cause for celebration.

As Keith was led from the courtroom she flashed him a smile broader and more genuine than those she'd mustered over these months of his incarceration. She was trying to communicate that they could handle this, which she said to him when they spoke on the phone later that day. He apologized, his voice breaking, as it had every time she had come to visit. This time felt different. They knew what they had to do and for how long they had to do it. "No more apologies," she told him. "We will manage. And I've made a friend at school. It helps." That was an understatement.

Chapter 52

It was quiet around the Bennie table that evening. Relieved as David and his family were, they were wrung dry from what they had gone through. Each of them had paid dearly in friends dropping away and people looking questions at them. "I wonder how long we'll be hearing, 'Is that your David Bennie who was before the bench for smuggling?'" Mam's question was rhetorical.

David was certain he did not want to remain in England, or anywhere in Britain for that matter. He would be receiving a check for the government payments he'd have received as an unemployed person had he not been imprisoned awaiting trial. He would take that money and go abroad, get away from this country that had unjustly incarcerated him and put his family through so much grief.

His barrister had suggested he send a formal request to Interpol right away to remove his name from their list as he had been found not guilty. They might not comply, and he might face layers of bureaucratic red tape as he traveled, but if they sent him paperwork that stated he'd been found not guilty, it could expedite his return to working the yachts, she had advised.

It took some weeks, but Interpol sent him a document that stated he was found not guilty. He was to carry it on his person, their letter said.

What surprised David most about his post-Brixton life was that he felt much the same as when he'd been in prison, burdened down with the nastiness of the experience and feeling guilty—or at least in some way responsible--despite knowing he was innocent. How long would it take that feeling to leave him? When would he truly have his life back?

Prison had showed who his friends were. His girlfriend had disappeared after visiting him once in Chelmsford jail the day after he was arrested. Other friends dropped him, also. But not his family and the friends who put up money toward his bail. He knew it had not been easy on Mam and Dad, not since back in October a year ago when Customs and Excise men had invaded their home while they were at work, searching mightily and messily, and needing no warrant to do so because this was a smuggling case. All the members of his family had been afraid of losing their jobs, though they never talked about it or about their former friends who passed them on the street without acknowledging them. Luckily, their employers stood by them. Trish handled it by telling her coworkers right from the start that, yes, it was her brother, and if he'd ever truly been involved bringing in drugs, she'd beat him within an inch of his life. They hadn't bothered her after that.

It had been a lousy ordeal for them all, but, as Mam reminded them, he'd been found not guilty. He—and they all—could now return to living their lives.

Within a few months Her Majesty's Government returned his passport, and a couple of months later he was offered a job on a boat owned by a wealthy couple who had employed him earlier to work on their yacht. The boat was leaving from Monaco and sailing to Turkey to pick up its owners, who were on holiday at the Black Sea. They wrote that they were happy to have David come back to their Moon Maiden.

When his unemployment check arrived, David bought a one-way ticket to Monaco, imagining his life from then on would be lived outside the United Kingdom, except for returning to testify for the defense at Sally's trial in a month or so and to see his family.

Being back at sea felt liberating, and David could imagine spending his life there.

Chapter 53

For the nearly five months before her case came to trial, Sally tried to focus on the fact that David had been found not guilty. It allowed her momentary optimism, a respite from anxiety. But by mid-December, when she heard the carolers outside the prison for a second year, even moments of optimism were hard to muster.

When her barrister paid her a visit and told her they would be going to trial the day after Boxing Day, she kissed him. He flushed and gave her a kindly grandfatherly look before reminding her that the jurors were weary of this case. She should stick to the facts and not wander in her testimony. "You never can tell what will happen with juries," he told her. "Someone gets out of bed with a headache—or hangover—or has an argument with their spouse, and they blame it on their jury duty, or, worse, on the defendant. But you are a likeable person and we'll hope they feel sympathy for you like I do." He smiled at her again, and she summoned her elusive optimism.

After he left, her cellmate Moira reminded her that bad times, like good times, always pass. Much as she had come to like Moira, Sally did not find that helpful.

On December 27th, Sally returned to court sharing the prison transport van with three other women whose cases were to be heard. No one spoke. It was raining, a cold rain that turned to mush when it hit the roadways and slowed traffic. She breathed deeply and focused on the view through the barred windows. Grey granite buildings, weeping, leafless trees, people tucked under black bumbershoots, taking long strides to reach their destinations with the least amount of damp. When she next rode this way, would she be returning to Wormwood Prison for half a decade or... Bad luck to expect the best outcome. She shifted her eyes to the other women, wondering what their situations were. She kept her attention on them until they pulled up to the courthouse.

She took her seat in the dock. This time her "partners in crime," as the newspapers put it, were not sitting with her, although she saw David below in the courtroom. He'd kept his promise to return to witness on her behalf.

The prosecutor made the case that she had to have known about the drugs because she was hired on in Rhodes before the cargo was picked up. It was as simple as that. The jury need deliberate no longer. It was a clear case of collaboration with those already found guilty.

In her October 4, 1984 deposition Sally had been muddled about just where she'd been hired on. At that time she'd said Palma. Then she back tracked and acknowledged that Keith had instructed her to say Palma rather than Rhodes. The court did not appreciate her initially lying to her interrogator. It was a mark against her that the prosecution reiterated. Why would she lie if she was innocent?

David was called to the stand to testify on her behalf. He looked different to her, stronger and hearty, but his eyes looked wary, which concerned her. Did this experience in prison change a person even six months after they were exonerated and released?

Her barrister called Niko and Keith to testify also, and she thought their appearances, also, had changed since she'd last seen them in July.

Mum was there in court both days. Brenda and Alfred could not get off work. She was grateful for Mum's presence.

Her trial was surprisingly brief. Her barrister had been worth waiting for, she decided. He was authoritative and calm, and his grandfatherly manner inspired trust. He described her as a brave young woman, out to see the world before settling down, and, after running a bar in Rhodes with no prior experience, wanting to return home to the U.K. to see her family. That was why she signed on with *The Robert Gordon*–missing her Mum. Several women jurors smiled at that. They must be mums, Sally thought. She liked him calling her brave. Maybe she was brave. She'd not thought of it that way. Certainly, none of her school mates had done anything as daring, although she admitted that marriage and children—what most of them had done—seemed to her to require its own bravery.

The prosecutor asked her again how it was she could claim innocence when she must have smelled the cargo. "I had a lot of responsibility, sir, cooking for five people three times a day. I had never been to sea before, never worked as a cook, never lived with four men in close quarters--it was all new to me. When I wasn't working in the galley cooking and cleaning up, Davy and I were drinking and singing karaoke, just relaxing. Oh, and smoking weed. Sorry, your honor, but it seems to be common among sailors." She feared it wasn't a good answer. But it was the truth.

A few minutes later, after the judge's instructions, the jury was dismissed to deliberate. They were back within an hour. Sally stood very straight when the judge ordered her to rise. She locked her knees waiting for the verdict. The foreman announced that they had found her not guilty and the verdict was unanimous. She had served fifteen months in prison and in two days they had found her not guilty.

She thanked her barrister and attempted to change what had become default depression. She was freed! It was nearly New Year's Eve, a symbolic chance to make a fresh start. On the ride back to Wormwood she was silent. She collected her things from her cell, gave Moira a hug, and left her a T-shirt with the name of Sally's bar in Rhodes silkscreened on it, "My Grecian Harbor!" She wouldn't be needing that.

David joined her family for a celebratory drink that evening, but when they parted she felt certain they'd never see each other again.

She moved in with her family for a few months and found work in a restaurant. It all felt very strange, and some days she missed Moira. No one including Mum and Alfred could understand her experience. They expected her to be her old self, but she didn't know where that self was hiding.

After a few months she located a one room flat in south London. She gave up her dreams of traveling to the Caribbean, gave up her interest in the sea, and decided to remain in London, especially after she met an international student from Greece who frequented her café. Within a month he moved in with her. Mum thought him a lovely man. So did Sally.

She was making up for lost time.

Chapter 54

There still wasn't much for Brian to do at the Hull ranch. Days would pass with no real activity. Then in a rush Oliver North or some other VIP would fly in with little warning and an overambitious agenda, especially considering that this was the tropics where road travel to Contra camps in Costa Rica and Honduras consumed an inordinate amount of time, especially during the rainy season. North was not unpleasant, but he was a Marine, used to things happening when he gave the order. Brian could tell North annoyed John Hull. He annoyed Brian also.

Hull had a lot of visitors to his ranch. Some of them seemed like they belonged in a James Bond film. Others, paunchy and over-dressed, seemed anomalous in the Central American jungle. Hull himself in cowboy boots and a broad Australian outback hat, a gaudy silver and turquoise belt buckle, and string tie, appeared to have stepped out of Bonanza. The whole scene was like a Wild West movie set. There even were "Indians," brown skinned Miskito Indians, their color the result of centuries of Africans marrying indigenous people, Hull told Brian. Like the Seminoles in Florida.

Hull was full of such facts and loved presenting himself as the resident expert on virtually any topic. He enjoyed entertaining visitors to the ranch with his knowledge and stories. Liquor lubricated conversations and Brian found that by sitting on the fringes listening, he was picking up a lot about how the CIA operated.

The Anglos who came through the ranch were mostly current or former agents, "assets," or Drug Enforcement Administration personnel working hand in glove with the FBI. The non-Anglos were not included in most of the informal conversations about Agency operations. Brian noticed that, though Costa Ricans and Hondurans might be fighting on the front lines of the Contra war, they were second class to the white inner circle that hung out at Hull's ranch.

It surprised Brian how fiercely anti-communist the agents were. That was about the only thing they all shared, as far as he could see. Some were beer-bellied sixty-somethings, some used every imaginable cuss word and racial smear, and some were family men who would trot out photos of the wife and kids. Most of them had served in several countries—Cypress, Chile, Guatemala, Afghanistan, the Dominican Republic, Angola, Ethiopia, Laos, Cambodia, Zaire, or various Eastern European nations.

One evening they'd gathered on the patio of the ranch house to drink and tell "war stories" about their cloak and dagger experiences. Two men had been part of the Bay of Pigs invasion. A couple of others helped overthrow the Allende regime in Chile in '73. Several talked about their secret missions in Cambodia and Laos. One man was attached to the intelligence agency of the apartheid government of South Africa. Another regaled the group with his assignment to assassinate Fidel Castro. As he listened Brian wondered if the U.K. government's Secret Services engaged in these sorts of activities.

They were clearly men dedicated to keeping leftists out of power. No one questioned that drug sales and arms sales were the winning tickets to keeping governments friendly.

November 3, 1986 dawned as an ordinary beautiful day on the ranch, but in the early afternoon Hull received a call from the National Security Council's Oliver North with news that obviously upset him. A newspaper in Lebanon had printed a story that the U.S. was illegally providing the Contras weapons and also selling arms to its alleged enemy, Iran. The money gained from the arms sales was funneled to pay for arms for the Contras, with Israel functioning as one of the middlemen.

The story would have sounded too fantastic to take seriously a year before, but now that Brian was living among CIA assets and privy to conversations where plans for aiding the Contras were discussed, he knew that having this story in front of the public around the world was cause for alarm to the U.S. government. It was likely to promote increased scrutiny by Congress. The operations here in Costa Rica could well be exposed by a Congressional investigation.

Hull told Brian that Oliver North, the Marine colonel in charge of the whole operation, maintained a close personal relationship with the director of the CIA. On their secure phone line North had insisted that his covert activities were untraceable. He had disguised the routing of the money made by drug and arms sales with many layers of laundering. Furthermore, the latest technology allowed virtually instantaneous movements of cash. Large amounts of money would be moved again and again, each time in seconds, bank to bank, country to country. The public would never be able to follow the money trail. North and others involved would argue that the CIA and Defense Department were not involved.

When Brian asked Hull about how the story would affect them, Hull said it would not have traction with the public because it was too complicated. Following the money was nearly impossible. Besides, nothing would stick to Ronald Reagan, who the press called the Teflon President.

But later that day Georgina told Brian that she heard Hull on the phone talking with someone in Spanish about buying a ranch in southern Mexico. She wondered if he had plans to leave Costa Rica.

Brian and Georgina agreed with press reports that said this was a scandal of historic proportions that might result in President Reagan being removed from office. Cabinet officials and the President had been violating U.S. law and conducting foreign policy through other governments—one, Iran, on the official terrorist list—and through wealthy private individuals. The operations were conducted illegally for the purpose of avoiding congressional oversight.

Brian himself had trouble following the intricacies of what the press was calling the Iran-Contra Scandal. It was hard keeping straight all the layers and players, even though he lived on its frontline. Maybe Hull was right about the American public. Maybe they would not be able to keep track of all the covert sales and deliveries, the money laundering and third-party channels. Maybe these revelations would not take down the President.

Frankly, Brian was getting bored with all the high drama. He was ready for a change.

A year later Brian and Georgina were living in a town in San Cristobal de las Casas, Chiapas, Mexico, both working for Coca Cola. It was their cover. Covertly they gathered information on the movements of the Zapatistas guerrillas. They passed the information to the CIA and to the chief financial officer at Coke.

One afternoon after they had lived in Chiapas almost a year, Brian received a circuitously routed message from his mother asking if he could meet her in Tegucigalpa, Honduras on Guy Fawkes Day. He sent a message back to her via a secure channel. He suggested they meet at a hotel in Tegucigalpa that was the favorite watering ground of "spooks," NGOs, and journalists. There they would not stand out among the other foreigners using the restaurant, bar, and pool for R&R.

Brian was struck at once by how much older his mother looked. It had only been three years, but that time had aged her. She held his hand as they sat under at an umbrella table beside the swimming pool sipping pints of ale. Questions poured out of her, but there was little he could tell her. Yes, he was well. Yes, Georgina and he lived in Mexico now, quite a nice house with a number of servants. They were talking about marriage. Mama perked up at this news. No, he couldn't talk about his work or give her more details about where he lived. For both of their sakes. He didn't know how long he would be there.

After an awkward pause Mama began to talk. Dad sends greetings and love. (Brian doubted this was true.) Life in Cambridge was much the same. She attended lectures that interested her, volunteered at the Kettle's Yard museum, and accompanied Dad to social occasions that were required attendance for faculty and spouses. She mentioned a few books she had read and a play they saw in London. The words came out of her in a long stream and then stopped. They were unsatisfactory.

The gap between them felt cavernous. Their lives no longer shared familiar places and people. When he glanced at his watch, he saw that only thirty minutes had passed. What more was there to say or hear? She seemed uncomfortable, even jittery, sitting there in the sun. It was obvious that she had something else she needed to say.

"I ran into Archie's mum a couple of weeks ago. She hasn't seen or heard from Archie for more than a year. I could tell she was worried. Of course, I didn't offer anything about you, but she said she feared Archie was dead. Have you heard from Archie?"

"No, Mum. Not for at least that long."

"I'm worried for her. She said other times over the past decade he would disappear for some months, telling her he had business deals in this or that country. Then he'd pop up and be full of his latest investment. Singapore, Brunei, Saudi Arabia, you name it. No matter where he was or how long he was gone, she'd always get a birthday card from him. But this year, nothing."

Mum's news shocked him and put a damper on their already awkward reunion. What could have happened to Archie? They ordered another round of drinks and sat mostly in silence. Then Mum said she thought she should lie down and rest for a while.

When they met up for an evening meal, her eyes were red and watery. When Brian told her that he would not be returning to the U.K., her face lost color. She looked like someone had died. They would not see each other for five years.

Chapter 55

While David and Sally tried to shape their new lives outside prison, and Niko, Keith, and Tom completed two years of their sentences inside prison, news of the Reagan Administration's illegal sales of arms to Iran and gifts of arms to the Contras met a receptive audience across the world. The U.S. government had violated U.S. law.

Three weeks after the Lebanese newspaper *Al-Shiraa* broke the story, the President acknowledged publicly that profits from the arms sales were diverted to support the Contras. A day later he appointed a special commission to investigate, and his Attorney General requested an independent counsel to lead the investigation.

A month later, in December 1986, William Casey, Director of the CIA, testified before a handful of Congressional committees. The Iran-Contra Scandal, despite its complexity, had captured public attention. It might bring down the President.

On the 18th of December while talking with his physician, William Casey had a seizure that required brain surgery. When the surgeon removed a piece of his skull, they found that the Director of the CIA suffered from lymphoma, a rare form of cancer in the lining of his brain. From that day on Casey steadily declined. As the cancer multiplied, so did speculation about his involvement in the Iran-Contra Scandal.

On May 5, 1987, joint hearings began of before House and Senate committees formed to investigate the scandal, the House Select Committee to Investigate Covert Arms Transactions with Iran and the Senate Select Committee on Secret Military Assistance to Iran and the Nicaraguan Opposition. The first witness was Richard Secord, who with Alfred Hakim, oversaw the operation of the Enterprise and reported to Oliver North.

By then William Casey lay in a hospital bed in his mansion, Mayknoll, on Long Island, New York. His wife and daughter were at his bedside to keep unwelcome visitors away from the dying man.

He had been amazingly energetic and fit for seventy-three. Now he was almost unrecognizable, grey and pasty-faced, his mouth slack and drooling, his speech so slurred it was impossible for him to be understood. In his hospital bed at home he drifted in and out of consciousness, sometimes lucid, sometimes not. During wakeful moments he scanned the room and its occupants, his eyes intent. He tried to communicate with those in the room, with Sophia and Bernadette, his wife and daughter, and with the men who worked under him who came to see him. His eyes showed frustration when they didn't understand him. He could tell they were pretending to understand, nodding and making sounds of assent or commiseration. Sometimes in the middle of a thought he simply gave up. What was the use?

His visitors updated him on the investigation. They appeared optimistic that the President would not be impeached. The inner circle of National Security Council staff and administrators of the Enterprise operation would be only minimally punished for breaking specific directives that the United States Congress had written into the law.

They'll never pin anything on the CIA or on you, they assured him. That set him to dry-coughing, then wheezing, his weary lungs reaching for air.

Casey hated Congress's perpetual questioning of his integrity. They'd investigated his stock dealings--whether he had engaged in insider trading as head of the Securities and Exchange Commission. They'd faulted him for refusing to put his investments in a blind trust. When, after two years of resistance, he had finally complied by putting some of his investments in a blind trust, the press discovered that he had left out of the blind trust his Capital Cities Communication stock, the company he had built from one to more than twenty radio stations, seven television stations and eight newspapers. Capital Cities was buying American Broadcasting Company (ABC), one of the three major national television networks in the United States. The revelation that it was not in a blind trust produced another investigation.

The intelligence committees of the House and Senate had hammered him for withholding information about covert programs. And those investigations had been conducted long before the Iran-Contra Scandal broke into the news.

Now, confined to a hospital bed, he obsessively reviewed his decisions in between fits of wheezing.

Okay. Thirteen months of selling arms to Iran had freed only two hostages. In fact, two more were seized. But I still believe in the plan.

Iran was cozying up to the Soviet Union. It might cut off sixty percent of the West's oil.

We were pragmatic to work with the Iranians.

Our arms sales courted Iran away from the Soviets and brought in millions of dollars to fund covert activities against the leftist governments in Nicaragua and Afghanistan.

They'll never convince me covert operations aren't the best way to conduct foreign policy.

Other times he couldn't focus. His hands would pick at the sheet, a sign he was feeling agitated.

As the special congressional committees began their investigation, he was trying to concentrate. He wanted to remember what he had accomplished at the CIA, but it was hard.

Review what I've accomplished.

Nearly tripled our secret budget.

Recruited three hundred individuals from businesses to the Agency's seminars.

Half of those businessmen.

Provide cover for our operatives.

Capitalism depends on
people making money...
Government needs
the private sector to....
He was having trouble assembling his thoughts.
...Lymphoma—was that it?--in the slipper(?) that covers my brain.
...President's letter. Not Director any longer.
...Sophia turning on the TV.
...Secord testifying.
...Can't.
...Can't
...Can't...
The Old Man turned his face to the wall.

The joint congressional committee had begun its investigation, but William Casey would miss it. He would escape what would have been the biggest public challenge of his integrity. The moment of his demise could not have been more fortuitous.

Chapter 56

When *The Moon Maiden*, the yacht David Bennie was hired to work on, was docked in Monaco about to begin its voyage to Istanbul, police came aboard looking for David. They arrested him and took him to the police station to be fingerprinted and photographed. They questioned him about *The Robert Gordon*. His paper from Interpol confirming that he had been acquitted gave him no protection.

When they finally released him, David knew his dream of a life at sea had disintegrated. *The Moon Maiden* was headed for Turkey. What if the same thing happened there? He might never get out of a Turkish jail. He had heard tales of Turkey's military and the power they had to make people disappear.

Reluctantly he told the captain of *The Moon Maiden* that he could not safely remain part of the crew. Despite the jury finding him innocent and despite his correspondence with Interpol, it appeared his name would be kept on the Interpol watchlist.

He had felt hopeful that he could get past *The Robert Gordon* and incarceration in Brixton Prison and start a new life doing the work he loved, but his life at sea was over.

He went on board to say goodbye to the crew of *The Moon Maiden* and agreed to fetch them some smokes before they left port. It was October 4, 1986, two years to the day after the crew of *The Robert Gordon* was arrested bringing a cargo of cannabis resin into Britain. God, how that day had changed his life.

As he walked down the gangplank, he noticed on his left a sleek black limousine with darkened windows parked on the quay facing the exit. Four men in dark suits, black shirts and ties, and wearing shades stood at the four corners of the limo, eyes invisible, heads swiveling slowly. It made him smile, the drama that accompanied self-important people. They were always protected by bodyguards supposedly costumed to look *inconspicuous* when in fact being *conspicuous* was the whole point of their presence.

Black limousines and beefy bodyguards were not a common sight in the Monaco marina but not unprecedented. David remembered several years ago, before *The Robert Gordon*, when he worked briefly on Mr. Adnan Khashoggi's yacht *Nabila* and met Mr. Khashoggi. The man had arrived at his yacht in an armored limo with a handful of bodyguards like these. He couldn't help being impressed, even though he found it pretentious.

He took in this limo and its squad of nearly identical protectors. The back, right window now rolled down to reveal a mostly bald, distinguished looking man, probably in his fifties, portly and impeccably dressed. The man was watching him. He looked vaguely familiar.

"David Bennie?"

"Aye." Curiosity trumped David's wariness.

"I want to speak with you."

David altered course, walking directly to the limo, his sandals beating a soft cadence on the dock. A bodyguard opened the door of the limo, and a short, nattily dressed man with a tonsure of black hair and a horizontal slash of black mustache across his round face stepped out. He was not wearing shades and his black eyes sparkled with intelligence as he scrutinized David.

"I think I owe you an apology." The bloke did not extend his right hand to David. Now David recognized him and remembered that he was from Saudi Arabia. He probably finds a lowly boat mechanic unworthy of his handshake, David thought. The man's comment about owing David an apology puzzled David.

"I'm Adnan Khashoggi. I hired you several years ago to ferry my yacht, *Nabila*. That was after you worked on *The Welsh Falcon* and before *The Robert Gordon*. I see you're still working the yachts despite all the trouble they brought you. I followed what happened to you in the papers two years ago. I'm right sorry about all that."

"I don't blame you, Mr. Khashoggi. I wish I knew who to blame. My mates were just ordinary dudes, not enough smarts altogether to organize a major drug heist."

"It's all right, lad. You won't be having any problems in the future." Adnan Khashoggi bestowed a half-smile, then turned and climbed back into the limo. "Good to see you." Their exchange had lasted no more than two minutes. Mr. Khashoggi rolled his window up and the limo slipped into gear and sped out of the marina.

Something very odd in that exchange, David thought.

The End

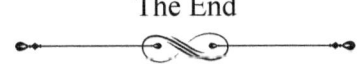

Afterword

This story is based on a real event. On October 4, 1984, the British government apprehended *The Sir Robert Gordon*, which was loaded with cannabis resin smuggled from Lebanon. The British government classified the records of the trial that took place in the summer of 1985 and extended the embargo of the records until 2064. Its response to my Freedom of Information request is included in the Appendix.

One of those charged gave me access to the depositions and court papers from the trial. I interviewed a retired Customs and Excise officer, a retired career sailor experienced in the Mediterranean, and one of the crew members of *The Sir Robert Gordon*, each of whom was working in the region during 1984.

Without access to additional court records, I took artistic license in creating stories for each of those involved and changed their names. With the exception of historical persons and the character David Bennie, the backstories of the characters in this novel are inventions of my imagination. There actually was a "Brian Baker," and he did disappear and did not appear during the trial. Archie is my invention. Any resemblance between my fictional crew members or their families and the actual people is coincidental.

There are historical figures in this book including Prime Minister Margaret Thatcher of the United Kingdom, U.S. President Ronald Reagan, Director of the CIA William Casey, National Security Council staff Oliver North, The Enterprise's Richard Secord and Albert Hakim, Miskito Indian Contra leader Brooklyn Rivera, Contra leader Eden Pastora, Casey's Hardy Boys (Bob Anderson, John Shaheen, Clark Clifford, Max Hugel, and Bob Rappaport), arms dealer Adnan Khashoggi, the CIA station chief in Beirut

William Buckley, and CIA-employed John Hull on his Costa Rican ranch. Scenes in which these historical figures appear or are discussed are imagined but informed by the historical record, e.g., the published reports of the Iran-Contra investigations and the studies listed in Discussion of Sources. Appended are excerpts from the Iran-Contra Report of the Congressional Committee Investigating Iran Contra, majority report, issued November 18, 1987.

In November 1986, during Reagan's second term and after a Lebanese newspaper broke the story of the Reagan Administration's violation of U.S. law by selling arms to Iran, President Reagan gave a speech explaining his actions: "My purpose was ... to send a signal that the United States was prepared to replace the animosity between [the U.S. and Iran] with a new relationship. ... At the same time we undertook this initiative, we made clear that Iran must oppose all forms of international terrorism as a condition of progress in our relationship. The most significant step which Iran could take, we indicated, would be to use its influence in Lebanon to secure the release of all hostages held there." (November 13, 1986)

Twelve days later President Reagan fired Oliver North, and his National Security Adviser John Poindexter resigned. The Attorney General Edwin Meese announced that $10-$30 million, revenue from the sale of U.S. arms to Iran, had been diverted to the Nicaraguan Contras. (www.npr.org/news/specials/obits/reagan/timeline.html) Oliver North was convicted of accepting a gratuity, aiding in the obstruction of Congress, and destroying documents. However, despite being found guilty after investigations by Congress and by Special Prosecutor Lawrence Walsh, who investigated the Iran Contra affair in 1987, North's prison term was suspended and instead he was given two years of probation, 1,200 hours of community service hours, and a fine. Nearly all of those found guilty in the Iran Contra investigations were given probation and suspended prison sentences. Five were pardoned by President George H.W. Bush, including the Secretary of Defense, Caspar Weinberger.

Brown University's website on Iran Contra contains details and film clips of the testimony of witnesses including North. (https://www.brown.edu/Research/Understanding_the_Iran_Contra_Affair/prosecutions.php#p_nss)

President Reagan escaped censure.

Two years after publication of Ronald Kessler's *The Richest Man in the World: The Story of Adnan Khashoggi (1986)*, Khashoggi was arrested in Switzerland, accused of concealing funds in the bankruptcy of the Bank of Credit and Commerce International (BCCI). After three months in jail, he was extradited to the United States, tried and acquitted, according to his obituary in the *New York Times*. A Saudi Arabian multibillionaire, Adnan Khashoggi once owned one of the world's largest yachts, *The Nabila*, which appeared in the James Bond film *Never Say Never Again*. Donald Trump, elected President of the United States in 2016, purchased the yacht for $30 million in 1988. Khashoggi was the uncle of Princess Diana's lover, Dodi Fayed, and of Jamal Khashoggi, the *Washington Post* journalist and U.S. resident who was murdered and dismembered by Saudi officials in Turkey in the fall of 2018.

Adnan Khashoggi made his fortune through international arms sales and was instrumental in the 1984-1986 arms sales to Iran that were part of the Iran Contra Scandal. He was rumored to be an asset of the CIA.

"David Bennie" really did have that strange exchange with Khashoggi that ends this book.

Discussion of Sources

This book began over dinner in Portsoy, Scotland in autumn, 2013. I had invited new friends to dinner and the man told me about his twenty-first year, when he went to prison, accused of participating in the largest importation of illegal drugs into the U.K. His story was riveting. "You must write it," I urged him.

"I've tried. I just can't. You are a writer. Why don't you write it?"

That was the beginning. I had worked on Capitol Hill during the Church Committee's investigation of the CIA and during the Iran Contra Scandal. As a former foreign policy lobbyist, I was familiar with what was happening in 1984, although it was a long time ago. I began researching.

I discovered a web of secret activity taking place in multiple places in that year and institutions like William Casey's "friends" who conducted foreign policy by raising money for covert operations against Nicaragua when Congress had banned government funds for the Contras.

I discovered the Bank of Credit and Commerce International (BCCI) and the hearings held in the U.S. Senate chaired by Senators John Kerry (Democrat) and Hank Brown (Republican) in 1990. That Senate investigation found that BCCI's criminality included 1) fraud by BCCI and BCCI customers involving billions of dollars; 2) money laundering in Europe, Africa, Asia, and the Americas and bribery of officials in most of those locations; 3) support of terrorism, arms trafficking, and the sale of nuclear technologies; 4) management of prostitution; 5) the commission and facilitation of income tax evasion, smuggling, and illegal immigration; 6) illicit purchases of banks and real estate; and 7) a panoply of other financial crimes limited only by the imagination of its officers and customers. (Senator John Kerry and Senator Hank Brown, The BCCI Affair: A Report to the Committee on Foreign Relations United States Senate, December 1992 available at https://publicintelligence.net/the-bcci-affair.)

Among BCCI's principal mechanisms for committing crimes were its use of shell corporations, bank confidentiality, and secrecy havens. It used front-men, buy-back arrangements, kickbacks, bribes, the intimidation of witnesses, and the retention of well-placed insiders to discourage governmental action against BCCI.

When BCCI closed on July 5, 1991, "some one million small depositors in BCCI around the world lost their deposits."

Because Operation Bishop brought drugs from Lebanon, I read about what was happening in the eastern Mediterranean-- in Cyprus, Lebanon, Syria, and Israel--during the years on either side of October 4, 1984. I read Robert Fisk's *Pity the Nation: Lebanon at War* (1990) and Kamal Salibi's *A House of Many Mansions: The History of Lebanon Reconsidered* (1988). I read Trita Parsi's *Treacherous Alliance: The Secret Dealings of Israel, Iran, and the United States* (2007) and John Loftus and Mark Aarons in *The Secret War Against the Jews: How Western Espionage Betrayed the Jewish People* (rev. 2017).

Loftus and Aarons found that William Casey met with the Brits in 1984 to pursue collaboration in arms sales to Iran. The first U.S. arms sale to Iran was scheduled for June 12, 1984, and Iran was to deposit payment for the arms into BCCI Iran. Jonathan Pollard, a U.S. intelligence officer later convicted of spying for Israel, acknowledged that he noticed shipments of arms in the Mediterranean in the spring and summer of 1984 and reported them to the Israelis, who notified Greece. Greece seized the first shipment of arms to Iran and a ship full of arms going to the PLO in Libya. Pollard had stumbled on part of the arms supply operation that had been arranged by the British secret service to ransom hostages in Lebanon.

According to Parsi, during the time Operation Bishop was being set up, Iran was following a two-headed policy of *verbal support for Palestinians*— in order to position itself as a leader in the Muslim world and court Arab states--and *covert relations with Israel*—to secure arms and protect itself from a hostile alliance of Arab states led by Iraq. Adnan Khashoggi, the Saudi arms dealer, and Manuchehr Ghorbanifar, the Iranian arms dealer, were instructed to contact the U.S. National Security Council (NSC) to pursue the possibility of acquiring U.S. missiles. On August 6, 1985, President Reagan approved the plan and two shipments of TOW missiles were shipped to Iran. The U.S. also followed a two-headed policy toward Iran: *verbal hostility and no U.S. relations with Iran while secretly selling Iran sophisticated weapons.*

I read Joseph Persico's biography of William Casey, *Casey: The Lives and Secrets of William Casey, from the OSS to the CIA* (1990) and Stephen Dorrill's *MI6: Inside the Covert World of Her Majesty's Secret Intelligence Service (2002).*

Gary Webb's *Dark Alliance: The C.I.A., the Contras and the Crack Cocaine Explosion* (1998), based on extensive research and interviews, examines CIA involvement in drug trafficking. Just how involved the CIA was in drug trafficking is disputed. The consensus is that the CIA at least turned a blind eye to drug trafficking by Contra leaders. Jonathan Winer, formerly U.S. Deputy Assistant Secretary of State for International Narcotics Matters 1994-1999, who investigated the Contras and cocaine trafficking, told PBS Frontline that, "Oliver North's diaries are filled with references to drug trafficking and people associated with his Enterprise drug trafficking-- filled with it. Oliver North can say, 'I never hired or worked with any drug traffickers.' His organization did."

Known drug traffickers testified to Congress that from 1985 they were working with the National Security Council. (https://www.pbs.org/wgbh/pages/frontline/shows/drugs/special/cia.html)

The Department of Justice's Office of Inspector General issued a report on its investigation of the CIA, Contras, and drug trafficking included the following:

"[T]hree "potential informants" provided information alleging that ranches in Costa Rica had been used to smuggle weapons to the Contras and cocaine to the United States.... specifically mentioned John Hull's ranch,

alleging that it was protected by the CIA and that Hull took advantage of this protection and allowed planes loaded with cocaine to land there, charging $10,000 per landing....

According to CIA records, Hull helped the CIA in its delivery of weapons and "humanitarian aid" (e.g. food and clothing) to the Contras and the families of Contra soldiers. Hull's ranch had airstrips which were used by pilots ferrying arms and other aid in CIA-subsidized operations to help the Contras....[C]onvicted narcotics pilot Gary Betzner testified before the Kerry subcommittee that he had used Hull's airstrips when he flew shipments of cocaine on behalf of the Contras. Jorge Morales, also a convicted narcotics trafficker, told the Kerry subcommittee, the DEA [Drug Enforcement Administration], and the CBS television program "West 57th Street" that the Contras used Hull's ranch as a transshipment point in the movement of cocaine destined for the United States.

The DEA did not conduct any formal investigation of Hull and he has never been indicted on drug charges in the United States....

In 1991, the Justice Department received a request from the Costa Rican government to extradite Hull [on charges that included drug trafficking based on]... informant information that, on at least three occasions between 1983 and 1985, planes carrying arms allegedly intended for use by the Contras landed on airfields owned by Hull, and allegedly were refueled and loaded with drugs for transportation to the United States with the knowledge of Hull...."

In January 1989, John Hull was indicted in Costa Rica on murder, narcotics, and "hostile acts." https://oig.justice.gov/special/9712/ch11p2.htm

"As the U.S. government investigated Iran-Contra, Hull left Costa Rica for Mexico and died there in 2017."

I personally met with Oliver North when he worked in the National Security Council keeping the Contras supplied. He bragged about his continued support for the Contras in violation of U.S. law when a delegation of national religious leaders I was part of met with him.

William Casey's Hardy Boys were real. According to a March 27, 1987 article in the *Los Angeles Times*, one of them, Bob Anderson, who had held several cabinet positions, was tried and found guilty of two felony convictions, tax evasion and operating an unregistered West Indian bank that solicited four million dollars from contributors between 1983 and 1985, funds that "disappeared." The bank, a BCCI affiliate, was frequently used to launder money from illegal activities including drug trading. Anderson was repeatedly named by a South African general as advising him in his sales of arms to Iran.

Civil asset forfeiture began in the 1980s. "The U.S. Congress rewrote the federal drug forfeiture statutes in two significant ways. First, it authorized the government to forfeit the proceeds of drug crimes. 21 U.S.C. § 881(a)(6) (1978). Second, it gave the government the ability to forfeit property used to facilitate drug crimes. 21 U.S.C. § 881(a)(7)(1984). Instead of forfeiting only contraband and property used to commit certain violations, the government suddenly had the ability to take the profit out of drug crimes and "any property that made the crime easier to commit or harder to detect." The U.K enacted a similar program in 2002 according to the U.S. Department of Justice, according to the November 10, 2015 *Washington Post*, Wonkblog by Christopher Ingraham, "New report: In tough times, police start seizing a lot more stuff from people" (See https://www.washingtonpost.com/news/wonk/wp/2015/11/10/report-in-lean-times-police-starttaking-a-lot-more-stuff-from-people/.) It was ended by the Obama Administration's Department of Justice as of January 16, 2015. (See Jay Syrmopoulos, "BREAKING: U.S. Department of Justice Ends Civil Forfeiture Program For State and Local Police" ((January 16, 2015)), http://thefreethoughtproject.com/breaking-u-s-departmentjustice-ends-civil-forfeiture-program-state-local-police/#ZeHYZuUVdIhIXKs3.)

The actual details of *The Sir Robert Gordon's* trip come from the depositions in the possession of one of those arrested and tried in Operation Bishop as do the photographs. I am grateful for these sources.

My Freedom of Information Act request for records on this case was denied. Files on this case were reclassified in 2013, public access to them denied until 2064, eighty years after the drug bust. The response to my request is included in the Appendix.

Throughout my research and writing I have puzzled over why the British government would embargo this case until 2064. Individuals who study the drug trade in Britain say the rarity of such a government action probably indicates government involvement at high levels. Matthew Atha of the Independent Drug Monitoring Unit UK responded to my email query with these words:

Certainly that bust coincided with the virtual disappearance of Lebanese resin from the U.K. market, which it had dominated for the previous decade. In the short term a drought could be explained by the dismantling of a major import and distribution network, however its failure to reappear after a few months suggests wider geopolitical forces may have been at work, noting that Lebanon was in a state of civil war at the time. I suspect if the matter is still classified that the security services may have had an involvement in the bust or more likely the trade, which could prove embarrassing to the U.K. government and/or its allies.

We know Margaret Thatcher and Ronald Reagan worked collaboratively on many areas of policy, especially foreign policy in the Middle East and the war on drugs. Hence my speculative take on what happened in the case of Operation Bishop and why the records were classified for eighty years.

The issues raised here concerning corruption in government, rogue operations, money laundering, and international shenanigans are familiar in the 2010s and 2020s. Even some of the names are the same. Adnan Khashoggi died in June 2017 and his journalist nephew was murdered and dismembered at the Saudi consulate in Istanbul October 2, 2018. In 2018, Oliver North retired from Fox News to become president of the National Rifle Association, later leaving that position. Robert Mueller, the Special Prosecutor for the investigation of Russia's involvement in the 2016 U.S. presidential election, was the lead investigator for the U.S. Senate investigation of the Bank of Credit and Commerce International (BCCI). The Assad regime in Syria continues to be led by an Assad, the son of the Assad whose army occupied much of Lebanon in the 1980s. Syria is still an ally of Russia, although Russia in the 1980s was the Union of Soviet Socialist Republics. Israel continues to exert considerable power over U.S. foreign policy.

This story is brought to you thanks to the records retained by one participant and my own research. I am grateful to be able to tell this story. I am also grateful to Laura Tillem, editor of Blue Cedar Press, who carefully read several versions of this book and made suggestions for how I could tell this story more effectively. Any errors are mine alone.

Appendix

1985 – Controlled Drugs (Penalties) Act. Increased maximum penalty for trafficking Class A drugs from 14 years to life imprisonment. Class A = heroin, cocaine, ecstasy, LSD (in 2002? LSD and ecstasy were reclassified as Class B like cannabis—the 1980s experienced a rising heroin addiction in Britain and he laws became tougher

Kew Gardens Archives' email response to my Freedom of Information request for the records of this trial:

Reference: J 265/107

Description:

[Names are redacted and only initials provided here: JGB, DJC, SLPE, TJG, BJH] and others: variously charged with conspiracy to be knowingly concerned in the fraudulent evasion of the prohibition on the importation of a controlled drug, being knowingly concerned in the fraudulent evasion of the prohibition on the importation of a controlled drug, having a firearm with intent to commit an indictable offence and being armed with an offensive weapon. Orderable at item level

Note: With photographs, maps and plans

Date: 1984 Jan 01 - 1985 Dec 31

The naming of a defendant within this catalogue does not imply guilt

Held by: The National Archives, Kew

Former   85/0208-85/0215 reference in its original department

Legal status: Public Record

Closure   Closed Or Retained Document, Open Description status:

Access   Closed For 78 years conditions:

FOI decision 2013 date:

Exemption 1: Health and Safety

Exemption 2: Personal information where the applicant is a 3rd party

Record   01 January 2064 opening date:

Context of this record

Browse by Reference

All departments

- J - Records of the Supreme Court of Judicature and related courts

Records of the Crown Courts

J 265 - Supreme Court of Judicature: The Crown Court at Chelmsford:

Case Files

J265/107 - [names deleted by author]

EXCERPTS FROM THE EXECUTIVE SUMMARY of THE IRAN CONTRA REPORT of the Congressional Committee Investigating Iran Contra majority report, issued November 18, 1987.

By December 1981, the United States had begun supporting the Nicaraguan contras, armed opponents of the Sandinista regime.

The Central Intelligence Agency (C.I.A.) was the U.S. Government agency that assisted the contras. In accordance with Presidential decisions, known as findings, and with funds appropriated by Congress, the C.I.A. armed, clothed, fed and supervised the contras. Despite this assistance, the contras failed to win widespread popular support of military victories within Nicaragua….

Congress prohibited contra aid for the purpose of overthrowing the Sandinista Government in fiscal year 1983, and limited all aid to the contras in fiscal year 1984 to $24 million. Following disclosure in March and April 1984 that the C.I.A. had a role in connection with the mining of the Nicaraguan harbors without adequate notification to Congress, public criticism mounted and the Administration's contra policy lost much of its support within Congress. After further vigorous debate, Congress exercised its constitutional power over appropriations and cut off all funds for the contras' military and paramilitary operations. The statutory provision cutting off funds, known as the Boland Amendment, was part of a fiscal year 1985 omnibus appropriations bill, and was signed into law by the President on October 12, 1984.

Still, the President felt strongly about the contras, and he ordered his staff, in the words of his national security adviser, to find a way to keep the contras "body and soul together." Thus began the story of how the staff of a White House advisory body, the N.S.C., became an operational entity that secretly ran the contra assistance effort, and later the Iraninitiative. The action officer placed in charge of both operations was Lieut. Col. Oliver L. North.

Denied finding by Congress, the President turned to third countries and private sources. Between June 1984 and the beginning of 1986, the President, his national security adviser, and the N.S.C. staff secretly raised $34 million for the contras from other countries. An additional $2.7 million was provided for the contras during 1985 and 1986 from private contributors, who were addressed by North.... The first contributions were sent by the donors to bank accounts controlled and used by the contras. However, in July 1985, North took control of the funds....

The Enterprise, functioning largely at North's direction, had its own airplanes, pilots, airfield, operatives, ship, secure communications devices, and secret Swiss bank accounts. For 16 months, it served as the secret arm of the N.S.C. staff,... North told the House Intelligence Committee he was involved neither in fund-raising for, nor in providing military advice to, the contras....

[I]n 1983 the Administration adopted a "public diplomacy" program to promote the President's Central American policy. The program was conducted by an office in the State Department [that]... disseminated what one official termed "white propaganda": pro-contra newspaper articles by paid consultants who did not disclose their connection to the Administration. Moreover, under a series of sole-source contracts in 1985 and 1986, S/LPD paid more than $400,000 for pro-contra public relations work... by law, appropriated funds may not be used to generate propaganda "designed to influence a member of Congress"; and by law, as interpreted by the Office of the Comptroller General, appropriated funds may not be used by the State Department for "covert" propaganda activities..... One series of advertisements was used to attack Congressman Mike Barnes, a principal opponent of contra aid, and one of the Congressmen to whom Administration officials had denied violating the Boland Amendment in September of 1985. ... $1 million was used for pro-contra publicity.

The N.S.C. staff conducting the contra covert action also took operational control of implementing the President's decision on arms sales to Iran. The President did not sign a finding for this covert operation, nor did he notify the Congress....

Israel shipped 504 TOW anti-tank missiles to Iran in August and September 1985. Although the Iranians had promised to release most of the American hostages in return, only one, Reverend Benjamin Weir, was freed. The President persisted. In November, he authorized Israel to ship 80 Hawk anti-aircraft missiles in return for all the hostages, with a promise of prompt replenishment by the United States, and 40 more Hawks to be sent directly by the United States to Iran. Eighteen Hawk missiles were actually shipped from Israel in November 1985...

North admitted that he and other officials lied repeatedly to Congress and to the American people about the contra covert action and Iran arms sales, and that he altered and destroyed official documents. North's testimony demonstrates that he also lied to members of the executive branch, including the Attorney General, and officials of the State Department, C.I.A. and N.S.C.

Secrecy became an obsession. Congress was never informed of the Iran or the contra covert actions, notwithstanding the requirement in the law that Congress be notified of all covert actions in a "timely fashion."....

Secretary Shultz objected to third-country solicitation in 1984 shortly before the Boland Amendment was adopted; accordingly, he was not told that, in the same time period, the national security adviser had accepted an $8 million contribution from Country 2 even though the State Department had prime responsibility for dealings with that country. Nor was the Secretary of State told by the President in February 1985 that the same country had pledged another $24 million.... The N.S.C. staff turned to private parties and third countries to do the Government's business. Funds denied by Congress were obtained by the Administration from third countries and private citizens. Activities normally conducted by the professional intelligence services - which are accountable to Congress - were turned over to Secord and Hakim....

the central figure in the Iran-contra affair was Lieutenant Colonel North, who coordinated all of the activities and was involved in all aspects of the secret operations....

[W]e believe that the late Director of Central Intelligence, William Casey, encouraged North, gave him direction and promoted the concept of an extralegal covert organization. Casey, for the most part, insulated C.I.A. career employees from knowledge of what he and N.S.C. staff were doing. Casey's passion for covert operations - dating back to his World War II intelligence days - was well known. His close relationship with North was attested to by several witnesses....

[T] he ultimate responsibility for the events in the Iran-contra affair must rest with the President[who]... told the public that early reports of arms sales for hostages had ''no foundation.'' He told the public that the United States had not traded arms for hostages. He told the public that the United States had not condoned the arms sales by Israel to Iran, when in fact he had approved them and signed a finding, later destroyed by Poindexter, recording his approval.... During the Iran-contra hearings, Oliver North, John Poindexter, Fawn Hall and others admitted to having altered and destroyed key documents relating to their activities. Such actions constitute violations of the Presidential Records Act.

Study Guide

Discuss the following, taking care to include each person in the conversation. It may help to pass a spoon or something you can hold while it is your turn to speak and pass to someone else.

1. What was the motivation for each of the five crew members for joining this trip?
2. Which of the five people on *The Robert Gordon* did you most relate to and why?
3. Discuss the differences in parenting that you see in the parents of Brian, Niko, Sally, David, and Janet.
4. How does prison affect Keith, Niko, David, and Sally?
5. This is a crime novel–both the crew and the government commit crimes. What crimes does the governments commit and how are government officials held accountable? (Oliver North, who oversaw that operation ,was given a suspended prison sentence, two years of probation, and community service. Others involved were treated similarly by the courts.) Should government officials be allowed to violate the law if they believe in what they are doing?
6. Sally has never been told much about her biological father. How does that fact of her life influence her during the year she is involved with the crew of *The Robert Gordon*?
7. Archie tells Brian that Queen Victoria took marijuana for menstrual cramps and that marijuana is less harmful to the body than alcohol, but the war on drugs means opportunity for people

like them to get rich by trading in drugs. What do you think of Archie's argument?

8. Janet felt suffocated by her ultra-conservative Plymouth Brethren parents and chose Keith for her partner. Should she continue committed to Keith through his years in prison? Why?

9. *The Set Up* tells the story of ordinary people caught in a scheme of international espionage. How are each of their lives changed by international events? (Brian? David? Keith? Sally? Niko? Janet?)

10. The Middle East became a major focus of U.S. interest during the 1980s and was the site of America's longest wars—Afghanistan, September 2001 to today, and Iraq, March 2003 until December 2011. What did you learn from *The Set Up* about the reasons this region still suffers so from war?

Chapter Summary

Part 1 The Set Up

Ch 1 David Bennie, a young, unemployed Scot, goes to London for a job interview and is hired to escort yachts in the Mediterranean.

Ch 2 Brian Baker, Greek mother, British father a don at Cambridge, must find a way to replace his lost inheritance from his grandfather. He visits his old school friend Archie at the Bentley Golf Club and Archie has a plan

Ch 3 At a meeting in London the Customs and Excise, CIA (The Agency), American Embassy, Chelmsford Police Chief Inspector, and MI-6 (British Intelligence) plan a drug heist (and bust) to assist British and American foreign policies.

Ch 4 Keith Brown, who boats as a hobby, tells his partner Janet Morris that his old chum Archie has invited him to bring inlaid furniture from the Middle East to Britain and will pay handsomely.

Ch 5 "Niko" Karras's, born in Lebanon in 1958 to Cypriot parents during Cyprus's war for independence from, became a refugee at 17, fleeing civil war in Lebanon and moving with his family Rhodes, Greece.

Ch 6 William Casey, Director of the CIA under President Ronald Reagan, sets up a way to conduct foreign policy without Congress knowing about his secret funding of anti-communist "Contra" guerrillas to overthrow the government of Nicaragua.

Ch 7 Brian Baker and his girlfriend Georgina Graves travel to Rhodes with Keith Brown and his partner Janet to buy a boat for Keith to use in his new "import" business. Janet, a teacher, has no idea what Keith and Brian are really planning.

Ch 8 While Keith finds a boat, Brian visits the Karras family that worked for his parents in Cyprus, meets their son Niko, and offers him a job bringing cargo to Britain for good money. Niko accepts. Back in London, Brian and Archie finalize their plans as US personnel are evacuated from Beirut.

Ch 9 A Customs and Excise agent at Heathrow notices Brian and Georgina flying to Larnaca, Cyprus, and monitors them.

PART 2 The Transfer

Ch 10 In Larnaca, Cyprus, Brian finds the house where Mrs. Karras had cared for him when he was a toddler. He checks Keith's progress readying the yacht and the timing and is reassured.

Ch 11 In Majorca, Spain, Keith has hired an acquaintance, Tom Hill, to build storage compartments in the hold of *The Robert Gordon* for the cannabis resin. He confirms the final plans.

Ch 12 Niko has flown to Majorca and works with Tom. They sale for Rhodes in the third week of July and Keith hires Sally Eliades to be their cook. Sally and Niko become mates. Keith gives her a long weekend off while the men sail to Tripoli, off the coast of Lebanon, to pick up the cargo.

Ch 13 On deck during their watch Niko talks to Keith about his anxiety about the political situation in Lebanon and what he's read about Israelis boarding boats off-shore as part of their occupation of Lebanon. Keith's anxiety grows. They have two nights to make contact. Nothing happens the first night.

Ch 14 Night two men in black board *The Robert Gordon* bringing the cargo onboard. Keith gives the leader something (key to safety deposit box?). The three men put the cannabis packages into the storage compartments and sail back to Rhodes.

Ch 15 In Rhodes Keith phones a number in South Africa and exchanges word codes. Keith reads in a newspaper about Islamic Jihad attacks in Lebanon. Sally returns and they sail from Rhodes amidst stories of the bombing of US Embassy Annex. Beset by mechanical problems, they put into Gibraltar for repairs.

Ch 16 David's return to UK is delayed. Homesick in Gibraltar, he meets Sally and *The Robert Gordon* and asks to join their crew. Keith hires him. She is sick with a cold as they take the boat through sheeting rain to the English Channel, getting stuck on a sandbar, calling the Coast Guard, but then getting unstuck.

Ch 17 Keith is eager to get home Oct. 3. The yacht moves into place and Keith gives the signal that they've arrived. In the middle of the night they will unload the cargo.

Ch 18 Janet prepares for Keith's return after Archie calls to say Keith will be home tomorrow. Teddy (4) makes a welcome sign.

Ch 19 Keith asks the drunk and happy David and Sally to remain in the galley while the other three work in the prow. He, Tom, and Niko bring cannabis packages to the deck and load the dinghy, then take it to the shore where three vans wait. They return to the yacht for another load.

Ch 20 David and Sally are drinking in the galley. David goes to the toilet, sees a spotlight, and hears a loudspeaker telling them it is the police. On deck they along with Niko are handcuffed, ordered into a police boat, and taken to police cars.

Ch 21 Police interrogate the drivers of the vans: Terrance Gale, John Benton, and Geoff Knowles.

Ch 22 Each of the crew is interrogated. Flustered, Keith lies and changes his responses. He says he doesn't know Brian Baker.

Ch 23 The day before the bust, Georgina gets Brian Baker to the airport to fly to Cyprus. He receives a new passport, new name, new credit cards for a BCCI bank, and waits for Georgina is to join him. Something has gone wrong, but he is in the dark what or why.

Ch 24 Bill Casey loves his covert Contra support operation. Casey, a serious Catholic, is disturbed by his church's attraction to liberation theology, radical priests, and nuns.

Ch 25 Casey has created a network of wealthy private citizens to supply the Contras in violation of Congress's ban of all aid to overthrow the Nicaraguan government. Directed by Oliver North, a Marine working in the National Security Council, "The Enterprise" launders the money through BCCI, the largest privately owned international bank.

Ch 26 Janet wakes up to an anonymous call telling her to say nothing. There has been a problem. The news reports a major drug bust and arrests, but what would that have to do with Keith?

PART 3 Prison

Ch 27 Janet's students can tell something is wrong. She gets home to find two police officers there who tell her Keith is in prison and ask her questions she has no answers to. They advise getting Keith a good criminal lawyer. Archie hasn't called.

Ch 28 At a congratulatory meeting of Operation Bishop organizers, someone asks what happens to the drugs and they are told about a new American pilot program called civil asset forfeiture.

Ch 29 Georgina arrives in Nicosia Oct. 5. A letter in her suitcase says to go to a restaurant in Argos and ask for Andreas Vasileiou. At the restaurant, they are sent off with a young man who drives them to a field where a plane awaits to take them to Tel Aviv and then Costa Rica with only their new passports.

Ch 30 Janet visits Keith at Brixton Prison. He is apologetic and tearful. At home papers shoved through her mail slot tell her to put the enclosed contracts in the car hire shop files and to not talk to anyone. She does as instructed.

Ch 31 Janet's fundamentalist parents didn't approve of her having a baby with Keith without marrying him. She doesn't tell them of Keith's arrest. The police have been around to interview her again. One officer said the police had been watching them for nine months. The press badger her at her home.

Ch 32 Sally's Greek father left when she was young. Sally went to Greece to find her roots. Her stepdad Alfred is fighting in the Falkland War. Her half-sister Brenda told the police Sally was paid a lot to cook, which was not true. Terrified of being found guilty and imprisoned five to ten years, Sally breaks down.

Ch 33 A man from the Greek embassy visits Niko in prison to tell him of his mother's constant efforts to get help for him and of his father's sudden death. He says Niko never took Greek citizenship when they left Lebanon as refugees so will be deported to Lebanon. Niko, devastated, grieves alone.

Ch 34 David's family and friends scrimped to put together bail money, but his inept court appointed lawyer can't get bail for David. David's cellmate suggests his own solicitor who is interested in David's case. It is Christmas and the family bring goodies for their standard 15-minute visit.

Ch 35 Sally receives a Christmas visit from her Mum, and Keith receives Janet and Teddy. Janet's anger is building, and she wants to know why Archie and Brian aren't in prison.

Ch 36 Niko is receiving a steady stream of letters from his mother who writes about her life with his father. The chaplain has come by with a Greek bible and a guard has showed him kindness.

Ch 37 New Year/Hogmannay leaves David depressed. His new cellmate is a junkie. David has a terrible night and is desperate to get out. Trish and Mam travel three hours each way to see him, but Dad won't return. More bad dreams. David asks the guard for paper and pencil and begins drawing.

Ch 38 Everything in prison is regulated. David is accumulating sketches. He turns 22 in February 1985 and acquires Mr. Bernard Carnell as his new solicitor. Carnell gets him out on bail. Mam has a Christmas tree up to receive him.

Ch 39 Sally's barrister is well known but working a high-profile case. She will not be tried till four months after the men. Niko is putting his mother's letters in a book and researching what she has lived with the aide of the friendly older guard. He is troubled by Brian Baker's disappearance but won't betray him.

Ch 40 Niko's mother writes about the 1960s in Lebanon. Niko recalls a happy childhood but is learning of the violence eclipsing the country. She writes Lebanon was occupied by 60,000 Syrian and Israeli troops and desperate refugees. Niko panics. Were their suppliers Palestinians? "Terrorists"?

Part 4 The Trial

Ch 41 In the courtroom for the trial are David's Mam and sister and Janet,. Niko is interrogated and the others learn he will be deported. When the judge questions him, Niko says the suppliers might PLO but he asks for time to recall what he heard them say. The judge adjourns court until the following day.

Ch 42 Niko in his cell thinks they said soo'ria, Arabic for Syria. Maybe the suppliers were a radical splinter off the PLO? Were the crew part of the Cold War and the fight against terrorism?

Ch 43 A Secret Service agent approaches the judge and asks him not to deport Niko. Give Niko a five-year sentence with probation after two years, releasing him to the Secret Service, who will supervise him. HMS government wants him not to permit questions about Baker. The judge is angered by this. That night at a party in honor of American Clark Clifford, in London for a BCCI board meeting, he meets other Americans who he suspects manipulate the law for profit.

Ch 44 The MI-6 Special Agent discusses the case with his supervisor. They want the judge to classify the case. The agent is hopeful.

Ch 45 Brian and Georgina live on the ranch of John Hull (CIA) on Costa Rica's border with Nicaragua, a transit site for arms and drugs. Oliver North and Contra leaders Brooklyn Rivera and Eden Pastora visit. Congress has lifted the ban on military aid to the Contras.

Ch 46 Casey is also selling arms to Iran and diverting the profits to Contra military aid and other covert operations. North's Enterprise operation lands flights at Hull's ranch.

Ch 47 The judge finds a legal loophole that would allow Niko not to be deported. Consulting with prosecution and defense he learns neither has evidence on Brian Baker's involvement. In court there are no further questions for Niko. That afternoon Niko's barrister brings surprising news.

Ch 48 After Keith's testimony Janet goes to her parents' for tea. They have invited a man from their church. She wonders if she can forgive Keith and survive his incarceration for probably ten years.

Ch 49 Sally talks with her Mum about her biological father and discovers Mum's affair with Alfred had caused the rupture in their marriage.

Ch 50 David is interrogated by his effective barrister, Anne Worrall. At school a teacher invites Janet for a pint or a cuppa after school the day before the verdicts will be given. She acquires a friend.

Ch 51 July 3, 1985 the verdicts are given for seven of the eight defendants. They are predictable except for Niko's. David's verdict is inaudible and his barrister asks to poll the jury.

Ch 52 David is sobered by the price each member of his family has paid for his incarceration. He tries to return to sea.

Ch 53 Sally's trial is uneventful. Outside prison she finds no one can understand what she has gone through. Her dreams and her life are profoundly altered.

Ch 54 Brian in Costa Rica learns of U.S. arms sales to Iran and their connection to supplying the Contras. Brian and Georgina move to Chiapas, Mexico to start their new lives. Brian has a rare and uncomfortable meeting with his mother in Honduras.

Ch 55 When the Iran Contra scandal becomes public, President Reagan acknowledges the trade with Iran. Investigations begin by a special prosecutor and by special committees of the House and Senate. Casey, ill, will miss them.

Ch 56 David in port in Monaco is arrested and must give up his dream of a life at sea. Adnan Khashoggi is waiting for him in his armored car and says he is sorry David had such a difficult time two years to the day ago, October 4, 1984. Khashoggi assures him it won't happen again.

About the Author

Gretchen Eick worked on Capitol Hill in Washington, D.C. for over a decade as a foreign and military policy lobbyist before earning a Ph.D. in American Studies from the University of Kansas and becoming a Professor of History. She was awarded two Fulbright Scholar awards--Latvia and Bosnia and Herzegovina (BiH)--and a Fulbright Hays grant to South Africa. She has lived in or visited over forty countries and is the author of two scholarly books, the award-winning _Dissent in Wichita: The Civil Rights Movement in the Midwest, 1954-1972_ (University of Illinois Press, 2001/2007) and _They Met at Wounded Knee: The Eastmans' Story_ (University of Nevada Press, 2020). Her other novels are _Maybe Crossings_ (2015), _Finding Duncan_ (2015), and The Hard Verge: Britain, 2025 (2019).